Dark Wings

Published by John J. Rust at Createspace

Copyright 2012 John J. Rust

This book is a work of fiction. Names, characters, businesses, organizations, events and incidents are either a product of the author's imagination or are used fictitiously. Any resemblance to actual persons, living or dead, events or locales is entirely coincidental.

D0746342

CHAPTER 1

Whose brilliant idea was this?

Jim Rhyne's round face twisted in annoyance, his eyes flickering between his cousins.

"You need to be realistic," Doug Rhyne said to his younger brother Chuck, who sat on the other side of the campfire. "Do you know how many people who play baseball actually make it the majors? It has to be less than one percent."

The skin around Chuck's nose crinkled. "I'm sure people said the same thing to guys like Albert Pujols and Ryan Howard. What if they'd listened to them?"

"So now you're comparing yourself to two of the best players in the game?"

Jim groaned. He knew another huge argument was coming. It always happened whenever his cousins Doug and Chuck entered the same air space. Before it simply annoyed him.

Now it pissed him off.

"That scout said I have good speed and he likes my plate discipline," Chuck said. "And making the all-conference team didn't hurt any."

"You're playing junior college ball." Doug leaned forward, the glow from the campfire washing over his smooth, chiseled features. "What major league team will want a player who isn't good enough to make a big-time college team?"

"That's bullshit. Plenty of major leaguers played for junior colleges."

"Will you two knock it off?" Jim's sister, Valerie, glowered at them. "We went on this camping trip to enjoy ourselves, not listen to you two have the same damn argument you've been having for the last two years."

"Well I'm sorry this is so inconvenient for you, Val. But if it was you, wouldn't you want to stop your brother from wasting his life."

"I'm not wasting my life." Chuck's voice rose.

"You want to make a living playing a game. Even if you do get drafted by some major league team, they'll stick you in the minors, you'll bounce around from one little town to another barely making enough money to live on. How long do you intend to do that? Three, four, five years? Those are years you could spend doing something more important."

"Like joining the Army?"

"Yes. Just like the rest of us. Just like our father did, and Jim and Val's father, and most of our family going back to the Civil War."

Jim rolled his eyes. *Please don't do "The Speech."* He'd heard it more times than he cared. Doug would drone on about the importance of serving the country, of being part of a cause greater than yourself, of the honor and privilege of wearing the uniform of the United States Army. Sure, he believed in all that. But when Doug said those things, he sounded overbearing, and acted like anyone who didn't serve in the military was somehow a lesser being, even if that person happened to be his brother. Plus, Doug tended to gloss over the sacrifices one had to make when serving the country, and the toll it took on people.

Hannah.

A beautiful, smiling face crowned by shoulder-length blond hair appeared in his mind's eye. His throat clenched. Part of him wanted the image to go away. Another part wanted it to stay there, forever. If it went away, he risked forgetting about her. But if it stayed, the pain would just dig into his heart.

"It's my damn life!" Chuck's shout brought Jim back to the here and now. "Maybe I'll make the big leagues, maybe I won't. But at least I'm gonna give it a try."

"And what happens when you don't make it?" Doug demanded.

"*If* I don't make it, then at least I'll know I tried my best."

"You tried your best. That's how a loser talks."

"I'm not a loser!" Chuck scowled, looking like he wanted to leap over the campfire and tackle his brother.

"Chuck, calm down!" Val's arm shot out toward Chuck, her hand up. She then turned to Doug. "Doug, that was uncalled for."

"You kiddin'?" Chuck blurted. "That's typical for him. Big Brother always knows best, don't you?"

"Someone has to care about your future since you don't."

Chuck opened his mouth to respond.

"That's it." Jim pushed himself to his feet. "I need some fucking peace and quiet."

Jaw clenched, he spun on his heel and marched into the darkened woods. He knocked a few branches out of his way, his anger building with each passing second.

He soon came to a small clearing and stopped. Hands on his hips, he drew slow, deep breaths, trying to calm himself.

Eventually, his cousins' fight faded from his thoughts. But other images replaced it. Camping trips he'd been on with Hannah. She'd been reluctant at first, but ultimately grew to love the great outdoors. He remembered how happy she'd been the first time she made pine needle tea, the time they fed one another s'mores, jamming them into each other's faces and laughing over it, or the nights they held one another in their sleeping bag. He drew a staggered breath, recalling the feel of her body against his, how much he enjoyed it.

How he would never experience it again.

"Jim."

He turned around. A compact, feminine silhouette strode toward him.

"I thought you'd like to know Chuck and Doug didn't kill one another," Val said as she stopped a few feet from him.

He grunted in acknowledgement and turned away.

"But, the night is still young." Val kept her tone light-hearted. "The way those two argue, it may still happen."

Jim said nothing, just clenched his left fist.

"Look at it this way. If it does happen, we'll finally get some peace and quiet. Though I don't want to be the one to tell Uncle Phil and Aunt -"

"I'm sick of it, Val." He spun around, throwing out his arms. "Those two are brothers. All they do is argue, and over petty shit. So Chuck doesn't want to join the Army. Yeah, maybe I would have liked to see him follow in the family's footsteps, too, but it's his life. But Doug rips him every chance he gets. They're supposed to be family. They're supposed to appreciate one another. They're supposed to support one another, be there for one another when . . . ." He bit his lip and lowered his gaze to the ground.

Valerie walked up to him and placed a gentle hand on his shoulder. "This is more about you than it is Doug and Chuck, isn't it?"

Jim sighed and looked up at her. He forced down a lump in his throat. "It's been a year. I still miss her. I still can't believe she's . . . that she isn't around."

"She was your wife. There isn't any time table that says you have to get over it by a certain date."

"It's affecting my job, Val. I'm making mistakes. Little ones, sure, and yeah they've all been in training. But in our line of work, it's those little mistakes that get people killed. That's probably why they want to make me an instructor."

Valerie shrugged. "Well, someone needs to train up the newest batch of Delta Force recruits. Preferably someone with as much real-world experience as you."

"I'd rather be out there, hunting down terrorists. Not back here, safe and sound, running guys through obstacle courses."

"I'm sure it's just a temporary thing. Maybe do this for a year and two, then you'll be back in the field."

"I doubt it," Jim grumbled.

"What makes you say that?"

He folded his arms across his chest, the corner of his mouth curling.

"Jim?" Valerie urged as the silence continued. "Jim." Her tone became more insistent.

"My CO thought I should see a shrink."

The whites of Valerie's bulging eyes shone through the darkness.

When she didn't speak, he continued. "He was concerned about the way I was dealing with Hannah's death. Thought maybe talking to a psychologist would help. Heh! Help how? What Delta trooper is going to follow an officer who's been on a shrink's couch spilling his guts? I sure as hell wouldn't. And what the hell's he supposed to tell me anyway? That I shouldn't blame myself? When Hannah needed me I was five thousand miles away, in the middle of fucking nowhere, trying to find some group of shit-suckin' Taliban assholes who got their jollies machine gunning schools." He shook his head. "I can protect a bunch of

Afghans I never even met. But when it comes to my own wife . . ."

"Jim . . ."

He backed away from Valerie. "No. My days in Delta Force are done. I'm damaged goods. Trouble is, I have no idea what the hell else to do."

"You can always go to work for Dad and Uncle Phil."

Jim worked his jaw back and forth, thinking about the company they owned in Lexington that made all sorts of combat accessories for infantrymen. "I don't know. I don't think I'm cut out for some nine-to-five desk job."

"Well, you're on leave for, what, another month? You've got time to figure out what you want to do with -"

A noise caught his attention. He tuned out Valerie and tensed, concentrating on the air around him.

There it was again. Above him. A deep flapping sound. He looked up, scanning the night sky, wishing for more moonlight. All he saw was darkness.

"Jim?"

He held up a hand to quiet her. "Did you hear that?"

Now Valerie lifted her gaze to the sky.

Flap . . . flap . . . flap.

"Is that a bird?" she asked.

"If it is, it's one hell of a big bird." He tried to peer through the darkness, hoping to see a shadow, something, anything to indicate what it was. Part of him thought he was overreacting. He'd spent a good chunk of his life hunting and camping. It was probably an owl.

But the hairs on the back of his neck tingled. Something about that sound didn't sit well with him.

Jim heard the flapping again, this time to his right. He turned, his eyes sweeping the sky and the tree tops. He saw nothing in the dark. What he wouldn't give for a nightscope. He had brought one with him, but it was back at the campsite. Fat lot of good that did him now.

He held his breath, straining his ears to pinpoint the flapping.

For God's sake, chill out, Rhyne. You're being ridiculous.

But he couldn't let go of this feeling. That flapping sounded too loud to come from any bird he knew. So what could it –

He heard a crackling of wood. One of the treetops bent to the left. His eyes widened. A large dark shape sat on the tree fifty feet above him.

"There," Jim whispered to Valerie and pointed up to the tree.

"What is it?"

Bear was his first thought, given the size. He pulled out the Ruger P944 from his hip holster. Out the corner of his eye, he saw his sister draw her little SIG Sauer P230. The pistols may not kill a bear, but they should at least scare it off.

Jim kept his eyes on the top of the tree. The dark shape stayed there. He screwed up his eyes, trying to make out some details. All he could see was a dark lump.

He kept backing up. Ten steps. Fifteen steps.

With his right hand, he signaled Valerie to start backing up. She did. Both of them watched the dark shape in the tree. It appeared to stay still.

It's a bear. It has to be a bear. No matter how many times Jim said it, he couldn't convince himself. But what other animal in Kentucky could be that big and be in a tree?

The shadow jumped from the top of the tree.

"Jim!" Valerie screamed.

The dark shape grew larger by the second. Glowing red eyes locked right on him.

CHAPTER 2

Shoot or dodge?

Jim had a split-second to decide.

He chose dodge.

He threw himself to the left. A dark shadow flashed in his peripheral vision. It hit the ground with a thump.

Jim rolled and came up on one knee, pistol raised. Shock paralyzed him when he saw the thing.

What the hell?

It had to be nearly seven-feet tall with thin arms and legs, both of which ended in razor sharp talons. A snout protruded from its dark hairy face, filled with jagged teeth. Above it was a pair of glowing red eyes. But the most astonishing feature had to be the large wings extending from its back. Basically, it looked like a human bat. And it carried something in its right hand, something sleek and tubular.

A gun.

The monster unleashed a high-pitched shriek and stepped toward Jim. Its gun came up.

Training and experience blasted through the shock. Jim squeezed off three rounds, aiming for the center of mass. The monster gasped and flinched, but did not go down. He swore it scowled at him before bringing up its gun again.

Three more shots echoed through the woods. The monster flinched and glanced over its shoulder. Jim peered around its legs. Valerie stood twelve feet away and fired twice more. The monster twisted around, leveling its gun at Val.

Jim sprang to his feet and launched himself at the monster's legs. He sensed more than felt a large mass tumble over him. The monster's gun fell on the ground.

Jim landed on his stomach and rolled over. He quickly got to his feet to see the monster on its back, shrieking, more out of anger than pain. He stepped toward it, pistol extended.

The monster's right foot lashed out. Jim jumped back, barely avoiding the razor sharp talons. The monster reached out and snatched its gun off the ground. Jim aimed his pistol. His finger froze when he noticed some sort of padding on its torso.

It was wearing body armor!

The monster let out another angry shriek and sat up. It swung its gun toward Jim.

Crack! Crack!

The monster's head jerked back. A dark mass burst from its skull. It dropped onto its back, arms and legs sprawled out.

Jim hurried over to it, covering it with his Ruger. The monster didn't move. The red glow faded from its eyes.

He fired two more shots into the monster's head. *I'm not taking any chances.*

"Jim!"

He turned, still keeping one eye on the monster.

Valerie slammed into him, her arms tight around him. "Are you okay?" she asked.

"Yeah, I'm fine." He slipped out of his sister's hug and looked down at the monster. His brow furrowed as he examined its humanoid bat features. *What the hell is this thing?* Moreover, how the hell could it be real? Things like this didn't exist outside of dumbass sci-fi movies. But here it was, right in front of him, or rather lying at his feet.

"What is this -"

Two distant shots cut off Valerie's question. Both their heads snapped to the left, toward the direction of the camp.

Chuck. Doug.

Jim sprinted through the darkened woods, Valerie at his heels. Worry slithered inside him for his cousins. Could another of these bat-things have gotten them?

He willed his legs to go faster. Adrenaline slowed the world around him. After what seemed an eternity, he reached the edge of their campsite.

Another monster stood a couple feet from the camp fire, holding out a boxy device with a handle the size of a lantern. On the other side of the fire, Doug and Chuck wobbled back and forth, doubled over, their hands over their ears.

That's when Jim noticed the high pitched buzz.

He raised his pistol. Something vibrated in his skull. His grimaced, fighting to concentrate on his aim. He glanced at his cousins. Chuck had already fallen to his knees.

C'mon, c'mon. Get it together.

Jim clenched his teeth, trying to fight of the tingling in his head. He leveled his pistol at the monster's head, but held his fire. In the glow of the fire, he noticed the monster wore a thick, dark-colored helmet. He had to assume it was bullet resistant.

He only had one other option.

A dizzy spell swept through him. He shook it off and aimed at the device in the monster's hand. Holding his breath, he focused on the target until it filled his vision.

Jim pulled the trigger until his Ruger P944 clicked empty.

The device jumped out of the monster's hand. The high-pitched buzz stopped. The monster glanced at its shattered device on the ground, then whipped its head toward him. It shrieked in rage.

A shot rang out next to Jim. Another. Another. He glanced at Valerie as she emptied her SiG Sauer at the monster. It stumbled back and fell to the ground, lying on its side.

Jim hurried toward it, ejecting his Ruger's empty clip and ramming home a new one. He covered the creature with his pistol and kicked it twice in the shoulder. It didn't move. He noticed a bloody hole just under the monster's right eye. He flashed a brief smile. For a chopper jockey, his sister was one hell of a shot.

"Chuck! Doug!" she called out. "You guys all right?"

He looked over to them. Valerie knelt beside Chuck, while looking over at Doug. Chuck was on one knee, holding his head. Doug sat on the ground, forehead pressed against his arms, which rested on his knees.

Jim jogged over to Doug and knelt beside him. "Doug." He rested a hand on his cousin's back. "You okay?"

"Uh, yeah. No." He lifted his head and blinked. "Aw man, I feel dizzy. Kinda feel like I'm gonna puke."

"What the hell was that?" Chuck asked in a groggy voice.

Jim looked at the device lying a few feet from the monster. "Some kind of sonic weapon." He had seen them demonstrated a few times with Delta Force, and the Rangers before that. But those devices had to be mounted on vehicles. He knew of no such man-portable weapons.

"Yeah, I kind of figured that," Chuck replied as he tried to get to his feet with Val's help. "I mean, that thing. What was it?"

Once they got Doug upright, they walked over to the dead monster.

"This thing can't be real." Doug shook his head. "It has to be a guy in a suit."

Jim looked at his cousin, then back at the monster. Drawing a deep breath, he knelt down and reached out with his free hand, his Ruger trained on the monster.

It's dead, man. It's not gonna jump at you like some horror movie monster.

Still, a paranoid voice in the back of his head told him not to take any chances.

His fingers hovered a few inches away from the monster's head. Part of him prayed Doug was right.

His fingertips felt coarse hair on the monster's cheek. He pressed harder, and felt no give like he'd expect from a rubber mask.

In all honesty, he'd expected this. From the way the monster he and Val encountered moved, and from its shriek, he couldn't imagine a guy in a suit being capable of all that. Still, he wanted to hold on to that faint hope. It would sure as hell be easier to accept.

"No suit. This thing's for real."

In the light of the campfire, he watched the color drain from Doug's face. "No. No way. This isn't possible. Things like this don't exist. They can't."

"Look for yourself. This thing is real. And another one just like it attacked me and Val."

"Really?" Chuck said. "Where is it?" He whipped his head around, as if expecting the monster to suddenly jump out of the darkness.

"Don't worry," Jim told him. "We killed it."

Doug's jaw trembled as he struggled to speak. His wide eyes stayed locked on the monster. "It can't . . . I mean, what the hell is it? Where did it come from?"

"I don't know," Jim answered.

"Well what did it want with us? Why did it attack us? Why is it here?"

"Calm down, Doug."

"Calm down? Look at that thing! It's a monster. A real fucking monster! How can I calm down when -"

"Dammit, Doug!" Jim shot to his feet and glared at him. "You're an officer in the 101st Air Assault Division. Start acting like it!"

Doug took a couple deep breaths. For a moment, he looked like he was about to yell back. Instead, Doug's shoulders sagged. "Yeah. Yeah, you're right. Sorry."

Jim nodded, then returned his gaze to the monster.

"You think there might be more of these things around?" Val asked.

"I don't know. We should probably assume there are."

Val snorted. "That makes me feel good."

"Hey, wait a minute." Chuck stepped closer to the dead monster. "I think I know what this thing is."

"You've got to be kidding me." Doug gave his brother a skeptical look. "How could you possibly know? No one's ever seen anything like this."

"Maybe not. I'm telling you, this thing looks just like the Mothman."

"The what?" Jim's face scrunched up.

"The Mothman. I saw a show about it on History Channel. A bunch of people from this town in West Virginia reported seeing it back in the Sixties. Some of them even said it caused this bridge to collapse. And they had this computer generated image of it and it looked just like this thing."

Doug rolled his eyes. "You have got to be kidding me. You know those monster shows are a bunch of bullshit."

"Well if they're a bunch of bullshit, why does thing look almost exactly like how every eyewitness described the Mothman?"

Doug's mouth hung open. His head trembled slightly, as if fighting to find an answer. When he couldn't, he pressed his lips together and scowled at his younger brother.

Jim's jaw moved back and forth as he pondered Chuck's explanation. He enjoyed sci-fi and horror movies as much as anyone. But he certainly didn't believe in "real" monsters like Bigfoot or the Abominable Snowman or anything like that.

But looking at the bat-thing lying on the ground, he figured he'd have to change those beliefs in hurry.

"So what do we do now?" Valerie asked.

"Ain't it obvious?" Chuck turned to her. "We gotta go to the cops."

"Like they'll believe this," Valerie scoffed.

Chuck shrugged. "Okay, then. We just take it back to your truck."

"You do know my truck's two miles away. It's gonna be a bitch to carry that thing."

"Chuck's right," Jim said. "We gotta get this thing and the other one back to someone in authority, not only to show them proof, but to find out what makes them tick, especially if there might be more out there. But I don't agree with taking it to the police. I don't think they're equipped to deal with something like this."

"The Army?" asked Chuck

Jim nodded. "Look at it. This thing isn't some animal. It's a soldier."

"How do you know?" Doug shot him a perplexed look.

He drew his head back in bewilderment. Doug was part of one of the best light infantry units in the Army, a company executive officer. How the hell could all his intelligence have completely abandoned him?

"It's pretty damn obvious. Helmet, body armor, rucksack, webbing, and the one that attacked me and Val had a rifle. I don't think they would have any of these things if they were botanists."

Doug narrowed his eyes, glaring at him. Jim glared right back. Seconds later his cousin turned away, his face twisting even more. But Jim sensed Doug's anger was now directed at himself, for not realizing that this monster must be a soldier.

He went through the monster's rucksack and webbing and examined the contents. "Looks like he's carrying the sort of things you'd expect a typical infantryman to have. Spare magazines, canteen, bags that look like MREs, entrenching tool, knife, something that looks like a PDA. Check this out. This looks like a throat mike."

"Great." Val frowned. "That means if there are any more of these things out there, these two may have told them about us."

Worry bubbled inside Jim. Two of these things had been bad enough. He didn't relish the idea of a whole squad or platoon dropping in on them. "I think that's safe to assume, which means hanging around here isn't a good idea." He got to his feet. "Leave the camping gear behind. We need to travel as light as possible, especially if were taking these things with us."

"We're really taking these things back to Fort Campbell?" Val asked.

"Yeah. That's the closest base from here. Even better, you and Doug are assigned there, so we won't have to worry about wasting time convincing everyone that this isn't a prank."

Valerie let out a breath and shook her head. "Man, are the people back there gonna shit a brick when they see these things."

Jim nodded, looking back down at the dead monster. He chewed on the inside of his cheek. What this thing was took a backseat to another question. These things were most definitely soldiers. And what is it that soldiers do?

A chill went up his spine. The sooner they got these monsters to Fort Campbell, the better.

CHAPTER 3

Ignore the pain. Ignore the pain.

Jim clenched his teeth. Invisible coils crushed and burned his arms and legs and back. He took measured breaths and concentrated on his steps, being careful not trip. Every few seconds he twisted his head around, making sure the path ahead was clear. Then he quickly scanned the trees and sky above them, wary of any more Mothmen.

His body screamed in pain as he continued to carry one of the dead monsters by the armpits, while Chuck carried it by the legs. Doug and Valerie carried the second Mothman just behind them. The wings of both creatures dragged on the ground.

Another step. Another. Check behind. A little bump in the ground. Shift right. Check above. All clear.

Tremors started in his shoulders and went down his arms. His body begged him to let go of the Mothman. They'd already carried this thing a mile, and still had another mile to go before they reached Val's truck.

Jim looked up at Chuck. The strain was evident on his angular face. The kid may be in great shape, his tall, lean frame hardened by years of running and weight training and other conditioning. However, Jim doubted any of Chuck's baseball practices required him to carry two hundred to two hundred-twenty pounds of dead weight a couple miles. Still, his young cousin didn't gripe about it once. He hoped Doug would take notice of that, maybe give Chuck a pat on the back for his effort.

Then again, he couldn't remember the last time Doug complimented his brother on anything. Why start now?

Focus.

He pushed the turmoil between Doug and Chuck out of his head and looked down at the Mothman. Who were they? Where did they come from?

He decided not to expend much thought on those two questions. Whatever he came up with would only be SWAGs, Scientific Wild Ass Guesses, not fact.

What facts did he have on the Mothmen? Obviously they were soldiers. Judging by the rifle and that sonic device, they seemed to be on par technologically with humans. They could fly. *How far? How fast?* They wore no night vision goggles. He recalled the glowing red eyes, and wondered if they had natural night vision.

One thing for sure. They were hostile. Very hostile.

That brought him back to the soldier part. He knew of only two reasons soldiers like these would be in Kentucky. The first, recon. The state hosted two of the Army's biggest bases, Fort Campbell, roughly forty miles east, and Fort Knox further north.

That dovetailed into the second reason non-human soldiers would be here. Just thinking about it turned Jim's stomach into a cold, lead ball.

Eventually, thankfully, they reached Valerie's black twin-cab pick-up, parked on the side of a dirt road. The white decal in the back window caught his eye. "Silly Boys, Trucks Are For Girls." They hefted the Mothmen corpses into the bed, then chucked their backpacks in there as well, along with the Mothmen's rifles and the wrecked sonic device.

All four groaned and stretched, trying to ease their aching muscles. Jim and Val then covered the dead monsters with a tarp. He didn't want to risk any civilians seeing these things.

"How long will it take to reach Fort Campbell?" he asked Valerie.

"If I go the speed limit, thirty, thirty-five minutes. If I don't, twenty minutes. Probably less."

Jim bit his lower lip. More often than not, his sister drove like she was qualifying for the Daytona 500. It made for some scary moments in his life, even scarier than firefights he'd been in with al Qaeda and Taliban dirtbags. But given the situation . . .

"Let's see if you can set a new land-speed record."

Valerie smiled wide.

Doug and Chuck exchanged nervous looks.

They piled into the cab, keeping their hunting rifles at their sides. Jim wanted them ready in case any more Mothmen popped up. He prayed that didn't happen. The monsters' rifles had to be semi-automatic or full automatic, or both. That put the four of them at a distinct disadvantage with bolt-action rifles and pistols. Jim had attempted to fire the Mothman rifles back at their campsite, but neither trigger would budge. His attempts to find the safety proved unsuccessful.

Valerie twisted the key. The big truck's engine revved to life.

"What the hell?" She scrunched her face at the dashboard.

"What is it?" Jim asked.

"The GPS didn't come on." She tapped the screen a couple times. It remained dark.

"Forget about it. You should know the way back to your own base without that thing."

Valerie nodded, put the truck in drive and stomped on the gas. The rear tires churned. Jim could feel streams of dirt flying into the air as the truck shot onto the road. Silhouettes of trees blurred past him. The truck bounced non-stop, his seatbelt the only thing keeping him from smacking his head against the roof, or the windshield.

Valerie twisted the wheel left at a hairpin turn. Jim swore the truck went up on two wheels. He glanced out the passenger side window. Trees passed within centimeters of the glass.

He looked over at his sister. She just smiled serenely as the needle rose past 60 mph.

He just shook his head. That was Val. Always the daredevil. Always pushing the limit with anything she rode. Skateboards, dirt bikes, motorcycles, cars, pick-ups. To civilians, she was reckless, a funeral waiting to happen. To the Army, it made her the perfect candidate for the 160th Special Operations Aviation Regiment, "The Night Stalkers."

The truck burst out of the woods and fishtailed onto a paved road. Valerie spun the wheel left to straighten out the truck, then shot down the road. In what seemed like an instant later, they were on Highway 68. The speedometer kept rising. 65. 70. 75. 80.

"Uh, Val?" Chuck's voice cracked. "Do you think you can slow down?"

"Of course I *can* slow down. But I won't."

The needle hit 85.

"Doug." Jim turned around to face him. "We should have good cell phone reception now. Get on the horn to Campbell and let 'em know we're coming."

Doug glanced out the back window, no doubt focusing on the tarp covering the Mothmen corpses. He then looked back at him. "What should I tell them?"

Jim tightened his lips. He couldn't risk a full report about something this extraordinary on an unsecured line.

"Just tell them we're en route with evidence of a national security threat, and we need senior officers on scene when we arrive."

Doug nodded and pulled his cell phone from his pocket. He dialed – probably the base's operations center, which was staffed 24/7 – and put the phone to his ear. Jim saw his cousin's face scrunch in puzzlement.

"What is it?"

"I don't know. All I'm getting is static."

"No way," Chuck said. "We should have good service here."

Doug pushed the END button and dialed again. "I'm gonna try Captain Rodriguez."

A minute later, Doug announced he couldn't get through to his company commander either.

Jim got his cell phone and dialed Brigadier General Monge, the CO of Delta Force.

Nothing.

Val also fished her cell phone out of her pocket and dialed with one hand, the other on the wheel as the truck exceeded 80 mph. Within seconds of putting the phone to her ear, frustration etched in her face. "I tried my Regimental CO. Nothing but static."

Chuck tried to call his parents and a teammate from his baseball team. He couldn't reach any of them.

Only the growling engine could be heard in the otherwise silent cab. Jim glanced at the faces of his sister and cousins. He sensed worry from Val and Doug, and borderline panic from Chuck given how wide and white his eyes had become. Cold needles dug into Jim's spine, then formed sharp daggers that pierced his stomach. His heart sped up. First monsters had tried to kill them. Now they had no cell phone service in an area where there should be a clear signal. He wanted to believe it was a coincidence.

There's no such thing as coincidence, the professional soldier in him declared.

His gaze turned to the dashboard, to the radio. He held his breath and slowly reached out for it. A small part of him hoped to turn it on and hear music playing, any music, even rap. A large part of him expected to hear an announcer say, "This is an activation of the Emergency Alert System. This is not a test."

After hesitating a second, he turned on the radio.

Static.

He moved up and down the AM and FM dials. His stomach twisted with each passing second.

Every single station broadcast nothing but static.

"What's going on, man?" Chuck demanded. "How come there's nothing on the radio? How come we can't call anyone?"

"We'll probably find out once we get to Fort Campbell." Jim said. His face stiffened, trying to hide any trace of the concern. Could there be other Mothmen out there? Were they responsible for what happened to their phones and the radio? Was only this part of Kentucky affected? The whole state? The whole country?

The whole world?

Tremors gripped his legs. He closed his eyes, willing them away. He couldn't afford to panic. He was Delta Force, for God's sake!

Fall back on your training. No matter how strange the situation, he had to rely on his training, his experience in the field, to see him through. Anything less, and he would die, and maybe take his sister and cousins with him.

Valerie raced across the bridge spanning Lake Barkley. A highway sign whipped past them on the right. CADIZ 10 MILES.

Jim continued to gaze out the window as dark, rolling fields flashed by. He'd been to the little town a few times in the past, usually to gas up or get food or other supplies going to or from the Land Between the Lakes.

He debated with himself. Getting those Mothmen back to Fort Campbell had to be top priority. But he didn't like speeding through the Kentucky night without any clue what was going on that would render cell phones and radios useless. They might find out the reason if they –

"SHIT!!!"

The truck suddenly swerved left.

Jim gripped the sides of his seat. He glanced out the windshield. His eyes widened as he spotted a station wagon sitting at an angle in the middle of the road.

Val barely avoided it.

Another car appeared in front of them. Val jerked the steering wheel. Tires squealed. A scrape of metal on metal filled the cab.

"Dammit!" Val hollered. She swerved to miss another stalled car.

Chuck cried out in terror.

Jim's heart threatened to pound through his chest. He glimpsed an SUV to the side of the road. Just past that, an old pick-up truck had rear-ended a Lexus.

The breath stuck in his throat. In front of them, two police cars were parked hood-to-hood, blocking the entire road.

"Hold on!"

The instant Valerie shouted, she cut the wheel to the right. She narrowly missed the cop car, went off-road, and into a small incline. Jim tensed, ready for the truck to tip over.

Instead Valerie gunned the engine, shot up the incline and back onto the highway.

"Stop!" Jim ordered.

Valerie jammed on the brakes. Tires squealed. Jim's seatbelt dug into his torso, keeping him from being hurled into the windshield.

Finally, all was still.

"Shit . . . shit . . . shit," Chuck gasped. "You're fuckin' nuts, Val. Fuckin' nuts."

She ignored him and turned to Jim. "Why did we stop?"

"Because I want to know why this highway suddenly turned into a parking lot. Come on."

He opened the door, grabbed his hunting rifle and got out. Val, Doug and Chuck followed suit. They advanced toward the cop cars. Jim scanned all around him, and above him. No sign of any Mothmen.

He slowed as he approached the cars. The windows had been shattered, as had the lightbar on top of one car. He walked around to the other side, and stopped.

Bullet holes riddled the sides of both police cars. Sizeable ones. 7.62mm, maybe? Could be as big as 8mm.

"I got shell casings here." Doug examined a small brass object between his thumb and index finger. "Looks like nine-millimeter."

Jim nodded. Most police departments in the country use 9mm pistols. "How many did you find?"

"A lot. Looks like the cops put up a good fight."

Jim groaned to himself. He had a bad feeling who, or what, those cops had been fighting. He also had a bad feeling what had happened to them.

"Jim," Valerie called out. "I think I got something here."

He strode around the police car. Valerie crouched a couple feet from the wheel well, staring at a dark patch on the asphalt. He knelt beside her and pulled out his Mini-Maglite. He made sure to lean over and hold the light close to his torso before turning it on, wanting to block out its glow as much as possible. The little beam swept over a dried patch of dark crimson. The corners of Jim's mouth twisted. He knew instantly what it was.

Blood.

Guess we know what happened to the cops.

They checked the other vehicles and found more of the same. Windows shattered, doors pockmarked by bullet holes. In the station wagon they discovered the driver's seat covered in blood and bits of gray matter. Jim clenched his jaw. Valerie and Doug cringed. Chuck turned away, a hand over his mouth, trying not to be sick.

Several items lay scattered around the highway. A purse. A couple cell phones. A flip flop. A golf club, of all things, which Jim figured had been used for hitting something else besides a little white ball.

They also found a real weapon, a Browning semi-automatic pistol. Jim checked the magazine. Half full.

Amongst those items, there were more patches of blood.

He slowly rotated his head, taking in the highway. Not a highway any more. A battlefield. On a small scale, but a battlefield nonetheless. It had shell casings, bullet-riddled vehicles, blood and signs of flight.

But there was one thing missing, one thing synonymous with all battlefields.

Where are all the bodies?

CHAPTER 4

The four drove along Highway 68 for a couple more miles, weaving their way around more abandoned vehicles, when Jim spotted a farmhouse to the left.

"Pull in there," he told Valerie, pointing toward the darkened, two-story home.

"Why? The place looks deserted."

"Or maybe there could be people hiding in there." Despite the conviction in his voice, Jim only half-believed it. Still the house bore checking out. They might find some clue as to what the hell happened.

The truck bounced along the dirt driveway. Valerie stopped near the front porch.

"Val, Doug. With me. Chuck, you stay here and guard the bodies."

Chuck's enlarged, blazing white eyes stood out in the darkened interior of the cab. "M-Me?"

"The three of us are better trained to search this house and deal with any problems that might crop up than you."

Chuck continued to stare at him, his breaths becoming audible.

"For God's sake, Chuck, it's guard duty." Annoyance laced Doug's tone. "Just stand there with a rifle and look like you know what you're doing. You can handle that, can't you?"

Chuck's head whipped toward his older brother. His breathing grew louder, though this time it was more from anger than fear.

Jim clenched his jaw. The last thing he needed was these two dumbasses going at it again.

"Chuck. Yes or no, can you do this?"

"Yeah. I'm good." Chuck never took his eyes off Doug.

"Good. You see or hear anything, give us a shout. Or better yet, fire off a round. We'll come runnin'."

"Got it."

They exited the truck. Hunting rifle in hand, Chuck took up position along the side of the bed. Jim led Doug and Valerie toward the wooden porch, each one carrying their pistols, which were more conducive to close quarter battle than a hunting rifle. His eyes flickered between the two darkened front windows, looking for any movement. Spotting none, he crept up the steps, taking controlled breaths, keeping his heartbeat steady. He took up position on the right side of the door, Doug and Val on the left. Jim held up a hand, telling them to wait, and slowly turned the doorknob.

It was unlocked.

He held his breath. Maybe the owners had to leave in a hurry. Or maybe someone, or something, had entered here. Maybe they were still inside.

Jim pulled out his maglite and pushed the door with his shoulder, letting it swing open. He turned around, leaning halfway inside. Silhouettes of furniture greeted him. He settled his gunhand on top of his left hand, the one clenching the little flashlight. Clicking it on, he swept both the beam and the Ruger back and forth. No one around. He stood still, listening for the faintest sound from inside.

All was quiet.

He entered the house. Doug and Valerie followed a second later, pistols extended, flashlights on.

Jim checked behind a couch and a chair. Nothing. They moved into the kitchen. All clear. Then they came to the basement. He bit his lip. If whoever lived here needed to hide from something, the basement would be the most logical place.

Or someone could be using it for an ambush.

Jim stood off to the side of the cellar door and opened it. He cringed when he heard the loud creaking. If anyone happened to be down there, they knew now someone was coming.

Please be friendly.

He played the beam of his light down the steps and to the floor below. Taking a quick breath, he started down the steps. He constantly swept the light around the basement, his finger tensing around the Ruger's trigger. He spotted garden tools, cardboard boxes and pieces of furniture that had to date back to the 1940s.

Nothing living was down here.

They checked the rest of the house. Deserted. But in the bedroom they did find several dresser drawers open, and the clothing that remained in them in disarray, like someone just scooped up shirts and socks and underwear as quickly as they could.

They also noticed the alarm clock on the nightstand showed no red digital numbers. The nightlight in the outlet by the bedroom door wouldn't turn on. Apparently whatever attacked those motorists also must have knocked out the power.

They returned to the kitchen, which also showed signs of people leaving in a hurry. Cabinet doors were open, with items from shattered coffee mugs to a carton of hot cocoa mix lying on the counters and the floor.

"Hey," Val called out from the breakfast nook. "I found some newspapers."

"So what?" said Doug.

Jim heard his sister let out an annoyed breath through her nose. "Well maybe there's a story on what the hell happened here."

Even in the dark, Jim could read Doug's body language. His cousin was clearly irritated with himself for not realizing that right off the bat.

Jim took one of the newspapers from Val and held his maglite up close to it. The banner read *The Cadiz Record*. He scanned the front page and frowned at the headline.

MAYOR DEDICATES NEW HOME FOR ANIMAL SHELTER.

He took the other newspaper from his sister. *The Daily News* out of Bowling Green.

SCHOOL SUPERINTENDENT TAKES HEAT OVER BUDGET SHORTFALL.

Jim shook his head. Whatever happened obviously occurred before either newspaper could put out their next edition.

Another thought hit him. He shown his light around the top of *The Daily News* and checked the date.

"What the hell?"

"What is it?" Valerie asked.

"The date on this newspaper. It's from two days ago."

"Two days?" Disbelief coated Doug's voice.

"This has been going on for two days?" Val said. "But we checked our messages every day. If anything major happened, our units would have called us."

"Unless those Mothmen have been jamming all communications for that long." Jim looked up at the others. "C'mon. There's nothing more we can do here." He started for the living room, then stopped. "No, wait. Go through the kitchen. Get whatever supplies you can. We may need them, just in case."

He let the sentence hang. But judging from Valerie's and Doug's expressions, they both knew what he was implying. *In case what happened here happened to Fort Campbell.*

The thought put a knot in his stomach.

They went through the cabinets and the pantry, but didn't find much. A few cans of beans and tomatoes, a package of crackers, a bag of lollipops. Jim figured the original owners took most of the good stuff with them when they left. The thought gave him pause. What happened to them? Did they get away in time? Did they suffer the same fate as those people whose cars had been abandoned on the highway? The bag of lollipops meant they probably had a young child. What happened to him or her? Jim prayed the child was all right. But after his time in Iraq and Afghanistan, he knew children suffered and died in war just as much as adults.

The three headed outside, Val with a plastic bag for the food, while Jim and Doug carried jugs of water. They piled in the truck and headed back to the highway. They stopped at two more farmhouses along the way. Both were also empty, and both also showed signs of the owners leaving in a hell of a hurry.

They continued down Highway 68, still weaving around abandoned vehicles. The buildings became more plentiful as they neared Cadiz itself. Jim instructed Valerie to take the exit to downtown, ostensibly to gather any intelligence they could. Mainly, Jim just wanted to see if there were any other people around.

There has to be.

"Holy shit," Chuck stammered as they entered the Cadiz Main Historic District.

Valerie gaped, while Jim stared out the window, his mouth in a tight line.

Several vehicles sat along the street, either riddled by bullets or blackened by fire. More than one building had been gutted by fire. Not a single light shone anywhere.

They also saw no people.

Valerie continued to drive through the downtown area. Town hall was nothing but a pile of charred rubble. The same with the police department.

Icy needles pierced Jim's spine and dug deep into his stomach. He clenched his teeth, scanning the night, hoping for some sign, any sign, of people.

What if we're the last people on Earth?

He tried to shake that thought off. It was illogical. Six billion people couldn't just disappear like that. There had to be others out there. They would find them.

But it would bring him much comfort if he could see another human being right now.

They stopped at a convenience store, hoping to get more supplies. The glass doors had been shattered, with numerous shards spread out in front of the entryway. Jim led Doug and Valerie inside while Chuck guarded the truck. His nose crinkled at the rank smell that hung in the air of the store. Spoiled food.

No power, no refrigeration.

The three of them checked the store. A rack had been knocked over, candy bars strewn over the floor. Two glass cooler doors, and several of the drinks behind them, had been shattered. A clear plastic case laid on the floor, some flies buzzing around the donuts inside.

"Looks like they left here in a hurry, too." Val stood by the counter, her flashlight illuminating a circular black bag. "No woman in her right mind would forget her purse. Uh-oh."

"What?" Jim walked over to her.

"Look." Val moved her light across the countertop. Jim noticed two dark stains on it.

Blood.

He leaned over the counter and shined his light on the floor. It wasn't long before he spotted a spent casing from a small-caliber pistol.

"I guess the clerk tried to put up a fight." Jim's eyes shifted back to the blood on the countertop. "Doesn't look like he was successful."

They took all the bottled water they could, along with food that hadn't spoiled like candy and granola bars. They also grabbed a few road maps. From here on out they'd take back roads to Fort Campbell. If the Mothmen were responsible for this, they'd probably have patrols on all the major roads. It made him wonder why they hadn't encountered any coming into Cadiz.

Jim acted as navigator while Valerie drove down one rural road after another without any headlights. Why attract attention? That forced Val to drive at a reasonable speed, which to her meant around 50 miles-per-hour.

Fatigue ebbed away at Jim's consciousness. He checked his watch. 5:15 a.m. He'd been up nearly twenty-four hours now.

Jim did what he could to stay awake, tickling the roof of his mouth with the tip of his tongue, sucking on some of the lollipops they got from the first farmhouse. But his eyes, and the rest of his body, felt so heavy, and the seat was so comfortable. Why not just close his eyes, doze for a little bit . . .

No! He snapped his head back, looking around the rural road, keeping alert for any threats. He then looked at the map, trying to figure out their position. Jim estimated they had to be ten, fifteen miles from Hopkinsville, probably another twenty miles from Fort Campbell. The thought sent a burst of energy through him. Soon they'd be at a secure location. Soon they'd find out what the hell was going on.

Unless there's no one at Campbell.

The first rays of the sun appeared on the horizon as they drove down a road with lots and lots of trees but very few buildings. Jim checked the map again, then looked out the window. On the right he spotted a church with blue wooden siding and a white roof. He leaned closer to the window, wide eyes locked on the parking lot. Or more specifically, the twenty or so vehicles sitting in the parking lot. None of them showed the slightest bit of damage.

"Val." He tapped her shoulder.

"Yeah, I see it. You think there are people in there?"

"Only one way to find out."

Val turned into the parking lot. Jim turned around and woke up Doug and Chuck. All four grabbed their rifles and exited the truck.

That's when he heard the sound. Faint, but audible. Tingles raced up his spine as he faced the church.

"Is that . . . singing?" A bewildered look came over Chuck's face.

Jim could only nod. A fear shot through him. Fear it could be a recording. But no. This sounded live.

He headed for the door, his gait increasing with each step. His sister and cousins followed just as quick.

The front door suddenly opened.

Jim's hand went for his holster. His Ruger came halfway out, then stopped.

A little brown-haired girl in a white dress walked outside. She stopped when she saw them.

"Um . . . hello," she said in a small voice.

"Hey there." Jim forced a smile and took a step toward her. "What's your name?"

The girl started to shrink away. "I'm not supposed to talk to strangers."

"Well that's good." Valerie came forward, flashing a wide smile. "But you don't have to worry about us. We're with the Army. We're here to help."

The little girl relaxed.

"So what's your name?"

"Amanda."

"Amanda, that's a pretty name. Are your mommy and daddy in the church?"

"Mm-hmm." Amanda nodded.

"So why are you here?"

"We're praying."

Valerie chuckled. "Of course. Why else would you be at a church?" She stepped closer to the little girl. "Amanda, can you tell me and my friends what's been happening? You're the first person we've seen in a long time."

"Oh. It's Armee . . . um, *Arm-ee-gidden*."

"You mean Armageddon?" Val asked. Jim drew his head back, surprised a little girl would know a word like that.

"Yeah. That's what Mister Preacher said. He said it's the end of the world."

CHAPTER 5

Leaving Chuck behind to guard the truck and the two dead Mothmen, Jim, Val and Doug followed little Amanda into the Second South Congregational Church. The singing grew louder as they walked through hallways lit by candles and the emerging rays of the sun filtering through windows. Amanda led them down a carpeted staircase and into a basement. Jim stared at a wooden double-doors in front of him. The sound of many voices singing a hymn came from behind it.

"Everyone's in there." Amanda pointed to the door. She then lowered her voice. "But you have to be quiet. We're all singing and praying."

Jim nodded and smiled at her. He gripped the brass handles and slowly drew back the doors.

A group of about forty people, of all ages, stood in a large room with a tiled floor. There were no windows, but well over a hundred candles flickered from one end of the room to the other to provide illumination.

Joy and relief burst inside him. How many times over the past few hours did he start to believe he, his sister and his cousins were the last people on Earth? He mentally kicked himself for having such a stupid thought.

Jim slung his hunting rifle over his shoulder. Valerie and Doug did the same and followed him inside.

The "congregation" wrapped up their hymn. At the front of the room stood a rotund, balding man tightly gripping a bible.

"Yes, brothers and sisters. Pour out your love to The Lord. Show him you believe in his power, in his love. For this is the only way we can be saved."

"Amen!" responded several people.

Jim stepped toward the aisle separating the rows of people and stared straight at the preacher. The large man opened his mouth, prepared to go on, when his eyes fell on him.

"Well, well," he smiled. "It appears we have more friends seeking salvation. Amanda, sweetheart. Did you find these people?"

"Yes, Mister Preacher."

The congregation turned to them. A pretty blond woman next to a square-jawed young man gasped. "Amanda! Were you outside?"

"Yes, Mommy."

"We told you not to go outside," said the man. "It's too dangerous."

"I'm sorry, Daddy. I just wanted to see the sun come up."

Head down, Amanda trudged over to her parents. Her mother wrapped her up in a suffocating hug.

"And what are your names?" Reverend Crawford asked.

"I'm Major Jim Rhyne. My sister, Lieutenant Valerie Rhyne, and my cousin, Lieutenant Doug Rhyne. United States Army."

The preacher smiled. "Well, you're all welcome to stay here and pray with us."

"Actually," Jim took a step forward, "we were hoping you could tell us what's been going on, Sir."

"It's Reverend Crawford, son."

"Sorry." Jim nodded to him. "Could you please tell us what's going on, Reverend?"

"I'm saving these people, saving them so we can all enter the Lord's kingdom when the time comes."

Jim cocked an eyebrow, gazing around at the congregation. Some smiled, apparently looking forward to salvation. Others looked very worried. No, that wasn't the right word. They looked downright terrified.

He turned back to Reverend Crawford. "Yeah. Okay. Actually, I meant what's happening in Kentucky? We drove through Cadiz a few hours ago. The place was deserted, there were signs of fighting, and it looked got the he . . . er, heck, out of there in a hurry."

"It's gotta be the demons," blurted out a tall, brown-haired man two rows away from Jim.

"Demons?" Valerie tilted her head as she looked at him.

The man nodded. "I saw 'em. Flying over the city, carrying people away."

"What exactly did they look like?" asked Jim.

"Well, there were different ones. Some looked like big bats, but some had horns and long tails. Just the way you'd expect demons to look."

Jim nodded. He had no idea where this guy came up with the horns and tail description. Then again, any cop or lawyer would tell you eyewitness testimony is never one hundred percent reliable. But that first description perfectly matched the two creatures lying in the bed of Valerie's truck.

"What city did you see this in?" he asked the guy.

"Hopkinsville. We're from Hopkinsville." The guy put an arm around a plump, dark-haired woman and stared down at a round little girl with black curly hair. His wife and daughter, Jim assumed. "We were lucky to get out of there alive. God must have been looking out for us."

"Hopkinsville," Doug said. "Did you happen to go by Fort Campbell? Was everything all right there?"

"We heard a lot of gunfire and explosions coming from there. Saw a lot of smoke, too."

Jim clenched his jaw. From the guy's account, it sounded like there'd been one hell of a battle at Fort Campbell. His stomach constricted in dread. Did the troops there manage to hold onto the base, or had it been destroyed?

The Hundred-First Airborne is there. Those are some tough dudes. If anyone can hold onto that base, it's them.

At least he hoped so. And since he was in a church, he prayed it was so.

"When did all this happen?" Doug asked.

"Two, three days ago," answered a heavyset, middle-age woman.

Jim stared at her, digesting her answer. That would explain why none of the newspapers they found in Cadiz mentioned anything about these Mothmen.

"Do you know if this is happening anywhere else in the country? Anywhere in the world?"

"Hard to say," replied a balding man with a noticeable paunch. "TV went out a little bit before those demons showed up. Same with the phones and the radio."

"I heard some stuff." A skinny teenager with glasses and acne blazing on his cheeks raised his hand.

"What kind of stuff, kid?" Jim stepped closer to the teen's row.

"Um, well, I was on a couple of blogs, and there were people saying there were lots of explosions in New York and Chicago. One guy wrote he saw these flying monsters over

Norfolk. I thought he was making it up until . . . well, until those demons showed up here."

"Anything else?" asked Valerie.

The teen shook his head. "No. Sorry. The whole internet crashed after that."

A chill coated Jim's spine. Fear clawed at his mind, threatening to consume it. He closed his eyes, fighting it off, trying to think rationally.

The Mothmen attacked Fort Campbell, a large and very important military base. They attacked New York and Chicago, two major metropolitan areas. They attacked Norfolk, Virginia, home to one of the U.S. Navy's biggest bases. All forms of communication had been disabled.

The picture had become crystal clear to him, and terrifying. The Mothmen had launched a full-scale invasion of the United States.

"So where did these things come from?" Doug asked.

"Isn't it obvious, son?" Reverend Crawford answered. "They come from Hell."

Doug snorted and rolled his eyes. "I mean how did they really get here? Some sort of, I don't know, spaceship or something?"

"This is not Hollywood make believe." Agitation crept into Reverend Crawford's voice. "There are no such things as aliens. These are demons from the very bowels of Hell come to feast on the flesh of man and carry their souls to the fiery pit for all eternity."

"With all due respect, Reverend," Jim approached him. "I seriously doubt there's anything demonic about these things."

Crawford's eyes widened. For a second he looked outraged at Jim. The expression quickly softened, changing to one of pity. "Major, are you familiar with the Book of Revelation?"

"A little. That's all the end of the world stuff."

"Then all you have to do is look around you to see that the prophecies have come to pass. All these years of turning our backs on The Lord, of becoming slaves to greed and depravity and unbound fornication and wickedness, He could take no more of it. The angel sounded the trumpets. The great earthquakes, rivers and oceans rising up and killing hundreds of thousands, the constant wars, the famines in Africa and Asia. These were preludes. The preparations are being made for the final battle between good and evil. As it reads in Chapter Six, Verses Seven and Eight, of the Book of Revelation, an army of two hundred million shall come and kill a third of the Earth's population. That army is here in the form of demons."

Many in the congregation nodded.

"Look." Jim turned to them. "I know you're all scared. Let's face it, what's happening is about as far from the norm as you can get. These things may look like demons, but I can assure you, they're not."

"How do you know?" shouted a man in the audience.

"Because I doubt any demon would go around wearing a helmet and body armor and carrying an automatic rifle."

"You lie!" a woman hollered.

"Are you mocking us, young man?" added an older gentleman.

Jim scanned the congregation. Concern flooded through him. Would these people charge him? Beat him for being a non-believer? Would they do the same to Val and Doug?

"Calm down, folks. Calm down." Reverend Crawford waved his hands up and down, quickly settling his congregation. He then looked to Jim. "Now, Major, I'm sure you and your kin here have served this country nobly, and for that we all thank you. And maybe all your Army training makes you want to think rationally. But no amount of rational thinking can change the fact, the absolute fact, that demons have been set loose upon this world. Armageddon has begun. Don't let them take your soul to Hell. Stay here with us. Give yourself over to The Lord. I am sure you fought bravely against human enemies, but against these demons, all your weapons and all your training will be for naught."

"Actually, that's not true, Reverend. We've got two of those demon things lying in the back of our pick-up truck, both with bullet holes in their heads."

Gasps went up from many in the congregation. Several people turned to one another and held whispered conversations. A few shouted at him, accusing him of lying.

"If you don't believe me, go outside and see for yourselves. If those things really were demons, with all the supernatural powers they're supposed to have, I doubt I would've been able to take out one with a regular ol' Ruger pistol you can get at any gun shop for a few hundred bucks."

The hushed conversations grew louder. A handful of people shook their heads, disbelieving looks on their faces.

"Listen," Jim continued. "It's not safe to stay here."

"Where do you want us to go?" asked Reverend Crawford. "Out there? You want us to leave this sanctuary and risk having those demons rip out our souls and drag them to Hell?"

"They're not demons. They're soldiers. I don't know where they came from, I don't know what exactly they are, but they're not demons from Hell. And you gave them one gigantic clue that there are people in this building."

"What are you talking about?" Crawford furrowed his brow.

"Your cars. You must have twenty parked out there. If a squad of those monsters comes by here and sees all those cars, they're going to investigate. What do you think made us stop here?"

Jim noted a more panicked tone in the congregation's not-so-hushed conversations. He spotted little Amanda in the crowd, her father clutching her tightly against his leg.

A horrible image formed in his mind. The Mothmen smashing their way into the church, grabbing Amanda, the little girl screaming as they dragged her off to God only knew where.

Anger replaced fear, then determination replaced anger. He couldn't allow Amanda, or any of these people, to be captured or killed by the Mothmen.

"You have got to believe me," Jim went on. "Reverend, you have to tell your people it is not safe here anymore. I told you we drove through Cadiz before we came here. There's probably, what, a few thousand people in that town? We didn't find anyone there. Not a single person. And before that, one of those monsters used some kind of sonic device to try and incapacitate Doug and his brother. It's making me think they don't want to just kill us. They want to capture us. For what, I don't know. To turn us into slaves or to study us or to suck out our brains. I don't know, and I don't want to find out first-hand."

"Out there you risk your eternal soul," said Crawford. "In here, at least, we can prepare our souls to join God in His kingdom."

Jim gritted his teeth and exhaled slowly, shifting his focus between Reverend Crawford and his congregation. He noticed concern and doubt on the faces of more than a few people. Maybe he was finally getting through. The vast majority, however, seemed like they believed staying here and praying would save them from the Mothmen.

He turned back to Crawford. The man appeared more concerned than angry. That was good. If the reverend became angry, Jim would be worried he had a cult leader on his hands. Thankfully, he didn't get that vibe from Crawford. From what he'd seen on History Channel documentaries about cult leaders, they didn't tolerate an ounce of dissent from anyone. Crawford allowed him to have the floor and speak his piece. Cult leaders also usually had armed thugs around their compound to discourage anyone from entering and, more importantly, to keep anyone from leaving. This church didn't have so much as a night watchman with a flashlight and a big-ass set of keys.

Another positive sign was the absence of any big bowls of cyanide-flavored fruit punch.

Good. I have a chance to convince them to –

A number of faint, high-pitched yelps from outside filtered into the basement. Jim, Val and Doug all lifted their heads toward the ceiling.

"You have dogs here?" Doug asked.

"Some of these people brought their pets with them when they fled their homes," Crawford explained. "We put them out back in our playground."

Jim held his breath, concentrating on the barking. Hinkey hairs went up on the back of his neck. The barks grew louder, and more panicked.

"Guys! Guys!"

He whipped his head to the open door, instantly recognizing Chuck's voice, shouting from upstairs.

"Guys! Get up here! Now!"

Jim unslung his rifle and dashed for the door. He glanced back to find Val and Doug right behind him.

They pounded up the stairs and emerged on the ground floor.

"C'mon!" Chuck waved at them from the other end of the hallway. "C'mon!"

They hurried toward him, catching up just as he pushed open the door leading outside.

"What is it?" Jim demanded.

"Look!" Chuck pointed a finger skyward.

Jim raised his head . . . and swallowed.

Twenty Mothmen appeared at treetop level, flying straight for the church.

CHAPTER 6

"Back inside! Now!"

Jim herded his sister and cousins through the door. He turned and slammed it shut.

"C'mon! We gotta hold 'em off!" He bounded over to a nearby window. Lifting his hunting rifle, he used the wooden butt to smash out the glass. His stomach turned into a cold ball as he watched the Mothmen soar over the parking lot. He glanced over at Valerie, Doug and Chuck, who also busted windows with their rifle butts. Fear grew inside him. They were outnumbered five-to-one. They had to take on flying, automatic rifle-toting monsters with hunting rifles. The odds were definitely against them.

Jim thought of Reverend Crawford's congregation down in the basement. Scared, defenseless. He thought of little Amanda. A chill went down his spine as he imagined one of those Mothmen carrying her away.

Fuck the odds.

He drew back the bolt of his rifle and stuck the barrel through the window. Peering through the scope, he drew a bead on a Mothman descending into the parking lot. He settled the crosshairs on the monster's face, then lowered the rifle, anticipating where its head would be.

Crack!

The Mothman's head jerked back. A spray of blood shot through the air. The monster dropped onto the roof of a car and bounced off it onto the ground.

More rifle shots rang out through the lobby. Another Mothman tumbled out of the sky. Jim chambered another round, aimed at a Mothman that landed next to a pick-up truck, and fired. It stumbled backwards, but didn't go down.

Musta hit its body armor, dammit.

Jim drew back the bolt again.

Deep rattles echoed from outside.

"Geddown!" Doug hollered.

Jim dropped to his knees as snaps and thuds burst around him. Bullets tore through the walls and the door. Splinters of wood and plaster rained down on him.

Shit! Shit! Shit! He scowled at his hunting rifle. This was not the weapon to have in a fight like this.

Well an M-4 or M-249 isn't gonna just appear in your hands. Make do with what you got.

Mothmen bullets continued to punch through the walls. Jim looked across the lobby. Chuck crouched, trembling, his hands over his head. Val and Doug risked firing one shot each through their windows.

Jim drew a quick breath and rose. He quickly scanned the parking lot. Three Mothmen weaved their way through the parked cars.

A stream of bullets ripped through the wall just above his head. He snapped off a shot in the direction of a Mothman and ducked back down.

"Reloading!" Doug shoved more rounds into his rifle.

Val fired through the window. "I'm out, too!"

"Chuck!" Doug shouted at his brother. "Lay down some fire!"

Chuck looked up at him, shivering, his eyes wide.

"Dammit, Chuck! Shoot those sons-of-bitches!"

Chuck's chest rose and fell rapidly. His unblinking eyes looked from Doug to the window, then back to his brother.

"Fire, dammit! They're gonna kill us if you don't fire!"

Jim rose and spotted a Mothmen setting up what looked like a light machine gun on the hood of a car. He took quick aim at its head and fired. The monster crumpled out of sight.

He drew back the bolt, saw two Mothmen running for the side of the church, and fired.

Missed. And his magazine was empty to boot.

More bullets tore into the walls and the door. Jim set down his rifle and drew his handgun. He fired five rounds rapid through the window. At this range the best he could hope was to keep the Mothmen's heads down.

He noticed movement over the parking lot. Four Mothmen flew up to the roof.

"They're gonna hit us from all sides!" Jim shouted to the others. He bit his lip. They couldn't hold off these monsters much longer.

"C'mon! Down to the basement!" He fired three more rounds through the window, slung his rifle over his shoulder, and dashed into the hallway. Val followed.

"Dammit, Chuck! Get your ass up!" Doug yanked his younger brother to his feet. Chuck trembled, the color drained from his face. Doug had to push him along as more Mothmen rounds tore apart the façade of the church.

They pounded down the stairs and burst into the basement. Many of the congregation held hands, their voices raised in prayer, or sobs, or a combination of both.

"Reverend!" Jim raced to the front of the room. "Reverend! The Mothmen are about to breech this place. We gotta get outta here. Now!"

Reverend Crawford looked up at him, tears glistening in his eyes. His jaw trembled before he spoke. "There's no place to go. But our souls will be saved, son. Our souls will be saved."

"Reverend, these things are going to kill you. All of you! You have to leave. Now!"

Crawford shook his head and continued reciting the "Our Father."

"Reverend!" Jim grabbed the heavyset man by the collar. He winced for a moment. Putting your hands on a holy man was just not something you did. But right now he didn't have time to be nice. "We have to leave now! Is there another way out besides the front door?"

Crawford just stared at him with wide, unblinking eyes.

Two deep thumps echoed above them.

"Reverend! How do we get out of here?"

"B-Back door. Over there." He nodded to the left. Jim spotted a doorway leading to a set of stairs.

He let go of Crawford and turned to the congregation. "Everyone listen up! We are getting out of here now. My family will give you covering fire. If we can't get to our vehicles, follow us into the woods. We'll try to lose them there."

Some of the people looked up at him. Jim tried to push down his anxiety. He willed the congregation to follow him.

No one moved. They just continued praying and crying.

"You're gonna die if you stay here! Now move it!"

The prayers and sobs just grew louder.

"Oh shit! They're here!" Doug used the open door as cover and fired his rifle. Several screams interrupted the praying. Doug chambered another round and fired.

Jim whipped his head around. His eyes fell on little Amanda, smushed between her parents, who prayed as tears streamed down their cheeks.

"At least let us get the children outta here!"

That prompted most parents to grip their sons and daughters tightly.

"Dammit, what is wrong with you people!?"

"Jim!" Valerie rushed over to him as Doug fired again. "They're not gonna leave."

"No shit, Val! Then we'll just drag 'em out of here."

"There's gotta be forty, fifty people here. You think we can do that with every single one of them?"

"We can't just leave 'em here to die!"

"And we can't hold off those Mothmen!" Val's shoulders rose and fell rapidly. "We're outnumbered and outgunned, and these people think staying here and praying is the only way they can save themselves. You can't change their minds."

"We're soldiers, Val. We took an oath to protect this country and its people. We're not gonna leave them."

"And we're not gonna accomplish anything by staying here and dying. We need to get to Fort Campbell, deliver those Mothmen bodies and their equipment, then link up with whatever units are still there and continue to fight these things."

Jim opened his mouth to argue, then stopped when he heard something. A high-pitched sound bleeding through the ceiling. His chest tightened when he recognized it.

The Mothman sonic weapon.

Nausea rippled through his stomach. Tiny hammers pounded the inside of his skull. He looked around. Several members of the congregation grimaced. A few sagged at the knees.

Panic bubbled inside him. How long before the effects got worse? Before they couldn't even stand? Before they'd be at the mercy of the Mothmen?

He had to get his family out of here. But how could he leave dozens of innocent people behind to suffer who knew what fate?

Val's right. You won't get them to leave.

We're soldiers. We have to protect them.

The nausea burned Jim's stomach. His knees buckled. He scanned his family. Val started to double over. Chuck pressed his hands over his ears. Doug swayed, dropping the rounds he tried to shove into his rifle. He judged they only had seconds before they were incapacitated.

I'm sorry. I'm so sorry.

"Go! Go! Go!" He pushed Val toward the back exit. She stumbled toward it as he staggered toward Chuck. He shoved him toward the door, while Doug hurried after him on wobbly legs.

Jim staggered down the aisle. His legs turned to jelly. His skull vibrated.

Move. Move. Move.

He clenched his teeth, forcing his feet forward, pushing down the bile threatening to rush up his throat. The room rolled from side to side. He tried to concentrate on the exit. Val, Chuck and Doug already made it through, using the wall to support themselves.

Jim stumbled. By sheer force of will he stayed on his feet.

Not far. Keep moving.

His head felt ready to explode. Now he saw two exits in front of him.

Grunting, he lunged toward what he hoped was the right one.

His foot hit something solid. He fell forward, banging his elbow on a step. The world blurred.

Someone grabbed him by the arm and hoisted him up. Panic swelled inside him. Was it a Mothman?

He looked up into the face of his cousin Doug.

"C'mon, Jim!"

He let Doug guide him up the steps. The buzzing started to fade, as did the nausea and disorientation.

"You okay?" Doug asked.

Jim took a couple deep breaths, trying to regain his senses. "Yeah. Yeah, I'm good."

Valerie reached the door first. She twisted the knob and threw it open.

A Mothman stood in front of her.

Val gasped. The monster stared at her. Even with its inhuman face, Jim could make out an expression of shock.

The monster brought up its rifle.

Val swung her rifle, the butt striking the Mothman weapon. It tumbled out of its clawed hands. She drew back the rifle butt for another blow. The Mothman swung its right arm, nailing Val in the gut. She slammed against the open door, dropped her rifle and crumpled onto the walkway.

"Val!" Doug vaulted up the stairs and tackled the Mothman. They both fell to the ground.

That's when a second Mothman appeared.

Chuck brought his rifle up to waist level, hands shaking. The shot exploded in the confined space, rattling Jim's skull.

The round missed, but it got the second Mothman to turn toward them. Jim raised his Ruger pistol and fired until it clicked empty. The monster's head snapped back. It staggered and collapsed.

Jim started moving before the Mothman hit the ground. He rushed out the door and spied Val on the ground, clutching her ribs. Doug and the first Mothman rolled on the ground. The monster shrieked and pinned Doug on his back.

Jim flipped his empty Ruger, clutching it by the warm barrel. He raised the pistol over his head and brought it down on the Mothman's shoulder. The monster turned to him. Jim pivoted to his side and kicked the Mothman in the face. It fell on its side.

Jim dropped his pistol and reached for his survival knife. The Mothman rolled on its back and tried to push itself up. Jim leapt on it and rammed the knife into its throat. The monster went rigid. He pressed his left hand on the Mothman's hairy cheek. Tensing, he snapped the monster's head to the left, and yanked the knife in the opposite direction. The Mothman's throat ripped wide open, spewing a river of blood.

Jim let out a long breath, the tension vanishing from his muscles.

You're not out of the woods yet.

"C'mon." He got to his feet, wiping his blood-stained hands and knife on his pants. "We gotta go."

Doug helped Valerie up, asking if she was all right.

"Yeah, I'm fine." She grimaced, rubbing her mid-section. Jim wondered if his sister might have some broken ribs. Not that he could do anything about it right now.

He ejected the spent magazine from his Ruger and inserted a fresh one. After scanning the area and finding no sign of any more Mothmen, he led the others around the church. He spotted Valerie's truck, then swept his eyes over the parking lot. No sign of any other sentries. Hopefully the two Mothmen he killed were the only ones outside the church.

Val quickly checked the front of her truck. "I don't see any bullet holes. Looks like we're in good shape."

Jim nodded. "Doug. You and me, in the back."

His cousin's brow furrowed. "Why?"

"Because if the Mothmen come after us, we can give Val cover fire."

He and Doug climbed into the bed of the pick-up just as the engine roared to life. Jim drew his Ruger P944 pistol as the truck shot forward.

That's when he noticed dark shapes to his left. He turned and held his breath.

Two Mothmen stood on the roof of the church. One of them pointed at the truck, then turned to its companion. They spread their wings, leaped off the roof and flew after them.

Jim slammed his palm on the truck's back window. "Go! Go! Go!"

Valerie gunned the engine. The truck tore out of the parking lot and made a sharp right, throwing Jim into Doug. The two untangled themselves and looked back toward the church. The two Mothmen banked right and kept after them, flying about twenty feet off the ground.

The wind whipped around him as the truck sped up. The Mothmen flapped their wings furiously. Jim's eyes widened. The monsters were gaining on them.

How fast can these things fly?

Doug crawled over the tarp covering the dead Mothmen and pressed himself against the hatch. He leveled his pistol and fired. Jim joined him seconds later. Accuracy with a pistol at this distance, and in a moving vehicle, was too much to ask for. Hopefully they could put enough lead in the air and get lucky.

The Mothmen fired back. Rounds zipped over their heads. A sharp crack sounded behind Jim. He turned and swallowed in fright. A round had shattered the back window.

Val. Chuck.

The fear that filled him faded when he saw two heads in the front of the cab turning to one another.

Jim turned back to the Mothmen, who were still gaining on them. Rage flared inside him. My God, he'd come so close to losing his sister and cousin.

He emptied his Ruger at the Mothmen, reloaded, and fired again. Doug added his pistol to the mini-barrage. One of the Mothmen jerked and dropped to the asphalt, tumbling over and over.

The remaining Mothman opened up with its rifle. Jim and Doug jumped as two rounds punched into the hatch. They fired back as the truck swerved left and right. No doubt Val was trying to throw off its aim.

"I'm out!" Doug hollered.

"Me too!" Jim felt around his waist, trying to find another magazine. The breath stuck in his throat when the realization hit him.

He had no more mags.

Jim looked over to Doug. The look on his cousin's face said it all. He, too, had used up his last magazine.

Jim gazed over the latch. The Mothman drew closer. Forty feet away. Thirty. It fired again just as Val cut to the left. None of the rounds found their mark.

Jim unslung his rifle and reloaded it. He had to keep firing at that thing. Maybe he'd get lucky and . . .

His eyes fell on the tarp that covered the Mothmen bodies. He then looked to the Mothman, then back at the tarp.

No way this is gonna work.

What choice do you have?

"Doug. Help me with the tarp."

His cousin scrunched up his face in puzzlement. "Huh?"

"Just grab it!"

Jim yanked the right side of the tarp off the Mothmen corpses. Doug grabbed the left side and pulled. Jim looked back at the pursuing Mothman, now twenty feet away.

The truck swerved left, then right. The Mothman tracked it with its rifle.

Jim held up his side of the tarp. Doug did the same with his side. The blue covering flapped in the wind.

"Let go!"

The tarp flew away from them, twisting and turning in the wind. The Mothman veered to the right. Jim clenched his teeth. It wasn't going to –

The tarp got tangled around the edge of the monster's right wing. It jerked to the right, flapping its wings like mad. Arms flailing, the Mothman rolled on its back and slammed into the asphalt. Its rifle skidded away as it rolled another thirty feet. When it finally stopped rolling, it lay sprawled on the roadway for a few seconds, then fought to push itself up.

Tires squealed. The pick-up suddenly slowed, throwing both Jim and Doug on their backs. The sky above him spun around. White smoke rose from the tires. The smell of burning rubber filled the air.

"Val! What the hell are you doing?"

His words were lost over the deafening roar of the engine. The pick-up sped down the road. Jim pushed himself up and peered over the cab, hurricane-like wind buffeting his face.

The Mothman slowly rose to all fours, the tarp still wrapped around half its right wing. It shook its head, bent its knees and tried to straighten itself in the middle of the road.

Suddenly its head whipped around. Jim swore its red eyes widened in horror as the pick-up bore down on it.

A solid *thump* shook the vehicle. He heard another thump a split-second later as the pick-up bounced over something. Jim turned around. The Mothman lay in the middle of the road, its body twisted at unnatural angles.

The tension around Jim's muscles dissolved. He exhaled quickly, loudly. His relief only lasted a few seconds.

If those things had radios, they probably told someone about us. And when those two didn't report back to their CO, the Mothmen would send out search parties, for both their missing soldiers *and* for him and his family.

He crawled across the bed and put his face up to the big hole in the back window. "You guys okay?"

"We're fine," Val said.

"Yeah. I'm . . . I'm okay." Chuck's voice quivered.

"Val, we need to get off this road."

"I'm way ahead of you, big brother."

Less than a mile later, Val turned left onto a forest road. The truck bounced over the dirt surface. Jim looked up at the canopy of trees. This should shield them from any aerial patrols the Mothmen might put up.

He pressed his back against the cab, the adrenaline wearing off. His heartbeat settled down. Relief flooded him. He was alive. He sister and cousins were alive.

But what about the people back at the church?

Anger swelled within him. That anger soon turned to guilt. He thought about Reverend Crawford. He thought about the acne-scarred teen.

He thought of little Amanda.

What would the Mothmen do to them?

Jim's face twisted in fury. Tears stung his eyes.

"Jim? Hey, Jim? What's wrong?"

He ignored Doug's question. All he could think of was the people back at that church.

He let out a tortured cry and pounded his fist on the metal bed. A tear slid down his cheek. He'd failed to save those people.

Just like he had failed to save Hannah.

CHAPTER 7

Jim and his family continued along the dirt road for another twenty minutes before he called for Valerie to stop.

"How much gas do we have?" he asked his sister after she pulled next to a clump of trees.

"Just under half-a-tank."

He nodded. That would be plenty to get them to Fort Campbell.

"Everybody check your ammo."

Jim sat next to one of the wheel wells, examined his rifle's magazine, then went through his hunting vest. What he discovered made him scowl.

He only had fourteen rounds left for his rifle. The number of rounds for his Ruger pistol, zero.

The news wasn't any better from Doug. He carried just twelve rifle rounds and nothing for his pistol. Valerie was down to eight rifle rounds and one full clip for her SiG-Sauer P230.

Dammit. Jim clenched his teeth. They couldn't afford to get into another firefight with the Mothmen.

"I guess I'm not bad."

Everyone turned to Chuck, who sat near the front of Val's pick-up.

"I still got twenty rounds for my rifle and all my bullets for my Colt King Cobra."

"Well that's not a surprise." Doug got to his feet and slowly walked toward his younger brother. "Considering you spent most of your time back at the church cowering on the floor instead of shooting those damn monsters."

Chuck lowered his head and cleared his throat. "Um, uh . . . look, man. I'm sorry about that, okay?"

"Sorry? You think sorry cuts it in a situation like that? We needed every gun back there, Chuck. Just sitting there pissing your pants didn't help any of us. You're lucky none of us got killed because of it."

"I said I'm sorry!" Chuck sprang to his feet. "Shit, what the hell do you want from me? Those fuckin' Mothmen were shooting up the whole church."

"It's combat, Chuck! That's what happens. They shoot at you, and you shoot back. And I know you can shoot. You've been hunting since you were six."

"Well deer and ducks don't shoot back, you dumbass!"

"Don't talk to me like that!" Doug shoved a finger in his brother's face. "Not after you turned into a pussy back there!"

"Get outta my face!" Chuck slapped away Doug's finger.

Doug's eyes grew wide. His cheeks burned red. He stepped toward Chuck, fists clenched. Chuck didn't back away.

Jim started toward them. His was about to shout when Valerie rushed between the brothers.

"Knock it off! Both of you!" She rammed both hands into Doug's chest. "Bad enough we have a bunch of flying monsters trying to kill us, we don't need you two doing their job for them."

"He started it!" Chuck stabbed a finger at his brother.

Val turned to him, eyes narrowed. "Oh, grow the hell up."

"What are you gonna do?" Doug's shoulders rose and fell with angry breaths as he stared down at Val. "Coddle him? He's gonna get us all killed if he doesn't grow a fuckin' set."

"Fuck you!" Chuck tried to lunge past Valerie to get at Doug.

"Chuck!" Jim barked, pointing to the ground next to him. "Over here."

"What for?"

Anger burst inside Jim. This kind of thing did not happen in his world. When a major told a subordinate, "come here," they obeyed, no questions asked.

But Chuck's a civilian.

"Chuck," he softened his voice. "Just come here, okay?"

With one last harsh look at Doug, Chuck stomped his way over to him.

"Let's take a walk." He placed a hand in his cousin's back and guided him down the dirt road.

"I'm sick of this shit, Jim." Chuck's face twisted into a mask of rage. "Two years he's been on my ass about this.

Two fuckin' years! So I wanted to play baseball instead of join the Army. It's a free country, and it's my fuckin' life!"

Jim just nodded. Chuck's decision not to enlist was a continuing source of consternation in the family. The Rhynes could trace their military service back to the Civil War. To them, America had given them freedoms and opportunities they never would have had in many other countries. Ever since Jim could remember, his parents and other relatives talked about their obligation to protect those freedoms and opportunities not only for themselves, but for everyone else in the country.

Doesn't that also include Chuck's freedom to decide if he wants to serve or not?

Jim would have liked to have seen him serve, but Chuck was an adult now. The decision to either join the military or play college baseball was his and his alone.

"What the fuck does he want from me!?" Chuck spun to face him, arms out to his sides. "There were bullets flying all over the place. I mean, how the hell can anyone think with all that shit going on."

"You just do, Chuck."

"Yeah, easy for you to say. You and Val and Doug have been through that shit before. I haven't!"

"Well now you have." Jim's tone grew a little more forceful. "Look, we are dealing with some serious shit here. We've got monsters from who-knows-where invading the country, maybe the entire world. If we're gonna get through this, we've got to keep it together."

Chuck let out a loud sigh and scowled at the ground.

Jim grasped his cousin's shoulder. "Chuck. I know you're pissed off at your brother right now, and you probably don't want to hear this, but in one aspect, Doug's right."

Chuck's eyes bulged in shock. "What? Doug's right? Bullshit. Doug's an asshole."

"No. He's right about what happened back at the church. Right now the only people we have to depend on are each other. If we get into another fight with the Mothmen, every one of us has got to do their part."

"I shot at that one Mothman, you know."

"And you did it totally scared. Your hands were shaking, you didn't aim properly, and you missed. We can't afford that in another firefight. I need to know, right now, that if we have another run-in with these things, you're gonna have our backs."

Chuck huffed, his gaze drifting toward the ground. "Yeah, yeah. I will." He turned away.

"Chuck, I'm serious here. I have to know that next time the bullets are flying, you are not gonna fall to pieces."

"I said I will, okay? What the hell else do you want me to say?"

Scowling, Chuck stomped back to the pick-up.

Jim sighed, fighting the urge to go after him. Chuck's answer did not satisfy him at all. It was the sort of affirmative answer a nineteen-year-old gave because he wanted to be left alone, not because he meant it. Any other time he would have dragged Chuck back here, civilian or not, and kept at him until he was firmly convinced the kid would do his job if and when the time came.

But right now Chuck's emotions had reached full boil. Hell, everyone was emotional. They hadn't had much sleep in well over twenty-four hours and they'd just been through a hellacious firefight with an enemy not even human.

They all needed a break.

He headed back to the truck. Chuck leaned against a tree pouting. Near the front of the truck Val talked to Doug, who looked just as pissed as his brother.

"Listen up, everyone," Jim said. "We've been on the go a long time, and we're in a pretty secluded spot. We should be okay for the time being. So let's take advantage of this and get some rest. Four hours. Everyone does a turn on watch, one hour each. I've got the first shift. The rest of you get some shuteye."

He unslung his rifle and stood guard. Val sacked out in the front seat of her pick-up, while Chuck laid down in the back seat. Doug found a patch of earth under a shade tree and fell asleep there.

Jim's eyes darted around the woods, scanning for any Mothmen. He also listened for any sounds out of the ordinary.

The minutes dragged on without any sign of Mothmen. Jim's tired mind struggled to stay alert. He forced himself to look in all directions for any monsters. Unfortunately, he couldn't stop his mind from wandering. Were his parents all right? Were Doug and Chuck's parents all right? Was the U.S. winning this war or getting its ass kicked? Was the war already over?

What happened to those people back at the church?

When his shift ended, he woke Doug up to take over for him. Jim then curled up on the same patch of ground his cousin had just slept on. Seconds after he closed his eyes, he fell asleep.

He found himself kneeling in some living room. It took him a moment to recognize it. Hannah's old apartment, the one she lived in before they got married.

He raised his head and saw a slender woman with shoulder-length blond hair and a round face sitting on the coach, tears streaming from her blood shot eyes.

"I tried," she sobbed. "Dammit, I tried. But I just felt so much better with each drink and . . . I couldn't stop. I wanted to stop, but I couldn't."

Jim held his breath. He remembered this day. One of Hannah's last big benders before she finally got sober.

"What do I keep telling you?" He took hold of her hand. "You don't need booze. If things get bad, you come to me, and we talk about it. Got it? We've done this before. You know you can always count on me. If you ever have a problem, I'll be here for you."

Suddenly Hannah vanished. Panic filled him. He swung his head in all directions. Where was she? She can't be gone. She . . .

"Jim."

The living room vanished. Jim's eyes flickered open. He found Chuck standing over him.

"Um, sorry, man. But you said four hours, and well, it's four hours."

Jim groaned and rubbed his crusty eyes. "Yeah. Thanks, Chuck."

His cousin nodded and headed back to the truck. Jim followed, the dream lingering in his mind. The words he'd said to Hannah rang inside his head. "You can always count on me." "I'll always be here for you."

Only he wasn't there for her when it counted. He failed her, just like he failed those people back at the church. And now they were probably dead, too.

He stared at Val, Doug and Chuck as they climbed into the truck. He stiffened with determination. *It's not gonna happen to them. I don't care what it takes, I'm getting all of them out of this alive.*

Jim rode shotgun, while his cousins sat in the back, both looking much calmer with a few hours of sleep under them.

"So what now, big brother?" Val asked from behind the wheel.

"Same as before. We head for Fort Campbell. But we stay off-road as much as possible. After that firefight back at the church, we have to assume the Mothmen have a description of this truck, and maybe the four of us. We took out about half that platoon, so those things probably have a hard-on to find us."

"Heh!" Val shook her head. "Monsters putting out APBs. What's next?"

"You know," Doug spoke up. "It might be a good idea if we head south into Tennessee."

Jim turned to him. "Why's that?"

"That's the back end of Fort Campbell. It's mostly woods. There's a bunch of back roads around there that go through the base."

"You think you can get me on one of those roads?" Val asked.

"Definitely." Doug nodded. "I've been on maneuvers with my unit in those areas lots of times."

Jim mulled over his cousin's idea. That was one good thing about Fort Campbell. The base was enormous, encompassing over 100,000 acres, much of it forests and fields to give the 101st Air Assault Division quality training grounds. They'd certainly stand a better chance reaching the fort that way than trying to go through a more built-up area like Hopkinsville.

"Let's do it." He nodded at Doug, then turned to Valerie. His sister smiled and started the engine.

The pick-up bounced over dirt roads and roared down small county roads. When on the paved roads, Jim's eyes constantly scanned the sky for any Mothmen. He prayed these roads were too small for them to patrol on a regular basis. This early in their invasion, they would likely concentrate on the highways and major city and county roads and streets.

Something niggled the back of his mind. *How would they know which roads were important and which ones weren't?*

The same way they knew to target Kentucky and Norfolk.

Human or not, all armies needed one thing before they commenced any invasion.

Intelligence.

The Mothmen had to know well in advance which places in the United States to hit first. But how did they acquire that intelligence? *Probably the same way we would.* They likely had electronic intelligence gathering capabilities. Intercepting radio or TV signals, hacking into the internet, possibly aerial drones. Satellites? He doubted they could launch one without some outfit like NORAD detecting it.

But if they're aliens, they could probably sit in their spaceships and scan the Earth from orbit. And if they had ships capable of interstellar travel, they'd certainly be advanced enough to shield them from any human means of detection.

But there was one critical element missing. Satellites and unmanned drones were fine. But they could be fooled. They couldn't gauge the mood of enemy troops. They couldn't spot small, unique features in the terrain that could prove critical in a fight. Only one intelligence asset could do that.

A living, breathing soldier.

That meant the Mothmen likely had had reconnaissance forces in the United States long before this invasion began.

That must have been difficult. For many of the world's special operations forces, their main job wasn't to fight, but to stay out of sight and observe and report. Most times the enemy never knew they had been there. But every once in a while something happened and a spec ops team got caught. Any Mothmen recon units would have had to get in close to targets like Fort Campbell or Norfolk, increasing the chance of being discovered. And seven-foot bat-looking monsters couldn't exactly blend in with the locals.

Then he remembered when Chuck had first brought up the whole Mothman thing last night.

"Hey, Chuck."

"Yeah?"

"When did you say people first started seeing the Mothman?"

"Um, according to that show I saw, back in the late sixties. Like '67 or '68, I think."

Jim nodded. "And how many people saw this thing?"

"Damn, I dunno. A bunch. I mean, people were seeing this thing for about a year until the bridge collapsed."

"What bridge?" asked Val.

"Oh. On the show, it said people saw Mothman flying over the Silver Bridge. Then one day it collapsed. Killed a lot of people, too. Some people said the Mothman was responsible because nobody saw it around town after that."

"And where was this?" Jim asked.

"Some little town in West Virginia. I don't remember the name."

Jim worked his jaw back and forth. He knew of no major military bases in West Virginia.

"Has Mothman been reported anywhere else? Anywhere recently?"

Chuck stared at the roof of the cab in thought. "Yeah. It's pretty weird, too."

Val cranked an eyebrow. "Weird how?"

"Like, they said some people saw Mothman around New York just before Nine-Eleven, and in Minneapolis before that bridge collapsed a few years ago. There was one guy on the show that said Mothman could be some supernatural being that shows up when something bad is gonna happen."

Any other time, Jim would have dismissed that as bullshit. He never believed in ghosts or hauntings or any sort other supernatural stuff. But now . . .

Well, as he told Reverend Crawford, he didn't think the Mothmen were demons. They sure as hell didn't cause 9/11.

But maybe they got advanced intelligence on it. Maybe they wanted to observe what our response would be to an attack like that.

As for the bridge in Minneapolis, he had no idea why the Mothmen would want to destroy it years before any invasion.

Whatever the case, the show Chuck saw seemed to indicate the Mothmen had been observing the U.S. for decades. And a good number of people had seen them.

So why did the Mothmen let those people live? For the sort of mission they'd been on, SOP would be to eliminate anyone who stumbled across them. Why let them go to blab about their encounter to the world?

Then again, it's not like everyone believed their story. Maybe these things knew about creatures like Bigfoot or the Loch Ness Monster and figured the vast majority of people would treat the Mothman as a legend, too.

Still, why take that chance?

They drove on into the forests of Tennessee. Using a compass, Doug's memory, and a bit of luck, they made it onto a dirt road that Doug was "pretty sure" would take them to Fort Campbell. Jim's plan was to drive as far as possible through the wilderness, then stop a couple miles from the main base and proceed on foot, just in case the Mothmen had taken it over. If that was the case . . .

The truck emerged from the thicket and into a clearing. Jim tensed. *Dammit, we're too exposed.* He eyed the treeline ahead of them. It had to be about three hundred yards away. He swallowed, scanning the sky.

Thankfully, he saw no sign of any Mothmen.

They continued on, getting closer to the treeline. Not fast enough, though, for Jim's taste. He kept looking up at the sky, searching for any –

A fiery comet tumbled from the sky.

"Whoa!"

"What?" Val turned to him.

"We got . . ." His face hovered inches from the window. The burning object spiraled through the air and into a mass of trees about two miles away. Seconds later a plume of flame and smoke rose.

He moved to the windshield and looked up. Several white contrails stretched across the sky.

"Looks like we're right under an air battle."

Val, Chuck and Doug all peered out the windows, trying to catch a glimpse of the action. When they got into the woods, Jim ordered his sister to stop. They exited the truck and hurried to the edge of the treeline, looking up.

Jim recognized two of the aircraft streaking overhead. The pointy nose, the small delta wings. They were F-16 Fighting Falcons. U.S. Air Force. He also spotted four other aircraft. Dark in color, squat, teardrop-shaped with swept wings and forward canards. Definitely not something in the U.S. inventory. It had to be Mothmen.

C'mon, c'mon, he silently cheered the F-16s. *Shoot those bastards down.*

His hopes were quickly dashed. A contrail extended from one of the Mothmen fighters and connected with an F-16. The American fighter vanished in a ball of fire. Anger flared inside Jim. On the edges came another feeling. Sorrow, for the pilot who'd just died.

"Yo, check it out!" Chuck pointed skyward. "That dude's on his ass!"

The remaining F-16 dropped behind a Mothmen fighter. Flashes of yellow appeared between the two aircraft. Fire and smoke trailed from the Mothmen fighter. It nosed over and plummeted toward the ground.

"Yeah!" Jim raised a fist. Val, Doug and Chuck also let out cheers of their own.

"Oh shit! Watch out!" Worry blazed across Val's face as she stared at the sky.

Another Mothmen fighter got on the F-16's tail. The American executed a series of tight turns, hoping to throw off the enemy pilot's aim.

A missile streaked from the belly of the Mothmen fighter. Jim tensed, praying for the F-16 pilot to dodge it.

His prayers went unanswered.

A flash of orange and black blotted out the F-16. Jim closed his eyes and hung his head. Dread grew inside him. Did he just see a microcosm of how the war was going for America? For all of humanity?

"Hey, look!" Val hollered.

Jim looked back up at the sky. He sucked in a surprised breath, elation bursting inside him.

A green parachute slowly descended from the sky.

Jim watched it fall closer to the ground. His eyes flickered from the parachute to the forest. He then scanned the field leading to the treeline and did some quick calculations in his head.

Two miles away, three at most.

"Mount up," Jim ordered, heading back to the truck.

"We leavin'?" asked Chuck.

He turned back to him. "No. We're gonna get that pilot."

CHAPTER 8

They drove in the direction of the parachute until the dirt road ended in a thicket of trees and brush. The four grabbed their rifles and exited the pick-up. A raw, musky stench hung in the air around them.

"Oh my God." Chuck scrunched his face. "What the hell's that?"

Jim looked to the bed of the pick-up and grimaced. "I think our friends back there are getting a little ripe." It didn't come as much of a surprise. It must have been nearly twenty hours since they killed those Mothmen.

He led them into the brush, twigs and branches snapping as they advanced. It made him wince. He was leaving one hell of a trail for any bad guys to follow, but right now speed was of the essence. By his estimates, they had a mile to go to reach the downed pilot. He had no doubt the Mothmen had dispatched soldiers to find him as well.

Burrs and sharp twigs tugged on his pants and sleeves and scratched his hands and cheeks. He ignored them, checking his compass to make sure they continued in the right direction.

The brush started to lessen, making movement easier. Soon they emerged onto a large patch of dirt, with trails branching off to the left and right. They found no sign of the pilot. Jim checked his compass, then recalled where he saw the chute fall.

"This way." He pointed to the trail on their right.

They jogged down it. Jim's head was on a swivel, searching for any sign of the pilot, or his chute. In these woods it must have gotten hung up in the trees.

They ran a half-mile. A mile. Still no sign of the pilot. Jim ignored the burning in his lungs and the leaden feeling in his legs. Desperation swelled inside him.

Where the hell is he? He bit down on his lower lip to the point it became painful. Had he messed up on his calculations? No way. The pilot should be around here somewhere.

So how come we can't find him? Fear grew inside him. He thought back to Reverend Crawford's church, thought about the man's congregation, especially little Amanda.

He also thought about Hannah.

How many more people could he let down?

Not this guy. I don't care what it takes, we're gonna –

"Look!" Valerie called out. "To the left."

Jim peered through the foliage and spotted something on a tree forty yards away. Something large and dark green undulating in the breeze.

A smile grew across his face when he recognized it as a parachute.

"C'mon!" He led them through the foliage, his eyes darting around for any sign of Mothmen. Finding none, they continued into a small dirt clearing. Jim looked up at the canopy of a parachute, which dangled high in the branches.

"Shit," Chuck blurted from the rear. "Where's the pilot? He couldn't'a jumped from there. It's gotta be, like, a forty foot drop."

Valerie strode past Jim and clutched a thick nylon rope with a bar attached to it that dangled from the chute and scraped the ground. "This is how. A PDL, Personal Lowering Device. You deploy it if your chute gets hung up in the trees, like this guy did."

"Okay, so we know the pilot's alive."

"Yeah, but he ain't around here." Chuck swung his torso from side-to-side, as if half-heartedly looking for the pilot. "Crap, he could be anywhere."

"Aren't pilots supposed to go into the weeds and lie low until a rescue chopper comes?" asked Doug.

"Depends." Val turned to him. "When I went through my SERE training," she used the acronym for Survival, Escape, Resistance and Evasion, "we were told the first thing to do is get as far from the crash site, or in this case, the chute, as quickly as possible, because it's a beacon to the bad guys. If the area's clear of hostiles, keep moving. If not, or if you're unsure, then hide and wait it out."

"So our guy could still be on the move," said Jim.

"Maybe. Especially if there aren't any Mothmen around."

Jim groaned. "If there aren't any Mothmen around now, there will be soon. Like you said, this parachute'll be like a beacon to them." He looked around at his sister and cousins. "Check around. If this guy was in a hurry, he probably left some sign."

It took less than a minute before Doug spotted a faint footprint and a couple broken branches leading into a thicket heading south, away from Fort Campbell.

The four plunged into the thicket. Jim spotted more broken branches, along with other sign most civilians would miss, but that screamed out to a man who'd been hunting since he was little and who'd been with the Army Rangers before joining Delta Force. Flattened strands of grass, slightly bent branches and foliage.

The trail took them left, then right, then left, then right, then back the way they came, then in a semi-circle. By this time the sign was harder to pick up, at least for those without years of hunting and special operations experience.

The guy's being careful, and smart, not going in a straight line.

After twenty minutes, traces of the pilot's flight on foot became few and far between. Jim called a halt, carefully scanning the brush around him. He thought back to Val's words. Maybe the guy was lying low. Maybe he heard them coming and feared they might be Mothmen.

"Pilot!" he said in a loud whisper. "Pilot, are you here? We're U.S. Army. We're here to help."

No response.

He waved his family forward. All four of them called for the pilot as loud as they dared.

Five minutes went by without a response.

Ten minutes.

What if the Mothmen got him? What if they can hear all the noise we're making?

He worked his jaw back and forth. Should he risk the lives of his sister and cousins to keep searching for a person they didn't even know? They could trek through these woods all day and all night and not find him.

No. I'm not giving up.

"Pilot!" He called out. "U.S. Army. We're here to help."

"Don't shoot," a soft, baritone voice suddenly cut through the air.

The Rhynes whirled to the right, rifles raised.

"Yo, I said don't shoot. I'm human. See?"

From behind a mass of foliage twenty yards away, a figure stood. He wore an olive flightsuit and clutched a handgun, a Beretta 9mm, the barrel pointing up.

Jim lowered his rifle. Val, Doug and Chuck did the same.

"Man, am I glad to see you folks." The pilot holstered his pistol, stepped out from behind the brush and headed toward them. As he approached, Jim took stock of him. The pilot was tall, at least 6'1, with a lean frame. His skin was black and his features chiseled. If a Hollywood producer needed to cast someone in the role of a fighter pilot, this guy would be the perfect choice.

"You said you guys are Army?" the pilot asked, stopping a few feet from Jim.

"That's right. Major Jim Rhyne." He extended his hand, which the pilot accepted.

"Captain Dan Williams, Ohio Air National Guard."

Jim introduced Williams to his sister.

"Hello." Williams drew out the "o" as he and Val shook hands. He tilted his head slightly, a twinkle in his eyes. "It's a pleasure to meet you."

"You as well, Captain." Valerie smiled, a very wide smile at that.

The big brother instinct flared inside Jim. His eyes flickered from his beaming sister to the pilot. *Watch yourself, buddy.*

After being introduced to Doug and Chuck, Williams stared at the weapons they all held. "I didn't realize the Army was so hard up. You gotta use hunting rifles now?"

"Actually," Jim answered, "we were all on leave and decided to go on hunting trip when . . . well, when the shithammer fell."

Williams let out a sardonic laugh. "Yeah. One hell of a shithammer at that."

"Can you tell us anything about what's been happening the past few days, Captain?"

Before Doug could get an answer, Jim spoke. "Tell us on the way back to our truck. We need to get out of here before any Mothman patrols show up looking for you."

Elation flashed across Williams' face. "You've got wheels? Sweet, I don't have to hike."

"Think again. The truck's a few miles from here. Let's go."

"Wait a minute." Williams brought up his hand. "What about Sandoval?"

Valerie's face scrunched in puzzlement. "Who?"

"Lieutenant Rafael Sandoval. He was my wingman. I know he got hit. Did any of you see his chute?"

Jim sighed. "I'm sorry, Captain. We saw his plane fireball. There was no way he could have punched out."

Williams closed his eyes and lowered his head. "Dammit," he whispered before stiffening his jaw.

"I'm sorry." Val offered her condolences, as did Doug and Chuck.

"Thanks," Williams muttered without looking at them.

"C'mon, guys." Jim waved for them to start moving. "We gotta get going."

He led the group further south, away from Williams' parachute. He planned to go about a mile before swinging to the southwest and back to Valerie's pick-up.

"So like I said before, Captain." Doug looked over his shoulder at Williams. "What can you tell us about these Mothmen?"

"Mothmen?"

"That's what we call 'em," Chuck explained. "You know, like that monster people saw in West Virginia back in the Sixties."

Williams shrugged. "I don't know about any Mothmen. We just call these things Man-Bats."

"Man-Bats?" Val turned to him. "Are you serious?"

"Hey, the reverse of that name was already taken. Besides, we had to call them something."

Val softly chuckled.

Jim groaned to himself. He could sense the vibe coming from Captain Williams, the "Ladies Man" vibe. He'd been around enough of those guys in college and the military to know one thing about them. He didn't want his little sister getting involved with them.

"So," Williams began. "I assume from the way you've been talking that you've already seen these Man-Bats, or Mothmen?"

"Oh yeah." Jim pushed aside his anger at this James Bond wanna-be in favor of his professionalism. "Two of them dropped in on our campsite last night."

"Really? And you got away from them?"

It was Valerie who answered. "Well, it was kind of tough for them to chase us with their brains lying on the ground."

"You killed them? Good for you." A slight edge poked through the admiration in Williams' voice. Jim figured the guy was remembering his dead wingman.

As they continued through the brush, Jim told Williams about their drive through Cadiz, the firefight at the church, and finally watching the air battle minutes ago.

"Man." Williams shook his head when Jim finished. "You don't have anything close to the whole story. Then again, I don't know if anyone has the whole story."

"Then just tell us what you've got."

"Well, it all started about three days ago. I was doing my civilian job, flying for an air cargo service out of Springfield-Beckley Airport. We were in the flight crew lounge watching the news when they had this special report about an explosion at the Pentagon."

"The Pentagon?" Doug's eyes widened. "How bad was it?"

"A lot worse than when the terrorists hit it on Nine-Eleven. Half the damn building was on fire."

Jim gritted his teeth, scowling. To the logical side of his mind, it only made sense. You had to take out the enemy's command and control before any invasion. But emotionally, he was pissed off, and worried. The Pentagon's destruction would make it difficult for the U.S. to coordinate an effective counter-attack against the Mothmen.

"Then," Williams continued, "they started getting reports of other explosions throughout Washington, including the White House."

"Aw, no fucking way," Chuck blurted. "Is The President okay?"

"I don't know. The reporters were trying to confirm his whereabouts when a bunch of other cities got attacked."

"Which ones?"

"New York, Los Angeles, San Diego, Chicago, Colorado Springs, Norfolk, Omaha, Tampa."

Jim's brow furrowed as he processed the information. He already knew about the attacks on New York, Norfolk and Chicago. As for why they'd hit the other cities, L-A was obvious. It was a major metropolitan area that boasted one of the world's busiest sea ports and airports. It also had another important asset most people didn't know about. Los Angeles Air Force Base, home of the USAF Space Command's Space and Missile Systems Center, which oversaw the military's network of surveillance, communications, meteorological and GPS satellites.

He kept going down the list. San Diego had several important Navy and Marine Corps bases in and around the city. Colorado Springs was home to NORAD, the North American Aerospace Defense Command. Omaha, Nebraska had Offutt Air Force Base, the headquarters for Air Force's Strategic Command. Tampa had MacDill Air Force Base, home to U.S. Central Command and U.S. Special Operations Command.

"They also hit a couple smaller towns, too. Little place in Texas. Um, Killeen I think it was. And Fayetteville, North Carolina."

Jim gripped his rifle tighter. Killeen was one of the towns around Fort Hood, home of the U.S. Army's III Corps. Fayetteville hosted Fort Bragg, home of the 82nd Airborne Division, the Green Berets . . .

And Delta Force.

He had to fight not to let rage and worry consume him as he thought of the men in his unit.

"Damn." Jim shook his head. "They hit us where it really hurt, didn't they?"

"Not just here," Williams said. "There were reports coming in all over the world. Britain, France, Russia, China, Israel, India, Belgium."

"Belgium?" A quizzical look formed on Chuck's face. "Why the hell would they attack Belgium?"

"That's where NATO Headquarters is," Jim told him. He also thought about the other countries Williams named. All major players on the world stage. They also had another thing in common.

All of them possessed nuclear arsenals.

I bet Pakistan, North Korea and Iran got hit, too.

"My God," Val said in a stunned voice. "It's all over the world."

Jim felt a chill run down his spine at the thought of millions upon millions of Mothmen swarming over the planet.

"So where do these things come from?" Chuck asked.

"Nobody knows," Williams replied. "About fifteen minutes after we heard the report about the Pentagon, the TV went out. Actually, everything went out. TV, radio, phones, internet. We couldn't get any news after that. Luckily, my Guard squadron's based at the same airport I work at. So I just walked over and reported for duty. Pretty soon the rest of my squadron filtered in one or two at a time. We couldn't contact anyone, so my CO on his own decided to set up Combat Air Patrols around central Ohio."

"So did you do any fighting?" Chuck asked.

"Not that first day. All we did was punch holes in the sky. The second day things got more interesting."

"How so?" Jim asked as he led the group out of the thicket and onto a dirt path.

"The TV came back on. I mean, from time to time. The first time we saw the Statue of Liberty with a bunch of those Man-Bats on it. All of us about crapped our pants. We didn't know if it was for real or not. The second time it was from London." Williams' lips tightened. He looked away for a moment.

"What's wrong?" Val asked.

The pilot took a breath before continuing. "Those Man-Bats were at Buckingham Palace. They had some of the Royal Family there and . . . and they killed 'em. Right there on TV. And believe me, it wasn't pretty."

"Oh my God," Val gasped.

"Shit," muttered Chuck.

Jim grimaced, sending up a silent prayer for the dead royals.

Williams stayed silent for several seconds before finally regaining his voice. "Every couple of hours they'd come on with something else. Man-Bats flying around the U.S. Capital or the Kremlin or that gold dome in Jerusalem. Then they showed Miami and Riyadh from distance, and both times these huge explosions went off."

"Nukes?" asked Jim.

"I don't think so. They didn't look like nukes to us. But they were damn big explosions."

"So, what?" Chuck shrugged his shoulders. "They want to show us how they're kicking our asses."

"That's exactly it." Williams looked over his shoulder at him. "At least, that's what our squadron intel officer thinks. He said it's probably a psy-op."

"A what?"

"Psychological operations. The Man-Bats are showing themselves flying around very powerful national symbols, or in the case of the Royal Family, killing a powerful national symbol. That's designed to weaken our morale. Blowing up Miami and Riyadh shows how easily they can destroy us, and that fighting them would be futile."

"Plus Riyadh's the capital of Saudi Arabia," Jim noted. "Knock that out, and you plunge one of the world's biggest oil producing nations into chaos."

"Great," Doug groaned. "So the only news we're getting is news the Mothmen are showing us. News that's good for them and bad for us."

"Not necessarily." Williams raised a finger. "Springfield-Beckley Airport happened to have a couple old shortwave radio sets on hand. Our squadron communications officer and one of the airport's engineers managed to get 'em working again. We got in touch with a few people. Some guys in Canada and New Zealand reported no fighting there, or at least in the cities they lived in. Another guy said he was from Deer Valley, just outside Phoenix, and saw a big cloud of smoke coming from Luke Air Force Base. Then another guy from Bhopal swore someone said a nuke went off somewhere in India. He didn't know if the Indian military dropped it on the Man-Bats or if maybe Pakistan took advantage of the situation and launched one. Of course, we have no way of confirming any of that."

Jim shook his head. Amazing that in the age of satellites and computers the only way they could communicate with people now was a piece of equipment invented around the turn of the last century.

"So how did you wind up over Kentucky?" Val asked Williams.

"The state adjutant general came to our base in person. He told us since we couldn't raise anyone in Washington or in one of the unified commands, we were on our own. He gave us orders to organize hunter-killer missions against the Man-Bats. Not an easy thing to do when communications are out, intel is almost non-exsitent, and there are no ground assets to coordinate an air strike. Still anything was better than sitting on our asses while those freakjobs attacked the country. So we went up and hoped for the best." A long silence followed. "We lost half our squadron yesterday. All we had to show for it was a convoy of Man-Bat vehicles a couple of our guys managed to shoot up. Then today me and Raffy fly over Kentucky and run into their jets. Damn things were fast, maneuverable, and stealthy as hell. I couldn't get any kind of lock from my Sidewinders or my AMRAAMs. I had to go with my gun to bring down that son-of-a-bitch, and I was damn lucky to do that."

"We saw," Doug said. "Nice shooting."

"Yeah, for whatever it's worth." Williams snorted. "I lost my plane, I lost Raffy, and those friggin' Man-Bats probably have a lot more of those jets out there."

"Did you get a look at Fort Campbell while you were up there?" Jim asked, hoping to steer the pilot away from the path of self-pity. "Did it look all right?"

"Sorry, Major. I couldn't tell you one way or the other. I was pretty wrapped up with those Man-Bat fighters to check out the scenery. Even on the way down I was facing away from the base. Couldn't really get a good look."

Jim forced himself not to frown as they continued through the woods.

It was late afternoon when they returned to the pick-up truck. Williams had to wedge himself into the back with Chuck and Doug while Jim again rode shotgun.

"So what's the plan, Major?" Williams asked as Val started the engine.

"We keep going toward Fort Campbell. We'll stop a couple miles from the base, then go in on foot and check and see if it's still in friendly hands."

"And if it's not?"

"Then we go with Plan B."

"And what's Plan B?"

The corners of Jim's mouth twisted. "I'll let you know when I come up with it."

CHAPTER 9

After parking the truck behind some brush, Jim and the others set out on foot toward Campbell Army Airfield. Doug took point for the two-mile hike, while Jim brought up the rear. Tension coiled around his insides. Would they encounter a Mothmen patrol? What would they find at Campbell? He thought back to what that one man from Reverend Crawford's congregation had told him, that he heard explosions and gunfire coming from the base. Did the Hundred-First hold on to it? Did the Mothmen destroy it?

"We should almost be there," Doug informed them, speaking only as loud as he dared.

Jim tried to breathe a sigh of relief. They'd hiked two miles without seeing any Mothmen. He prayed that was a good sign.

The woods thinned out. He peered through the branches and bushes and could make out two long asphalt runways.

"Oh my God," Val's voice cracked.

Doug's right hand shot up. Everybody halted. Doug waved his hand toward the ground. They all crouched. Jim, however, went one further, getting on his belly and snaking his way up to his sister and cousin.

"What is it?" he asked in a whisper.

Valerie stared straight ahead, her jaw clenched, her hands clutching her hunting rifle so tight her knuckles went white.

Jim followed her gaze. He bit his lip as he took in the sight.

The airfield had been decimated. Huge craters pockmarked both runways. Buildings sported holes and scorch marks, or lay in charred rubble. Burnt out Humvees and aircraft littered the field, which was completely deserted.

He turned to his sister. A tick had formed under her right eye.

"Val, I'm sorry."

She swallowed, her face tightening even more, as if fighting back the urge to cry. "Some of them had to have gotten away. They had to. We're the best. They couldn't get us all. No fucking way could they get us all."

Jim reached out and clutched his sister's shoulder. She turned her head slightly toward him. He tried to keep his face as stoic as possible. Val's worries about her friends in the 160th Special Operations Aviation Regiment probably mirrored his own about his Delta Force brothers back at Fort Bragg.

"What now?" asked Doug, his voice as flat as Valerie's. No doubt he had to be thinking about the men in his unit who likely took part in this battle.

"We check it out. Maybe there's someone alive here and they're just hiding. Maybe we can find some more weapons and supplies. Come on, and stay alert."

They hurried across the field until they came to the ruins of a building. They crouched behind it, Jim peering around the corner and checking things out before they moved on.

The destruction looked worse up close. A faint smell of burnt rubber and metal hung in the air. Chunks of asphalt were strewn over both runways. Buildings left somewhat intact had windows shattered or their interiors gutted by fire. Empty shell casings lay all over the place. Dried blood stained the ground and any walls that remained standing.

"Man, they did a job on this place." Williams shook his head.

Valerie sighed and lowered her head.

"Yeah, but they put up one hell of a fight," Chuck added as he walked past the charred remains of a twin-prop airplane.

"Yeah." Doug's jaw stiffened as he continued to gaze around at the devastation.

A few things survived the battle. Two Blackhawk helicopters sat on the tarmac unscathed, at least from a distance. Upon closer examination each one had several bullet holes. They also found a few Army Sedans and trucks intact. The biggest find, and the one that brought a brief smile to Valerie's face, was a bulbous MH-6 Little Bird helicopter sitting in one of the hangars. The chopper didn't appear to have a single scratch on it.

As with Cadiz, they couldn't find a single body, human or Mothman, anywhere. Neither could they find any weapons.

"Well, I guess it was a waste of time coming here." Williams frowned.

Anger lines dug into Jim's face. Williams' word stung him, fueling his misery. Fort Campbell had been one of the few hopes he could latch onto since they first encountered the Mothmen. He desperately wanted to believe everything would be all right if they reached the base. They could hand over the Mothmen bodies to doctors and scientists who could examine them.

Now that hope had been crushed.

"No!" Val spun around to face Williams. "We can't give up. This is just one small part of Fort Campbell. Between military and civilian employees and their families, there's about a hundred-ninety thousand people on this base. It's practically a small city."

"Valerie's right," said Doug. "There's no way the Mothmen could have gotten them all. There have to be survivors, people who are hiding."

Jim tried to use their words to fan the dying embers of hope inside him. But given what they'd seen in Cadiz, given the level of destruction here at Campbell Army Airfield, he didn't hold out much hope for survivors.

But like Val said, we can't give up. We have to try. If there were survivors on this base, he would not let them down. He would find them.

"But there ain't no way we can cover this whole base on foot," Chuck stated.

"We won't have to," Jim said. "Some of those Sedans look in good shape. We'll use one of them."

"Are you sure about that?" Williams looked leery of the idea. "It'd make it really easy for the Mothmen to spot us."

"They may not even be here. If this airfield is any indication, then Fort Campbell is probably too damaged for them to use. And if they captured or killed most of the base personnel, they may have moved on." *God, I hope so.* "If there's even the chance there could be survivors around here, then it's a risk worth taking."

Both Valerie and Doug nodded. Chuck and Williams appeared uncomfortable at the thought, but kept their concerns to themselves.

They commandeered an undamaged Sedan. With Valerie behind the wheel, they drove away from Campbell Army Airfield and proceeded to the Sabre Army Heliport. That, too, had been destroyed. Next they headed to the main post. There the destruction had not been as uniform. They'd go for three or four blocks, mainly in the residential areas, without seeing any hint of fighting. Then they'd travel down Bastogne Avenue and discover Blanchfield Hospital, the base library, the PX, and the Fellowship Chapel all in ruins. The same with the Headquarters Building. Even the base's four elementary schools all showed signs of battle damage.

They continued driving around, staring out the windows for any sign of survivors. Guilt and frustration stabbed at Jim's soul. On a base this large, there was no way they could search every single building. The best they could hope for is that any survivors would see their car and come out of their hiding place.

So far that had not happened.

"There has to be someone around here." Valerie shook her head, her expression wavering between anger and sorrow.

"Wait! Stop here!" Doug ordered.

Valerie slammed on the brakes.

"What the hell, Doug?" Jim furrowed his brow.

"Look." He pointed to a utilitarian brick building. "That's the MP station. Shit, I can't believe they didn't take out that place."

"So?" Chuck scoffed. "You really think there's anyone in there? Like it'd matter. I doubt they could arrest any Mothmen."

"Moron. This is a military police station. We can get some more weapons here."

Chuck's face reddened. Jim expected some angry retort. Instead Chuck turned away from his brother and scowled.

"Doug's right." Jim opened his passenger side door. "Let's check out the place and see what we can scrounge. Chuck, you stand guard outside."

He led Valerie, Doug and Williams inside. They swept the building from top to bottom. As expected, the place was deserted.

They located the armory in the basement. The door had been left open a few inches. Jim held his breath, fearing they'd walk inside and find that the Mothmen had cleaned out the entire room.

Gripping the door, he bit his lip and swung it open. They entered with weapons raised.

The place was empty . . . of any humans or Mothmen. As far as weapons went . . .

"About time something went our way." Jim let out a sigh of relief as he eyed racks of M4 carbines and Mossberg 590 shotguns, and shelves containing Beretta 9mm pistols, tasers, tear gas canisters, flash-bang grenades and bulletproof vests.

"Christmas time, people," Jim said. "Grab what you can carry, and make it quick."

"We have to leave the tear gas, though," Doug stated.

Jim scrunched his face in puzzlement. "What the hell for?"

"C'mon, Jim. You know as well as I do tear gas is banned in warfare by international treaty."

He rolled his eyes. Earth was being invaded by creatures from who-the-hell-knew-where, and Doug still wanted to go by the book?

"Well if the UN has a problem with me, they can kiss my ass. Now come on."

Doug chewed on his lower lip, eyeing the tear gas canisters warily.

Whatever. It was a stupid rule anyway. The US Army could use tear gas on its own people, but not in a hostile country?

Since when are politicians logical?

They snatched up M4s and Berettas, along with extra magazines. Jim also removed his hunting vest and strapped on a bulletproof vest. He had no idea if it would stop the big high velocity rounds the Mothmen used, but he figured it was better than nothing.

The others followed his lead, strapping on bulletproof vests. They also took a few flash-bangs and tear gas canisters.

Next time we meet the Mothmen, we'll be on even terms.

"You sure you know how to use that thing?" Doug nodded to the M4 in Williams' hand.

"Yeah, I think so."

"Think or know?"

"Hey, come on. I fight with missiles and bombs. I haven't fired a rifle since basic."

Doug groaned. "Do you need a refresher course?"

Williams glared at him. He held up the M4 and pointed to different parts. "Safety. Trigger. Sights. Aim. Shoot. I think I can handle it, *Lieutenant.*"

He narrowed his eyes at Doug as he walked past him. Valerie shook her head at her cousin and followed the fighter pilot out of the armory. Doug just scowled at the floor.

"Never did read that book *How To Win Friends and Influence People,* did you?" Jim slapped him on the shoulder.

"I just don't want Mister Top Gun here to get us all killed because he doesn't know which end of a rifle is which."

Jim said nothing as they walked out of the armory. He, too, had similar concerns about Williams. Though he would have voiced them in a less abrasive way. He also decided not to correct Doug that Top Gun was the school for Navy fighter pilots, not Air National Guard. He didn't need him moping more than he was already.

Once they got upstairs, they busted open some vending machines and grabbed armfuls of soda, water, Gatorade, candy bars and chips. They exited the building and told Chuck to run in and grab whatever he could from the armory and the vending machines. All four of them chowed down quickly while they waited for Chuck. When he returned, they piled into the Sedan and continued driving around the base. A half-hour passed without seeing another human being.

"Um, I hate to say it, gang," Williams said. "But I think we need to write this place off as deserted."

Jim looked over his shoulder at the pilot. "Not yet. There have to be some places we haven't checked out. Right, Doug?"

Doug tightened his lips. His gaze lowered to his lap.

"Doug. Where else haven't we checked yet?"

His cousin looked up at him and slowly exhaled. "I think Captain Williams is right. You'd think by now we would have seen somebody."

Jim narrowed his eyes. "You said it yourself, Doug. The Mothmen couldn't have gotten every single person on this base. You did too, Val."

Valerie's shoulders sagged. "Jim, I . . . I want to believe there are still people out there, but we've been here for, what now? Two hours? We haven't seen anyone. I think . . . I think we have to accept the reality. Everyone at Fort Campbell is gone."

He scowled, frustrated breaths shooting out his nose. He looked out the windows, scanning the rows of houses they drove past. He couldn't bring himself to give up yet, not when there might be people he could save.

"We need to leave," Doug stated. "What if a Mothman patrol comes by?"

"Yeah, man," Chuck added. "We're just wasting our time here."

"Trying to save people is not a waste of time." Jim swung around in the passenger seat, glowering at Chuck.

"Jim." Valerie looked over, her expression pleading with him to see things their way.

The skin crinkled harshly around his nose. He stared back at the houses, willing someone to come out.

No one did.

He closed his eyes, the same sense of failure he felt back at the church returning.

You still have four people here depending on you to get them through this alive.

"All right. Val, head back to the airfield."

"And what do we do then?" Anxiety tinged Chuck's voice. "I mean, the whole base is trashed, nobody's here. Where do we go now?"

"The only other major base near here is Fort Knox," Doug said. "But if they took out Campbell, then they probably took out Knox, too."

"Maybe there's, like, some National Guard armories we can go to," Chuck offered.

Jim shook his head. "After everything we've seen today, I think we have to assume all of Kentucky is enemy territory."

"What about Tennessee?" Val suggested. "Arnold Air Force Base is about a hundred and twenty miles southeast of here."

"She's right," Williams said. "Plus Arnold's not a combat base. They mainly test jet engines there. The Mothmen may not have considered it a priority target."

"What about Mothmen activity in Tennessee?" asked Jim. "Do you have any intel on that?"

Williams shook his head. "Negative."

Jim sighed. Arnold sounded like a good place. They probably had scientists there who could analyze the Mothmen's weapons and gear. But for all he knew, Tennessee could also be in enemy hands.

"What about Ohio? What have the Mothmen been doing there?"

"Not much, as far as we can tell. We've had some scouts drive around the state and report back to us. So far it doesn't seem like the Mothmen have hit us in force . . . yet."

Jim leaned back in his seat, staring out the windshield in thought. From here it was about 160, 170 miles to the Ohio border. Williams' Air Guard base was in Springfield, another 200 miles north. A much longer trip than to Arnold Air Force Base, but . . .

"I think we should make for Ohio."

"What?" Val shot him a surprised look. "But Arnold is closer."

"I know. But we have no idea if the Mothmen are in control of Tennessee. We know from Williams the Ohio Guard is fighting back against them. The way I see it, Ohio's our best bet."

Valerie bobbed her head from side-to-side. "Okay, I see your point. But there's no way my truck has the gas to make it to Ohio."

"I'm sure we can find some fuel around here," Doug suggested. "The Mothmen didn't take out all our armories. It stands to reason they didn't take out all our fuel tanks."

"Or, why bother driving when we can fly?"

"Fly?" Chuck's face scrunched up.

Valerie glanced at him. "There's a beautiful, undamaged Little Bird sitting in a hangar back at Campbell Airfield. It means leaving my baby behind." She frowned for a moment. Jim knew how much his sister loved her pick-up truck.

She continued. "But, I can get us to Ohio a hell of a lot faster. Not to Springfield. That's out of the Little Bird's range. If we're lucky, I can get us close to Cincinnati, then we can lay our hands on some transport there."

"Or we might run into other people who can help us," Jim said. "Police, local government."

"That may work out even better," Williams said. "Cincy's about an hour's drive from Dayton, and that's where Wright-Pat is. That's the Air Force's top research and development base. Probably the best place you could take those dead Mothmen and their equipment."

"So long as the Mothmen haven't bombed it," Doug muttered.

"Yeah, but you saw what those Mothman jets did to those F-16s," Chuck said, causing Williams to grimace. "What chance are we gonna have in a little helicopter?"

"Excuse me." Val's voice developed an edge. "Night Stalker here. We're trained to fly through enemy territory undetected, and we do it better than anyone in the world. I'll get you to Ohio without the Mothmen knowing shit about it."

Jim grinned. Having worked closely with the 160th SOAR on many occasions, he knew what his sister said was no idle boast.

Before heading back to Campbell Army Airfield, the group stopped at Old Clarksville Base, where much of the fort's munitions and supplies were stored. Not surprisingly, most of the buildings had been blown apart. Still Jim and the others managed to find several intact items in the rubble. MREs, blankets, fresh tan-gray-green pixel pattern Army Combat Uniforms, or ACUs, underwear, socks, a couple flashlights, night vision goggles, some toiletries, and MOLLE packs to carry it all. In the remains of one of the munitions bunkers they came across two very useful items for Val's Little Bird. M134 six-barrel miniguns. They also found belts of 7.62mm ammo to go with them.

When they returned to the airfield, Jim sent Doug and Chuck to get the pick-up, and more importantly, the Mothmen bodies in the bed. Val asked Williams to get one of the undamaged fuel trucks.

"It would be my pleasure," the pilot said with a grin and a twinkle in his eye. It made Valerie blush, and made Jim want ram one of the miniguns up that loverboy's ass.

While his sister checked over the Little Bird, he went about attaching the miniguns to each of the chopper's side doors. He'd finished feeding the belt ammo into the weapon on the left door when he noticed Val standing a couple feet away, arms folded, head tilted, and frowning.

"What's on your mind, Val?"

"What makes you think something's on my mind?"

"Because you have that look. So what's bothering you?"

She sighed, looking down at the concrete floor. Seconds later, she lifted her eyes back to him. "It's not going to change anything, you know."

"What are you talking about?"

"This need you have to save everyone. Back at the church, going after Captain Williams, wanting to search every square inch of Fort Campbell on the chance someone might still be here."

"We're in The Army, Val. That's what we do. If people need saving, we save 'em."

"True. But it's different with you. It's more than a duty, it's like . . ."

"Like what?"

Valerie bit her. She turned away, drew a deep breath, and looked back at him. "It's like you believe the more people you save, it'll make Hannah's death easier to deal with."

The words struck him like a boxer's punch. He went numb, staring unblinkingly at his sister.

She licked her lips, as if hesitant to continue. But continue she did. "You know what one of the big rules is of special operations. Don't make the fight personal. But that's what you're doing, and I think it's affecting your judgment."

"That's bullshit."

"Bullshit it's bullshit. You could have saved everyone back at that church, and it still wouldn't change what happened to Hannah. You have to quit blaming yourself. It wasn't your fau-"

"I'm not having this conversation, Val." He focused his attention on the minigun.

"Well I am. What happened to Hannah was horrible. But you couldn't -"

"I said this conversation is over. Got it?"

Val glared at him. "Fine. It's over . . . for now."

She stomped off toward the front of the helicopter.

Jim snorted, checking over the minigun again, more to keep his mind off the argument than anything else. *She doesn't know what she's talking about. Saving people comes with the job, and I was doing it long before Hannah died.*

He ran his eyes over the ammo belt, making sure it fed properly into the M134. All the while Valerie's words echoed in his mind. He shook his head, trying to dismiss them.

Deep down, however, he knew what his little sister had said was spot on.

CHAPTER 10

Night was setting in by the time Doug and Chuck returned with Valerie's truck. The men carried the Mothmen corpses and their equipment to the Little Bird, while Val hung back.

"So long, baby." She kissed her hand and placed it on the hood of her pick-up. "I hope to see you again someday." By the tone of her voice, she doubted that would happen.

"Jeez, Val," Chuck rolled his eyes. "Quit being so damn dramatic."

She fixed him with a death stare, one that made Chuck wince and cast his eyes to the ground. That glare soon turned toward Jim.

"If anything happens to my baby, you owe me a new one." She strode toward the Little Bird's cockpit.

Jim's lips tightened as he helped secure the corpses in the chopper's hold. *If you get us to Ohio in one piece, sis, I'll buy you a frickin' monster truck.*

"Aw shit." Chuck grimaced. "These things stink even worse now."

Jim just nodded, trying his best not to inhale deeply. That musky, raw odor permeated the Little Bird's interior. He also noticed the corpses had become bloated.

Chuck pressed his arm over his mouth and coughed. The grimace on his face deepened. Jim wondered if his cousin might puke.

"Too bad you couldn't get some of the other ones." Williams said.

Chuck scrunched his face. "What other ones?"

"Sorry. When we looked back at some of the footage we recorded off the TV, we spotted some differences in these things."

"What kind of differences?" Jim asked.

"Some of them looked like they had beaks. Some had little stubs on their head that looked like they might be horns. Then there was this one at Buckingham Palace. Real freaky-looking thing. It had a long neck, big horns on its head, and a tail."

Jim stiffened. "Wait a minute. You said it had horns and a tail?"

"That's right."

"Didn't one of the people back at the church give that same description?" Doug noted.

"Yeah. He did." Jim's brow furrowed in thought. Why would there be such dramatic differences in the Mothmen's body type?

Well, not all humans look the same. To an extent, anyway. Sure there were differences in height, weight, skin color, hair color, etc. But nothing as drastic as having horns and a tail or not having them. He wondered, could they be dealing with more than one species? Could these things have formed some sort of alliance? An intergalactic version of NATO?

Considering the way they're acting, an intergalactic version of the Axis Powers would be a better analogy.

He shook his head. Even after all the information Williams had given them, they still had more questions about the Mothmen than answers.

Hopefully that'll change when we get to Ohio.

"All right," Val announced from the Little Bird's cockpit. "Pre-flight checklist is done and we're looking good. Let's mount up and get outta here."

The four men settled into the helicopter, Jim and Doug manning the miniguns, Chuck sitting in the rear.

"You don't mind if I join you, Lieutenant?" Williams asked in a smooth tone as he entered the cockpit.

"Not at all." Val smiled at him.

Jim's jaw clenched. It was a shame. He might have thought Williams a cool guy if he wasn't putting the moves on his sister. The bitch of it was he really couldn't do much about it. If he said anything to Val, her response would be, "I'm not ten-years-old anymore, so mind your own damn business."

He grunted. Times like these he hated the fact Val had become an adult and not stayed his baby sister forever.

"So how much do you know about helicopters, Captain?" Val asked Williams as he sat in the co-pilot's seat.

"Just that they can hover, they look like they're standing still compared to an F-16, and they can pick us up if we get shot down. But if you're asking me to fly one, forget it."

"Then how about being my navigator?"

"It would be my pleasure." Williams gave her a friendly wink.

Val smiled.

Jim scowled.

The five of them strapped on their night vision goggles. After securing themselves with harnesses to prevent falling out the doors, Jim and Doug put on flight helmets plugged into the chopper's internal communications system, or ICS, so they could speak to Valerie and Williams over the noise of the rotors. After a quick mike check, Val fired up the engines. The Little Bird lifted off the concrete floor, flew out of the hangar and climbed into the night sky. Though it didn't climb very high. Valerie kept the chopper just above the forests that surrounded Fort Campbell. Jim watched the treetops pass just underneath the skids, so close he could reach down and touch them. Some slight tingles of nervousness went through him, but he quickly shook them off. This wasn't the first time he'd flown at treetop level with a pilot from Valerie's unit. As crazy as those chopper jocks were, they were the best in the world, and Jim had every confidence in them, his sister included.

He constantly scanned the sky, his NVGs turning the black of night into a phosphorescent green. He saw no sign of any Mothman soldiers or aircraft. There was also something else he saw no sign of.

Lights.

Even from this low altitude, he should have been able to see a myriad of lights blazing from Hopkinsville, or further in the distance, the smaller towns of Gracey and Kelly. At least he would have under normal circumstances.

The world stopped being normal three days ago.

They continued north over Kentucky. Valerie kept the Little Bird just a few feet over the trees, or hugged the contours of hills and valleys, or skimmed the surface of rivers. In-between scanning the sky for any threats, Jim glanced at his watch, trying to calculate how much longer they had before reaching Ohio, before reaching what he hoped was a relatively safe haven.

Yeah. Just like you thought Fort Campbell would be a safe haven.

Doubt crept into his mind. Should they have taken the shorter route and gone to Arnold Air Force Base instead? For all they knew it might still be in human hands.

But we definitely know Ohio is.

At least it was when Williams left his base earlier in the day. What if the Mothmen had dropped an entire combat division into the state in the last few hours?

Jim closed his eyes, forcing those thoughts out of his mind. He had made the best decision possible based on all the information he had available. He had to feel confident it had been the correct one.

"Okay, gang," he heard Valerie over the ICS. "We should be crossing the Ohio River in ten minutes."

Jim fought the urge to relax. They still had a ways to go before they reached The Buckeye State. Even then, he wouldn't be able to relax, not with the world under siege by . . .

He tensed as he looked north. Five small, dark shapes dove out of the sky toward them.

"We got company! One o'clock high!" Jim swung the minigun toward the approaching Mothmen.

"I see 'em!" Val shouted. "Hang on!"

The Little Bird jerked to the right. Tracers streaked across the sky from Mothmen assault rifles. Jim's thumbs mashed the firing button on the minigun. A deep *Grrrr* erupted from the weapon, along with dozens of 7.62mm rounds. The chopper dropped to the deck before he could see if he hit anything. He searched the sky for any more Mothmen when the Little Bird pulled up and soared over the forest. Valerie suddenly yanked the chopper right and descended into another clearing.

"More Mothmen!" Doug shouted. "Coming in at four o'clock!" He fired a couple bursts from his M134.

The Little Bird jerked left and climbed over the trees. Wind screamed around Jim as his sister gunned the engine.

He scanned behind them. Dark shapes of the Mothmen appeared in the distance, coming in at a steep angle. He recalled the fight back at the church, how the Mothmen had been able to keep up with Val's truck. He doubted that would be the case with a helicopter that topped out at 175 miles-per-hour.

Yet the monsters drew closer to them, to the point they fired several bursts from their assault rifles. All the tracers fell short of the Little Bird. Jim gritted his teeth, remembering something he saw on an Animal Planet documentary, how some falcons could reach speeds up to 200 miles-per-hour in a dive.

Could the Mothmen do that?

He triggered the minigun. Orange tracers lashed out toward the Mothmen. All his rounds missed.

The Little Bird banked right, sped over a gully, then climbed over another clump of trees.

"Mothmen! Eleven o'clock!" Jim fired the minigun. The first burst missed. So did the second. On the third one he saw one of the dark shapes spin around and drop like a stone to the ground.

"Got one!"

Something flashed among the remaining Mothmen. Jim held his breath, fear shooting through his veins. A fiery contrail streaked toward them.

"Missile! Missile! Port side! Port side!"

"I got it!" Val yelled.

He braced himself, expecting his sister to throw the helicopter into a series of gut-wrenching evasive maneuvers.

Instead she continued flying straight and level.

"Val!"

"Shut up! I know what I'm doing!"

The Little Bird maintained its course and speed. The missile sped toward them. Every muscle in Jim's body tensed. Fear turned his skin to ice as he pictured the missile striking him right between the eyes.

"Dammit, Val! It's gonna -"

"Hang on!"

Before she even finished the short sentence, the Little Bird made a sharp bank to the left, *into* the missile's envelope. Jim held his breath, bracing for the impact.

The missile flashed past them, unable to adjust in time to Valerie's tight turn. Jim's clenched teeth loosened ever so slightly as he leaned out the door as much as he dared.

A brief flash lit up the treetops.

Jim's muscles loosened. The missile had been going too fast to compensate for its lost target and plowed into the forest.

"Good flying, Val," he said breathlessly.

"Good?" Chuck blurted. "That was fucking awesome!"

"I'll second that," Williams chimed in.

Another squad of Mothmen dove at them.

"Can the celebration," Jim ordered. "We're not out of the woods yet."

He fired his minigun. One of the Mothmen spiraled toward the ground. Seconds later Doug called out another Mothmen sighting and opened fire.

Jim scowled. No way could they have just blundered into an enemy patrol. This was a coordinated attack. Those monsters must have spotted them earlier. How? Radar? A scouting party they failed to see?

It didn't matter. All that mattered was getting out of this alive.

Val climbed over another mass of trees. Doug fired more bursts. Jim scanned for any more targets. Nothing behind them. Nothing to the side. He turned toward the front.

A Mothman burst through the trees, clutching a light machine gun.

"Shit!" both he and Valerie barked at the same time.

Jim swung the minigun around. Val jerked the chopper to the right.

The Mothman leveled its machine gun and fired. Loud, metallic thuds echoed through the Little Bird.

"Holy shit!" Chuck screamed. His head whipped around in all directions, eyes wide with panic.

More expletives burst over the ICS from Valerie and Williams.

"You guys okay?" Jim demanded.

"We're fine!" Val hollered back. "The aircraft isn't."

As if on cue, he heard strange growling sounds coming from the engine. Even more disturbing, he smelled smoke.

"This bird's had it," Val stated. "Hang on. This won't be gentle."

The chopper bucked and groaned. The trees vanished underneath Jim, replaced by an expanse of grass and bushes. The Little Bird heaved to the left. Even with his harness securely attached, he reached out to grip the edge of the door on instinct.

The engine sputtered. The ground rushed up toward them. Jim let go of the minigun and rolled toward the center of the hold, next to the Mothmen corpses. Doug did the same thing. Chuck covered his head with his arms.

"Brace for im-"

A sharp blow rocked the Little Bird.

CHAPTER 11

Jim found himself crumpled against the rear of the Little Bird's cockpit. The cord for the ICS dangled from his helmet, ripped in half. His shoulder felt sore. He raised his left arm. Pain squeezed it, but not too badly.

Looks like nothing's broken, Thank God.

He checked around the hold. Doug also lay against the cockpit, grimacing. Chuck had wound up lying between the Mothmen bodies, sucking down quick, panicked breaths.

"Everyone okay?"

Doug, Valerie and Williams all answered in the affirmative. Chuck just nodded, struggling to get his breathing under control.

Jim pushed himself to his knees, noticing the Little Bird listing to the right. The skid must have shattered on impact.

"Sorry, everyone," Val said. "This bird's grounded permanently."

"Yeah, well, you know what they say about any landing you can walk away from," Williams added.

"Everyone out! Now!" Jim pushed himself up into a crouch, unslinging his M4 from his shoulder. "The Mothmen are probably inbound right now. Move! Move!"

Valerie and Williams grabbed their MOLLE packs and M4s and exited through the pilot side cockpit door, since the co-pilot's door was jammed against the ground. Chuck swallowed and jumped out of the hold, followed by Doug and Jim.

"What about them?" Doug nodded to the Mothmen bodies.

Jim bit his lip. He'd made delivering these things and their equipment to someone in authority his top priority. But with Mothmen soldiers on the way, could they afford to take even one body with them?

You have to complete the mission.

He opened his mouth to reply to his cousin.

Something flashed in his peripheral vision. He snapped his head to the sky. A trail of fire descended toward them.

"No time!" He smacked Doug on the back. "Go! Go!"

The two pounded across the darkened field. The others were about twenty yards ahead of them, making for the treeline.

"Incoming!" he shouted, then looked behind him. The missile whined as it closed in on the Little Bird.

"Shit. Hit the deck!" He grabbed Doug by the shoulder and shoved him to the ground.

A thunderclap tore through the air. Moments later sharp whistles sounded overhead. Shrapnel from the Little Bird.

Jim raised himself a couple inches off the ground and looked over his shoulder. He scowled at the sight of the little helicopter consumed by flames. Anger boiled inside him. Another damned failure. First his wife, then the people at the church, now this.

He spotted movement in the sky. At least half-a-dozen objects, all with wings flapping, dove toward the ground.

No time to feel sorry for himself. Now he had just one mission. Keep his family and Williams alive.

"Go! Go!" He yanked Doug to his feet. Both ran toward the treeline. Jim watched Val, Chuck and Williams disappear amongst the trees when he heard several cracks behind him. Little geysers of dirt sprouted nearby.

Jim spun around, raised his M4 and fired. Doug joined in a second later. Tracers streaked across the field. Two looked like they connected with a Mothman coming in for a landing. It twitched, but didn't go down.

Damn body armor.

He signaled Doug to go, fired two bursts, then took off. Doug dropped to a knee and fired. Jim rushed by him and slapped him on the shoulder. Doug took off running as Jim laid down more fire.

Orange strobes erupted from the woods as Val, Chuck and Williams also covered them. It wasn't long before Jim and Doug charged into the treeline. He dropped behind a tree and looked around the trunk.

At least ten Mothmen advanced across the open field.

Jim stared down the sights of his M4, placing them on the nearest Mothman. He pulled the trigger. The monster's head snapped back. Moments later it fell to the ground.

The steady crackle of M4s erupted all around him. Mothmen fell prone to the ground and fired back. A steady chatter cut through the small arms fire. A Mothman light machine gun.

Rounds slapped into the trees. Bark splinters jumped off the trunks. Severed branches spiraled through the air and onto the ground. Jim and the others crouched and pressed their backs against the trunks. When he sensed a slight break in the machine gun fire, he leaned around the tree as much as he dared and fired until his magazine ran dry. He shoved in a fresh mag as Doug and Williams continued firing. Tracers criss-crossed the field. More rounds smacked bark and leaves and dirt. No flesh, so far. At least not human flesh.

Mothmen soldiers crawled along the ground, their light machine gun still spraying the woods. Four more Mothmen landed near the burning Little Bird and loped toward their comrades. Jim noticed Valerie fire one burst after another at the new arrivals. One of them twisted and fell. It did not get up. The other three threw themselves to the ground.

Jim spotted a steady flash close to the ground. Tracers streaked from it and drilled into the trees. Everyone huddled for cover.

"Doug!" He shouted to his cousin, two trees down from him. He used a series of hand signals to communicate his plan.

MG. Thirty yards out. One o'clock position. Lay down fire.

Doug nodded. Jim held up his hand and counted down. *Three, two one.*

They leaned around their trees and opened fire. Tracers laced the ground around the Mothman machine gun. Jim burned through half his magazine before he ceased fire. Doug halted a couple seconds later. Jim held his breath, trying to tune out the buzzing in his ears, listening for the distinct chatter of the MG.

Five seconds passed. Ten seconds. Nothing.

Looks like we got –

A deep *pop* sounded from the field.

"Grenade!" Valerie shouted.

"Down! Down!" Jim shouted. He threw himself flat on his stomach, tension gripping his body.

A sharp explosion went off above them. A huge clump of branches fell near Doug. Shrapnel whistled and thumped into the ground.

"Doug!" Jim lifted his head, the fallen branches blocking his view of his cousin. "Doug!"

An arm appeared over the branches, giving him a thumbs up.

"Sound off! Sound off! Everyone okay?"

"Okay!" Val shouted and fired off two bursts.

"I'm good!" This from Williams.

"I'm fine!" Chuck hollered. "I'm fine!"

Jim checked around the tree. The Mothmen still crawled toward the treeline, the closest about ten yards away. Each soldier would slither forward for a bit, then fire a couple bursts from its rifle. Jim fired back, as did the others. He scanned the field for any sign of the grenadier. They got lucky the last time. He wasn't going to count on luck again.

"Flash bangs!" Jim turned left to right, making a throwing motion with his right arm. "Flash bangs!" He fired his M4 and signaled to Doug. His cousin fired a couple bursts before looking at him.

"As soon as the flash bangs go off, you and me are gonna chuck tear gas at 'em."

Mothmen rounds smacked into the trees around them.

"What about the treaty?"

Jim's head trembled in rage. *He's bringing that up in the middle of a firefight?*

"Fuck the stupid fucking treaty! Now do what I say!"

Doug looked reluctant, but nodded.

Jim fired at the Mothmen. When Doug let loose a burst he checked on the others. All of them signaled they had a flash bang ready to throw.

"Do it!" Again he made a throwing gesture, then turned to Doug. "Cover fire!"

He and Doug fired as Val, Chuck and Williams threw their flash bangs. Jim counted to three and turned away. He caught sight of Doug doing the same thing.

Three deep thumps shook the air. He sensed bright flares over the area, which dimmed seconds later. Painful shrieks went up from the field.

"Doug! Now!" Jim took out one of the tear gas canisters, pulled the pin, and tossed it toward the Mothmen. Doug threw his a couple seconds later. Jim pressed his lips together, wondering if tear gas would affect non-human lifeforms.

Even if it doesn't, the cloud should at least blind them even more.

"Move out! Move out!"

Jim led them deeper into the woods. It would take the Mothmen a few minutes to recover from the effects of the flash bangs and the gas. They had to put as much distance between them as possible.

He checked over his shoulder. The cloud of tear gas blocked his view of the Mothmen. But if he couldn't see them, they probably couldn't see –

Something buzzed to his left. Three small geysers of dirt sprang up near him. Jim dove to the ground, rolled and took cover behind a tree. He scanned the woods. No sign of any Mothmen. Where - ?

"In the trees!" Doug yelled. "The trees!" He raised his M4 and fired. Williams joined in a second later.

Jim lifted his head. Through his NVGs he picked out three large, dark shapes among the high branches. The Mothmen troopers fired down on them. Bullets chewed up the ground around them. He saw Valerie get off two bursts from her M4 before turning and crouching behind her tree, Mothmen rounds punching into the trunk. Jim fired into the trees. That drew some of the enemy fire toward him. He pressed his back against the trunk, wincing as he heard, and felt, the bullets striking the thick bark.

"Shit! Shit!"

He looked to the right. Chuck crouched into a ball, his M4 visibly shaking in his hands.

Jim swung around and fired another burst. That's when he noticed two more Mothmen through the breaks in the forest canopy, flying toward their rear.

Dammit! They were about to get hit from two sides, and from the high ground. No way would they last long.

Another burst of fire raked the tree and the ground around it. Jim fired back, as did the others. They had yet to hit any of the Mothmen.

That's when the idea hit him.

"Chuck!"

As soon as his cousin turned to him, Jim yanked out a flash bang grenade and tossed it to him.

"When I tell you, get in the clear there." He pointed to a patch of dirt a couple feet from the tree Chuck used as covered. "Then I want you throw that grenade straight up in the air, as high as you can."

"What!? Are you nuts? I'll get killed!"

"We'll give you cover fire."

Chuck's mouth opened and closed wordlessly. His eyes widened with fear.

"Chuck, you're a baseball player. You've got the best arm of all of us. If you don't do this, we're all dead. Understand?"

Chuck took a ragged breath and nodded.

"Good." He looked at the others. "Cover fire! Cover fire!"

Jim, Valerie, Doug and Williams all opened up with their M4s. Tracers cut through the tall trees.

"Throw it!" He hollered at Chuck.

Chuck rose, his back still against the tree, legs shaking.

"Dammit, Chuck! Throw it now!"

Chuck's body tightened. He took a breath and pulled the pin. In one motion he jumped out from behind the tree and threw the flash bang. Dread coursed through Jim. Chuck was at least a good two feet from where he wanted him. To make matters worse, he had thrown the grenade without even checking above him.

The flash bang hit a branch about twenty feet above them and fell back to the ground.

"Oh shit!" Jim whipped his head left to right. "Down! Down!"

He threw himself on his stomach, and spotted Chuck doing the same. Jim covered his ears and opened his mouth to try and lessen the –

A thunderclap slammed into his body. His ears rang. His skull vibrated. He tried to push himself up and was hit by a dizzy spell.

No. No.

He grabbed for his M4, but his fingers refused to work. He then noticed Chuck nearby, writhing on the ground in agony. To his left he spotted Doug with his hands over his ears.

Something moved in front of him. He looked up, pain hammering his head. Four dark shapes bounded toward him. Mothmen, all with their stubby assault rifles raised.

Jim tried to fight through the disorientation. He managed to snatch his rifle.

The Mothmen were ten feet away.

Would they capture them? Kill them? Either way, they lost. He failed. Again.

The Mothmen slowed their pace, rifles aimed at them.

Suddenly the lead monster jerked. A dark mass flew out the side of its head. It toppled to the ground.

The remaining three Mothmen froze in momentary shock. Before they could recover, yellow tracers tore through the air. Jim pressed himself against the ground as the monsters spasmed and fell.

The other side. Jim rolled on his back, scanning for the Mothmen attacking the front of their little makeshift line. A white flash lit up the tall branches. Instead of dimming, the white mass hovered in the trees.

A Mothman fell out of the branches, swatting at his body. A second one plummeted to the ground, also thrashing wildly.

White Phosphorus? It had to be. Nasty stuff. The moment it made contact with skin, it burned like a motherfucker.

Another white phosphorus round burst in the woods. More tracers streaked between the trees.

Who the hell's firing?

A minute later the chaos ended. Jim just laid on the ground, willing the hammering in his skull and the ringing in his ears to go away. It didn't. He took a breath and looked around. Four large dark lumps rested on the ground behind him, and two more in front of him. Mothmen bodies. All unmoving.

Something shimmered to Jim's right. He swung his head around, grimacing from the pain. At first he thought he was seeing things, a side effect from the flash bang. A tall figure suddenly appeared out of thin air. It wore a sleek motorcycle helmet, and its body was covered in some sort of thick padding. Or was it some sort of metal?

It also clutched a compact, futuristic-looking assault rifle. Jim fumbled for his pistol.

The figure raised its hands, gripping the rifle by the barrel and pointing it to the sky. It slowly made its way toward him. Jim managed to sit up as the figure stopped a foot away and bent down. Its helmeted head bobbed slightly, as if it was talking. Jim scrunched his face in confusion.

The figure set down its rifle and removed its helmet. *Da'hell?*

"It" turned out to be a woman, a woman with smooth, classic features and her hair braided in pigtails. Her mouth moved, but to his battered ears she sounded as though she was talking underwater. Jim pointed to his ears and shook his head.

The woman reached into a compartment of what he assumed had to be a combat vest. She pulled out a notepad and a pen, wrote something down and handed it to him. As he read it, his brow furrowed. A quizzical look formed on his face as he looked at the woman, then back down at what she had wrote.

Major Myra Kenaevya. 95th Recon Battalion. League of Alternate Worlds Armed Forces. We are here to help.

CHAPTER 12

Am I trusting her too quickly?

Jim fixed his eyes on Major Kenaevya, who walked point five yards ahead of him. So many questions raced through his mind. Where had this woman come from? What the hell was the League of Alternate Worlds? Was she really an ally, or did she have an ulterior motive for helping them?

She and her squad did kill all those Mothmen, so I guess the enemy of my enemy is my ally.

At least for now.

Kenaevya hadn't given him time to ask questions, insisting they move ASAP in case more Mothmen were on the way. Jim felt he had no choice but to follow the major and her squad of futuristic-looking warriors.

He glanced around at them. One had a stocky build and carried a tubular, six-round grenade launcher. The second was short and wiry, the third tall and thick, almost like a football player. Both carried a rifle similar to Kenaevya's.

They kept walking. As time passed, the ringing in Jim's ears faded. He fought the urge to start asking Kenaevya questions. Right now they needed to be alert for any enemy patrols. Plus sound traveled farther at night, and for all he knew, the Mothmen's sense of hearing might be keener than a human's.

Kenaevya's right arm snapped up, her hand closed in a fist. The infantryman's signal for *stop*.

Everyone halted. Kenaevya turned around and stared at the big soldier. "Mackanin. Break out your gear. Deathswipe . . ." She paused. "Deploy the Dragonfly. Let's make sure the area's clear."

Jim watched the big soldier, Mackanin, remove a rucksack and pull out a laptop. He then thought of the other name Kenaevya mentioned, Deathswipe. *What the hell kind of name is that?* Since he didn't see the other two soldiers deploying anything, he figured this Deathswipe guy must be further behind them, covering their withdrawal.

"So what exactly are you doing?" Valerie peered over Mackanin's shoulder at his laptop.

"Lieutenant Deathswipe's launchin' a mini UAV." He used the acronym for Unmanned Aerial Vehicle. "I can monitor its sensors here on my screen."

Jim's eyes widened. Mackanin's accent was unmistakable. Texas through and through.

Jim made his way over to Mackanin. So did Kenaevya, Doug and Williams. Chuck sat against a tree stomp, brooding. Probably thinking about throwing that flash-bang that blew up in their faces.

I should have thrown the damn thing myself. But Chuck was the baseball player. He had the best throwing arm out of the five of them. He had been the logical choice to throw it.

Jim just didn't take into consideration Chuck would panic under fire. That oversight almost cost them all their lives.

The corners of Jim's mouth twisted. Chuck had become the weak link in their group. In his experience, weak links got other people killed. Unfortunately, he couldn't just tell Chuck to go home. They were stuck with him. Jim had to find some way to turn him into a dependable member of this group. And he needed to find a way quickly.

"No sign of any bad guys." Mackanin looked up from his computer. "We're safe, for now."

"Good." Kenaevya nodded. She then spoke into her radio. "Deathswipe. No enemy activity in the area. You and Duguid rejoin us . . . copy that."

Kenaevya turned back to Jim. He started to open his mouth, ready to ask a long list of questions.

The others beat him to it.

"Who are you?" both Valerie and Doug demanded.

"Where did you come from?" Chuck asked. "What the hell's that stuff you're wearing?"

"Do you know about those things?" This from Williams.

The questions all flew out at once, followed by more before Kenaevya could answer any one of them. Plus their voices grew louder.

"Quiet down!" Jim snapped his hand down in front of him. "This isn't a damn post-game press conference. I'll ask the questions. Me and me alone."

He swung around to face Kenaevya again. She took off her helmet and flashed him a quick smile. Jim's gaze lingered on the woman's face. Even with the sweat shining on her skin and her hair matted down, she still looked very attractive.

An image of Hannah floated through his mind. He shut his eyes for a moment. *Focus.* "First off, thanks for saving our lives. We appreciate it. Now, who the heck are you?"

"I already told you. My name is Major Myra Kenaevya."

Jim now took note of the woman's accent. Definitely foreign, and an accent he recognized. He'd cross-trained once with special ops forces from that particular country.

Kenaevya was Israeli.

"You know what I mean. You show up out of nowhere, wearing a uniform I've never seen before, carrying a rifle I've never seen before, claiming you're with some group called the League of Alternate Worlds. I wanna know what your story is."

"I am sure you do. But first, I would also like to know who I am talking with."

"Major Jim Rhyne, U.S. Army." He then introduced his sister, cousins and Williams.

"In what units do you serve?"

Jim hesitated, then figured if they got into another firefight with the Mothmen, the woman may want to know they could hold their own.

Most of us, anyway. He glanced at Chuck.

"Doug's with the Hundred-First Airborne, Valerie's with the One-Sixtieth Special Ops Aviation Regiment, Williams is Ohio Air Guard, and Chuck . . . well, he plays college baseball."

"And you?"

Again, he hesitated. "I'm Special Forces." Not exactly a lie, since Delta Force had been originally designated 1st Special Forces Operational Detachment Delta. But because of their anti-terrorist mission, Jim and his comrades did not publicize the fact they belonged to Delta Force.

Kenaevya cranked a thin eyebrow. "Three soldiers, all related, a pilot and a civilian. That doesn't sound like the sort of special operations squad your military would put together."

"My family and I were on a hunting trip when those monsters invaded. We met up with Captain Williams after his F-16 got shot down."

"Ah." Kenaevya nodded. She went around and introduced her men. Mackanin was Senior Trooper Craig Mackanin, the stocky soldier First Centurion Namayxotl, or just "One Cent," and the wiry man Centurion Errol O'Neal.

Centurion? Senior Trooper? Who the hell used those ranks? And what the hell kind of name was Nama . . . Nama . . . that One Cent guy?

"There. Now we all know one another." Kenaevya gave Jim another brief smile and stepped over to him. He craned his neck a little to stare into her eyes. "I know you have many questions, but first, I would like to know how much you know about what has happened to your world."

"We know that the whole world's been invaded by these things that, according to Chuck, look like a monster called the Mothman. They seem more advanced than us, and they don't like us very much."

"Mm. Mothman. So you call them that, too."

Jim's brow furrowed. "What do you mean 'too'?"

Kenaevya paused. "What I'm about to tell you may sound . . . far-fetched."

"Lady . . . I mean, Major, the Earth's been invaded by monsters. I don't know what else can be more far-fetched than that."

"Very well." She took a breath before continuing. "The League of Alternate Worlds is an alliance made up of different Earths."

A bewildered look fell over Jim's face. "Different Earths?"

"Wait a minute," Chuck blurted. "You mean like parallel Earths?"

"That's correct."

"Parallel Earths?" Doug shot puzzled looks at his brother and Major Kenaevya. "What the hell is a parallel Earth?"

"You know, like in *Star Trek*," Chuck answered. "There was this universe and the mirror universe that existed side-by-side. In our universe, Captain Kirk was a good guy, and in the other one he was a bad guy." A satisfied grin grew on his face, as though he was glad he knew something his older brother didn't. He then looked to Kenaevya and the other League troopers. "I am right, ain't I?"

Mackanin let out a short chuckle. "Good thing that episode's been done on a lotta other Earths. Makes explainin' the whole concept easier."

"He is right," Kenaevya said. "Your Earth is one of many that exist side-by-side in the multiverse. Some things are similar, others are radically different. In One Cent's world, the Aztec Empire still exists. Mackanin comes from an Earth where Texas is a sovereign nation, not part of the United States. On O'Neal's Earth, his native Barbados was occupied by the Japanese during their Caribbean campaign in World War Two."

Jim just stood silent, his mind trying to accept Kenaevya's words as reality. Was she serious? He remembered reading a book a few years back of essays from historians that explored the what ifs of a Confederate victory at Antietam and an American defeat at Midway. But that had been all speculation. Now, according to Kenaevya, worlds like that really existed.

"So what about your Earth?" Chuck asked Kenaevya.

"On my Earth, my Amazon sisters spread throughout the world. And there are countless other Earths, where the Roman Empire never fell, where neither world wars happened, where the Germans won the Second World War, where technology is at a Seventeenth Century level . . ."

"Okay, we get the idea." Jim raised a hand, urging her to stop. "So how did you come to be on our Earth?"

"Trooper Mackanin can answer that. He went to Texas Technical Institute after all."

The Texan looked to Jim. "See, there's naturally occurrin' portals throughout the Earths where the fabric of space/time is weak. Ya might know 'em as The Bermuda Triangle, The Alaska Zone, The North Sea Vortex. Sometimes ships and planes and people go into 'em, and don't come out. Turns out in some cases they've gone through these portals and wind up on alternate Earths. We have the technology to make our own portals." Mackanin launched into an explanation involving electromagnetic fields, quantum physics and multiple dimensions. Jim tried to keep up, but gave up after less than a minute. The only possible way he'd be able to understand Mackanin's scientific babble was if his name had been Stephen Hawking.

Kenaevya briefly chuckled. "I graduated in the top ten percent of my academy class, and I still cannot follow all that."

Mackanin let out an audible sigh. Jim sensed a vibe coming from the Texan, one he'd seen before from other very intelligent people. *I understand it. How come no one else can?*

"So the Mothmen. Are you people in some kind of war with them?"

"Yes." Kenaevya nodded to Jim. "We have been for many years."

"Who . . . what are they? Where do they come from?"

"Earth."

Jim drew his head back. "You gotta be kidding me. How can those things be from Earth?"

Kenaevya frowned. "Forgive. What I mean is, most Earths in the multiverse developed the same way, in terms of geology and climate and evolution. But there are other Earths that are still in a Jurassic or Cretaceous stage of development, or are nothing more than large balls of molten rock. There are also Earths where humans did not evolve into the dominant species on the planet."

"And the Mothmen came from one of those Earths." Jim fought off the urge to wince. He couldn't believe he was seriously discussing the existence of other Earths with an armored woman who claimed to be an Amazon.

"Correct. Though their actual name is the Shreth'kil. At least, that is the rough English translation of their name."

"Mm-hmm." Jim folded his arms, eyes still locked on the tall woman. "You said we call them Mothmen here, too. What did you mean by that?"

"The Shreth'kil have journeyed to many Earths, including yours, for hundreds of years."

"What? How?"

"Interdimensional portals. Not as large or as famous as the Bermuda Triangle or the North Sea Vortex. But all over Earths, there are small portals in forests and deserts and mountains. Sometimes, a Shreth'kil has wandered into those portals and ended up on other Earths. A few managed to make it back to their own world and tell of their experiences. But those . . . wanderings to other worlds resulted in legends like the Jersey Devil, Big Bat in New Zealand, and your Mothman."

Jim slowly worked his jaw back and forth. He looked over his shoulder. "Chuck. How long have people been reporting things like Mothman and the Jersey Devil?"

"Um, Mothman was back in the 1960s. The Jersey Devil . . . uh, I saw a show about that thing, too. I think people started seeing him in, like, the 1700s. Oh! I do remember there was this one time, 1910 I think, when there were all these sightings in Southern New Jersey and Philadelphia. People were, like, freaking out. They actually closed schools and offered rewards to anyone who killed it."

Jim mulled over Chuck's words. Before today he would have chalked up a story like that to mass hysteria and the sensational journalism of the time. Now . . . could there have been something to that story?

"All right." He turned back to Kenaevya. "So these things drop in on our Earth from time to time, and people see them and report them. My question is, why don't the Mothmen . . . er, Shreth'kil, kill them? Why let them escape and tell the whole world of their existence?"

"Sometimes they do kill them. Every Earth has their missing hiker or hunter or camper stories. Some of them are likely Shreth'kil victims. But a few of them they let go because they feel those stories will make people afraid of them. Shreth'kil use fear as part of their tactical and strategic doctrine. On some Earths, whole areas of land have been declared off limits, even destroyed, because the fear of whatever the locals call the Shreth'kil is so great."

"I bet that's why they did what they did with the TV," Williams chimed in.

Both Jim and Kenaevya looked at him. "Excuse me?" asked the Amazon.

"Well, Ma'am, back at my base we made it a point to monitor the television. Most of the time we picked up nothing but static. But every once in a while we'd get a picture, like the . . . Shreth'kil, murdering the royal family in Britain or these big explosions in Miami and Riyadh. Any idea what those might be? They didn't look like nukes."

"Orbital kinetic energy rounds," answered Mackanin. "Shreth'kil bring in these mobile gantries and launch the satellite into orbit, where it fires a tungsten rod that can travel 'bout twelve thousand feet a second. When you take into consideration the speed of the rod, its weight, and the height it was launched from, the force of impact, and the amount of energy released -"

"Basically," Kenaevya interrupted him. "The rod hits with the force of a sizeable meteorite."

With his helmet still on, Jim couldn't see Mackanin's face. But his body language showed he was not happy being cut off before he launched into his impromptu physics lesson.

"Rods from God," Williams said. "That's what we call them. But that system is still on the drawing board. It's probably fifteen, twenty years away from actually being built and deployed."

"So was that another scare tactic of theirs?" Jim asked. "Turn on the TV long enough so we can watch them kill the Royal Family and blow up a couple of our cities?"

Kenaevya nodded. "Whenever something out of the norm happens, people want information about it. But when all their sources of information are taken away, they panic. Then the Shreth'kil will broadcast images from time to time of them destroying famous landmarks and cities or killing well-known people. All with impunity. The population will believe all is lost. They will flee or hide or riot or pray or even take their own lives. They will do everything but resist the Shreth'kil."

"Not everyone does that." Jim's face stiffened with determination.

"Obviously." Kenaevya gave him a quick, appraising gaze, then flashed him a smile. A tingle went through his stomach.

Jim cleared his throat and regained his composure. "So, um, the Shreth'kil. We need to know what -"

Valerie suddenly gasped.

"Holy shit!" Chuck cried out.

"What the hell is that?" Williams blurted.

Jim spun around, clutching his M-4 tight. Shock slammed into him.

A figure appeared in the darkness. Tall . . . *very tall*. Over eight feet in height. It wore a version of the armor

Kenaevya and her soldiers had, but the helmet only covered part of the face, which ended in an elongated snout. It carried a sleek light machine gun, and its slender legs ended in three-toed, taloned feet.

Jim Rhyne was staring at a dinosaur. An honest-to-goodness armor-clad dinosaur.

He raised his rifle. Doug did the same. An instant later, Mackanin and O'Neal brought up their rifles, while the One Cent drew a huge pistol.

"Stay your weapons!" Kenaevya shouted. She then clamped a hand on Jim's shoulder. "Lieutenant Deathswipe is on our side!"

"What?" He didn't take his eyes, or rifle, off the dinosaur.

"Remember what I said about some Earths following a different evolutionary path? Deathswipe is from one of those worlds. Dinosaurs, not humans, became the dominant species. They're part of the LAW. Deathswipe is my XO."

Jim took a calming breath and lowered his M-4. He signaled Doug to do the same. Mackanin, O'Neal and One Cent also lowered their weapons.

"You owe me five, Craig," O'Neal said to the Texan. "I told you one of them would scream when they saw the lieutenant."

"That wasn't a scream. It was a gasp. So you owe me five."

"Bull. One Cent, what's your ruling?"

First Centurion Namayxotl said something Jim couldn't make out. *What the hell language is that?* Aztec, he figured.

Whatever the One Cent said, it made O'Neal groan and Mackanin say, "You'all heard the man. Pay up."

Deathswipe snorted and turned to another new arrival, a soldier carrying a long, slender sniper's rifle. Duguid, he assumed. The dinosaur emitted a series of grunts and clicks. Duguid shook his head and muttered something in very harsh French.

"What did they just say?" Valerie asked.

"Oh. Forgive." Kenaevya reached into her combat vest and pulled out five small devices that resembled hearing aids. "We always carry a few of these in case we wind up working with locals." She lifted her hand to her face, said, "English," then handed out the devices to Jim and the others. They all stuck them in their right ears.

"Good. Now, you three." Kenaevya pointed to One Cent, Deathswipe and Duguid. "Repeat what you said."

One Cent went first, again speaking in his native tongue. But a computerized voice burst from Jim's earpiece. "I said that a gasp and a scream are two different things. The woman gasped, so Mackanin wins the wager."

Deathswipe spoke next. "I wagered Trooper Duguid that you locals would draw your weapons upon seeing me."

Duguid groaned. "And I lamented the fact this makes it the third wager in a row I have lost to the lieutenant."

Jim turned back to Kenaevya and pointed to his ear. "Well this is handy."

"The LAW is made up of countless nationalities and languages. We had to find some way for everyone to understand one another."

Kenaevya waited for her executive officer and sniper to get closer before continuing. "Now, it sounded like you had some other questions before Deathswipe and Duguid arrived."

"Yeah, I did. We already know the Shreth'kil can fly. I want to know how fast."

"The fastest speed on record is eighty-nine miles-per-hour. That's flying straight and level. In a dive, they can reach a maximum speed of one hundred sixty-five miles-per-hour."

"Any other advantages they have over humans?"

"They see very well at night. Of course, they are primarily a nocturnal species. They're also stronger on average than humans, and have keener hearing."

"Any weaknesses?"

"They don't like bright light. When they operate during the daytime, they'll wear special goggles to protect them from the sunlight."

Jim thought back to the fight at the church. None of the Mothmen . . . Shreth'kil, had worn any goggles. Of course, the attack had happened just as dawn broke. It was probably when the sun was fully up that they'd need eye protection.

"And," Kenaevya continued. "They also have a poor sense of smell compared to humans."

"Okay, now for the big one. Why are they here?"

"The same reason most empires and countries invade another. To expand their territory. And . . ." Kenaevya bit her lip.

Jim leaned forward slightly. "And what?"

"And for food."

"What kind of food?"

The corners of Kenaevya's mouth twisted. "You."

CHAPTER 13

Food. We're actually food for these things.

The surreal thought echoed in Jim's mind, as it had ever since they resumed their hike through the Kentucky wilderness half-an-hour earlier. It seemed too ridiculous to take seriously, like something out of a bad sci-fi movie.

Then again, the last twenty-four hours have been like a bad sci-fi movie.

His mind's eye bombarded him with images of Reverend Crawford's congregation. He replayed those last few minutes in the basement, pleading in vain with them to leave.

I should have grabbed one of them. Just one.

Little Amanda could have been that one.

Instead he left them all there. For all he knew, every last one of them had been chopped up into a stew and served in some Shreth'kil mess hall.

A cold, dark hole opened in his stomach. He wished Major Kenaevya never told him about that.

He wished the Shreth'kil had never come to Earth.

He wished Hannah was alive.

Jim snorted. Like wishing for all that would make it come true. It was just a waste of time.

He scanned the woods around him. All clear. He then checked on the members of their eclectic little group. Sister, cousins, fighter jock, alternate Earth people . . . dinosaur. All present and accounted for.

His eyes lingered on Doug and Chuck, taking note of how the older of the two moved his head. Sweep left. Glance at Chuck. Sweep right. Glance at Chuck.

He's keeping an eye on him. Making sure he doesn't screw up again. Jim grimaced. If you had to keep tabs on the weak link of the group, then you couldn't watch for the enemy, which could ultimately prove fatal, for all of them.

They kept walking, south. Away from Ohio. Deeper into enemy territory. It didn't surprise him. Kenaevya's bunch belonged to a recon battalion. That's what they did. Sneak around the bad guys' real estate and gather intel. Hell, he'd done that himself, first as a Ranger, then with Delta Force.

It also made him realize something. If Kenaevya's squad was doing recon here, did that mean a much larger LAW force planned to come in and deal with the Shreth'kil?

As liberators . . . or occupiers?

Jim frowned. He hated not being able to fully trust Kenaevya and her squad, especially since he and his family might have to depend on them to get through this alive. But he'd only known them for, what, an hour at best? Nowhere near enough time to trust them implicitly. In his gut, he felt the LAW soldiers were being sincere. But feeling was not the same as knowing.

The corners of his mouth twisted. For the first time, he truly understood how a good number of Iraqis must have felt during Operation: Iraqi Freedom.

We knew our intentions were just. But how could they be one hundred percent sure?

Fifteen minutes later, Kenaevya called a halt, and a chow break. She assigned Duguid to stand sentry for fifteen minutes, at which time he'd come back to eat while Deathswipe took his place.

Jim grabbed an MRE from his MOLLE pack. He groaned when he read the package. Vegetable Lasagna. Not his favorite, by far. Not like he had a favorite MRE anyway. The stuff was only meant to provide sustenance and give a soldier enough calories to get him through an active day. So what did taste matter?

At least his package came with a little bottle of Tabasco sauce. Dump it on the vegetable lasagna and that would help make it edible.

Barely.

He looked around at the LAW troopers. They, too, had rations similar to MREs. Like most of the soldiers on this Earth, they didn't look thrilled by the contents, or the taste. Deathswipe had the most "interesting" MRE of all. Jim watched the dinosaur scoop out stuff that looked like intestines and shove them into his mouth. After swallowing the first mouthful, Deathswipe grunted, a dissatisfied grunt at that.

Maybe he prefers his food alive.

Williams also watched Deathswipe eat. A grimace came over the pilot's face as the dinosaur shoved another clawful of intestines into his mouth. Looking like he was about to puke, Williams scooted away from Deathswipe and turned his back on him. He stared into his own MRE, but looked like his appetite had been destroyed. Valerie and Doug also made faces as they watched the dinosaur eat. Chuck, judging from his expression, thought it was the coolest thing.

"What's that you're eating?" he asked.

Deathswipe turned to him and snorted. "Pig bladders and livers. Freeze dried, of course, and barely edible." The dinosaur scooped out more intestines and ate them.

Valerie's face scrunched in disgust. The LAW troopers, however, didn't bat an eyelash. They had probably grown used to seeing Deathswipe chow down on uncooked animal parts.

Mealtime also gave them the chance to ask the LAW troopers more questions. Valerie got the ball rolling. "So how long have you been fighting the Mothmen . . . I mean, Shreth'kil?"

"Technically, since 1980," Kenaevya answered. "That's when the LAW was formed, after the Roman Empire defeated the Shreth'kil invasion of their Earth. But the Romans had been fighting them for five years prior. And long before that, the Shreth'kil invaded and conquered other Earths."

"When did all that start?" asked Williams.

"Back in the Fifties." This from Mackanin. "That's when the Shreth'kil scientists managed ta create the first artificial portal by causin' fluctuations in the local electromagnetic field and injectin' a stream of -"

Kenaevya cut off the trooper by clearing her throat, loudly. Jim figured this was necessary to keep the Texan from going into an MIT-type lecture.

Mackanin frowned and looked away.

"This invention did not just give the Shreth'kil the means to create artificial transit portals that were inherently more stable than naturally occurring ones," Kenaevya said. "It also had another result. It helped unite their race."

"How did that happen?" asked Valerie.

"Before the advent of what we call transit technology, the Shreth'kil were divided among three major nations and several smaller ones, all in conflict with one another over territory and resources. But with the means to open stable inter-dimensional portals, multiple Earths were open to them."

"Earths mainly populated by humans," said the One Cent, a trace of bitterness in his voice. "Who the Shreth'kil feared might one day discover how to create stable portals themselves and attack their Earth. There is nothing like a common enemy to make a divided people band together."

"They started out invading Earths far less advanced than they were," Kenaevya continued, "such as Neanderthal Earth, Bronze Age Earth, an Earth still in the grip of the Dark Ages. When they discovered Roman Empire Earth, they learned the Romans were doing what they had feared most . . . research into their own transit technology. So the Shreth'kil invaded. Luckily, the Romans defeated them, perfected their own transit portals, and made alliances with other Earths to fight the Shreth'kil."

Jim just stared at the Amazon, taking in this latest batch of information. *That explains the Centurion stuff.* Roman Empire Earth must be a major player in the League of Alternate Worlds, like the U.S. was in NATO.

"How many Earths have the Shreth'kil invaded?" Doug asked before spooning some chicken and rice from his MRE into his mouth.

"Currently, they rule thirty-three Earths. We are fighting them for control of ten other Earths, eleven now if you count this one."

"So I guess that's why you're all here." Jim did a quick scan of the Kenaevya's troopers. "Doing recon for a much larger LAW force."

Williams sat up straighter, his eyes widening. "Is that true? Are your buddies going to come here and kick these bat things the hell off our world?"

A determined look came over Kenaevya's face. "That is correct."

"So when's that gonna happen?" Anxiousness laced Chuck's voice.

"I cannot say for certain. There are several land, sea, and air forces deploying at various locations around the multiverse preparing to liberate this Earth." Kenaevya's lips tightened. Silence hung in the air for several seconds.

Jim's brow furrowed. "What?"

Kenaevya sighed harshly. "I am sorry to tell you this. For months the LAW has gathered intelligence that showed the Shreth'kil were planning to invade another Earth, though they had no idea which one. It wasn't until a week ago they learned for certain it was your Earth the Shreth'kil had targeted. My understanding is the League was preparing to contact many of your world leaders and alert them of the threat when the Shreth'kil attacked."

Valerie gasped. Chuck's jaw dropped. Doug snorted and crossed his arms.

Jim clenched the plastic spork from his MRE tight in his hand. Anger boiled up inside him. If the damn LAW intel assholes had been on the ball, they could have discovered this Earth was the target a lot sooner. They could have stopped the invasion. They could have saved thousands, millions.

His eyes narrowed at Major Kenaevya. He took a breath, ready to lash out at her.

But he didn't. It wasn't her fault. Kenaevya was just like him. A soldier. During his Army career, Jim had been the victim of bad decisions and sloppy work by people who sat in comfy, air conditioned offices thousands of miles from the desolate, uncomfortable patches of earth where he worked. He doubted things were any different with Kenaevya.

"I'm sorry." She fixed her gaze on him. He could see in her eyes a glimmer of remorse, as though the invasion of this Earth had been her fault, and hers alone. He noted the woman's body language, the tone of her voice as she apologized. He detected no insincerity.

Some of his suspicions regarding Kenaevya and the LAW began to vanish. In their place appeared something else. Hope. Hope that Kenaevya's LAW friends would arrive soon and defeat the Shreth'kil.

They quickly finished their meals. Jim managed to get in one more question before they resumed their hike.

"When we first encountered the Shreth'kil, we took their rifles and tried to fire them, but they wouldn't work. Do they have a different kind of safety than our weapons?"

"That they do," answered Trooper Mackanin. "They got biometric chips in their rifles, all their weapons systems, as a matter of fact. It scans the DNA of the person, or being, holding it. They'll work for the Shreth'kil fine, but not for us."

Jim nodded. He'd heard of similar technology being developed on this Earth, but none of it had gotten beyond the testing stage.

They hiked for about three more hours before coming to a main road. Kentucky Route 79, according to One Cent, who got the information from his armor's built-in computer.

"All right." Kenaevya looked around at her squad. "We'll set up here and see how active this road is."

She deployed her men. O'Neal guarded their rear. Duguid was sent a mile to the south, while Deathswipe headed a mile north, each trooper to give advanced warning of any approaching vehicles. The rest of them found bushes or trees to hide behind and waited.

And waited.

And waited.

An hour passed without any activity. Then two hours. Kenaevya, One Cent and Mackanin switched positions with O'Neal, Duguid and Deathswipe.

Three hours. They didn't see so much as a rabbit hopping down the road.

Jim checked around. Chuck kept shifting his position behind his tree, his eyes more on the ground than on the road. A bored look on his face.

Val's head dropped, then snapped back up. She rubbed her eyes, poured a handful of water from her plastic bottle and splashed it on her face.

Tabasco sauce in the eyes is better. He'd learned that trick to stay awake when he went through Ranger School.

Doug was doing a little better, but Jim could see his cousin's attention wavering from the road to the ground.

Hell, even he had to fight off the boredom and tiredness that threatened to overwhelm him. But he did. Unlike Val, Doug and Chuck, he'd done this before. Sit in one spot, wait for the enemy to show up, then report it to someone higher up the chain in command so they could either launch an air strike or file it away for future consideration. Hollywood and the public probably thought that special ops types just mowed down a hundred bad guys a la Rambo or Chuck

Norris, and walked away without a scratch. The truth was less exciting. A good portion of special operations involved a group of highly trained men doing what they were doing right now. Hide, observe and report.

Part of him wished something would come down the road. A Shreth'kil convoy maybe. They had to have vehicles, didn't they? How else could they move large amounts of supplies from Point A to Point B?

Next break we get I gotta ask Kenaevya about –

"Shreth'kil vehicles approaching from the north," Deathswipe hissed.

Val, Doug and Chuck brought their full attention to the road. Jim gripped his M-4 tighter and crouched lower behind his bush. The armor-clad LAW troopers shimmered and vanished in the darkness *Predator* style.

Damn, that is cool.

Jim concentrated, listening for the growl of multiple engines. He heard nothing. He held his breath, straining for any trace of sound.

A minute later he heard something. Not the typical growl of a vehicle engine. More like a low hum.

Rectangular shapes appeared down the road. No headlights. The Shreth'kil probably didn't need them from what Kenaevya said about their night vision.

Jim tensed, quickly checking on the others. Everyone was hidden.

Well enough to not be seen by creatures with night vision?

His teeth clenched. The convoy would have to have guard vehicles. How many? What weapons did they carry? How many soldiers were there? What sort of training and experience did they have?

What were their chances of survival if the Shreth'kil spotted them?

The steady hum increased. Half-a-minute later the first vehicle drove past. Big, boxy, with six wheels. A Shreth'kil poked out of the roof, manning some sort of large caliber machine gun.

The vehicle continued on.

Jim breathed a little easier.

Three more vehicles passed, all resembling large tour buses, only with battleship gray armor plating and no side windows. Next came another combat vehicle, this one packing what looked like a grenade launcher. Three more bus-like vehicles went by. Transports? The Shreth'kil versions of the Army's venerable deuce-and-a-half truck? A third combat vehicle brought up the rear. This one had no Shreth'kil soldier in a pintel mount manning a weapon. Instead a small quadruple missile launcher sat near the front cab. To the rear was a turret with ten stubby barrels. Jim worked his jaw back and forth in thought. Could it be an anti-tank vehicle? Anti-air? Both?

The convoy hummed along and eventually disappeared from sight. The tension dissolved from Jim's muscles. They hadn't been seen.

The LAW troopers disengaged their *Predator* camouflage. Jim turned to the closest one, Duguid. "What's up with those engines?" he whispered.

"Pardon?"

"I mean the noise they made. They don't sound like normal engines."

"They are powered by hydrogen fuel cells. We have them as well."

Jim nodded, his eyebrow cranked as he noted Duguid's accent. Two years ago he spent time cross-training with GIGN, France's elite counter-terrorist unit. Duguid's accent sounded nothing like those men's. It sounded rougher. In fact, he'd heard it before. In an enormous organization like the U.S. Armed Forces, made up of people from every state and territory, one can became adept at identifying accents.

And Duguid's accent sounded more Cajun than French.

I wonder what his story is.

He'd have to find out later. Right now their priority was watching the road.

When the sun came up, another convoy passed by, north to south. Same as before. Six transports, three combat vehicles. A couple hours later a squadron of helicopters flew high overhead. Four large, boxy ones and two sleek, shark-like ones. The big ones had to be transports. The sleeker ones were probably attack helicopters flying escort.

"It's weird, man," Chuck said after the choppers faded into the distance. "The freakin' Shreth'kil have wings, but they still use helicopters and jets."

"There is a limit to how far and fast they can fly before they tire," Deathswipe responded. "They certainly cannot fly as fast as combat aircraft, or carry large amounts of supplies."

"Even so, those boys hate flyin' in aircraft," Mackanin jumped in. "Kind of a pride thing with 'em. That's why all their aircraft are remote controlled."

Around mid-morning more Shreth'kil vehicles appeared. Jim counted twelve main battle tanks with flat turrets and guns with angled shrouds to reduce radar reflection. Also mixed in were six rectangular vehicles with sloped hoods. Infantry fighting vehicles, probably used as scouts. Four had rounded turrets with a pair of thin gun barrels. One had small missile tubes. Anti-air defense, he assumed. The last carried something that looked like a spotlight. He'd seen devices similar to it on some shows on The Military Channel.

It was a laser.

All eighteen vehicles headed north.

Jim bit his lower lip. Could the Shreth'kil be making a push into Ohio?

Morning gave way to afternoon, and no other vehicles appeared on Route 79. Kenaevya decided to move on. After making sure the road was clear, the group sprinted across to the other side. They hiked another two miles before Kenaevya called a halt. She ordered Mackanin to switch his laptop to communications mode so she could make her report. Kenaevya informed whoever she had contacted about their engagement with the Shreth'kil, the new additions to her group, including their names and units, and the enemy activity on Route 79.

"We were unable to confirm if those transports were carrying supplies or if they were meat wagons."

Jim scrunched his face at the term Kenaevya used. He turned to O'Neal. "What does she mean by meat wagon?"

"It's what we call vehicles the Shreth'kil use to transport human prisoners. Some they'll just send through transit portals to different Earths, while others will stay on this Earth to feed the Shreth'kil soldiers deployed here."

A heavy feeling formed in Jim's chest. The guilt returned, guilt at abandoning Reverend Crawford's congregation. Had they been shipped off to some other Earth? An Earth dominated by Shreth'kil, with no hope of rescue?

An image of little Amanda formed in his mind's eye.

I'm sorry. I'm so sorry.

"Major Rhyne."

Kenaevya's voice snapped him out of his misery. He looked up to see the Amazon waving him over.

"What is it?"

Kenaevya folded her arms and gave him a half-frown. "You've been keeping things to yourself."

A perplexed look came over his face. "What do you mean?"

"You told me you were Special Forces. But now I find out the truth. You're really Delta Force."

Jim held his breath and widened his eyes. "How did you know?"

To his surprise, Kenaevya chuckled. "Nothing to fear, Major. I've worked with you Deltas on other Earths. I know how secretive you like to be. A necessity in your line of work. But when my superiors ran a check on your name, they discovered someone you will be most interested to talk to."

"Who?"

Kenaevya just grinned at him and looked down at Mackanin, who sat in front of his laptop. "Mackanin?"

"Link's established." The Texan waved Jim to kneel down beside him. He then tapped the mouse pad.

The screen flickered. A stout man with a craggy face and a shaved head appeared.

It took all of Jim's self-control to keep his jaw from dropping.

"General Monge?"

"Major. You have no idea how glad I am to see you alive and well," replied the commanding officer of Delta Force.

CHAPTER 14

A flicker of hope sparked inside Jim, the first one he'd had since he'd learned about the Shreth'kil invasion. He'd feared the worst when he heard Fort Bragg had been attacked. But seeing General Monge's face, knowing his CO was still alive, reassured him that not everything had gone completely to hell.

"Glad to see you're all right too, Sir," he told Monge. "I assume you've linked up with some of these LAW people as well?"

"More like they linked up with us. We made contact with one another after Fort Bragg was attacked."

"How did you guys come through it?"

A thin smile traced Monge's lips. "Well, we taught those ugly bastards one lesson. When you come to a post that has three of the best units in the United States Army, you're gonna be in for one hell of a fight."

Now Jim smiled, thinking about the 82nd Airborne, the Green Berets, and his Delta Force all slugging it out with the Shreth'kil. "Did we hold the base?"

Monge's smile turned into a grim expression. "Unfortunately no. We fought 'em hard, but without outside support or reinforcements, our situation became unattainable. Bragg was pretty much destroyed."

Jim lowered his head. Images of familiar buildings and landmarks turned into charred rubble formed in his mind's eye. Fear grew inside him, turning his stomach into a cold lead ball. "Casualties?"

"For all combat forces at Bragg, around sixty-five percent. We also lost over half the Deltas based here. As for our boys overseas, we haven't been able to get in touch with any of them. If they're still alive, they're all on their own."

A lump formed in Jim's throat. Delta Force was a small unit. Not even a thousand operators total. And he knew many of them. Some in passing, some rather well, and some were like brothers to him. Who had died? Who had survived?

I should have been there with them. Maybe his leadership could have saved some of his friends. Maybe he could have helped turn the tide of battle.

Another thought struck him. "General. What about the dependents living on base?"

"We did manage to evacuate some of them. The rest . . ." A sullen look formed on Monge's face. "The rest were captured by the Shreth'kil."

The lump in Jim's throat grew. He forced his words past it. "General. The Shreth'kil, they . . ."

"I know, Major. The LAW folks here told us what those sons-of-bitches do to their prisoners."

"We've seen evidence of that on this end. Fort Campbell was deserted when we got there. Same with Cadiz."

"Cadiz?"

"A little town west of Campbell. We saw signs of battle, but no people."

Monge nodded. "That seems to be the MO of these things. They send in shock troops to take care of any military or police units, then follow it up with what they call sweeper units to incapacitate the civilian population, collect them, and haul them off to . . . well, you know."

"Any idea why the Shreth'kil don't just use those sonic weapons to take down military forces?" Jim glanced between Monge and Kenaevya. "Seems it would be a lot easier for them instead of having to fight it out with us."

"I asked our LAW friends about that, too," Monge said. "The Shreth'kil did try that years ago. The problem is those sonic devices have a limited range. Even the big vehicle-mounted ones only have a maximum radius of about a mile. So an army could just sit back out of range and hit them with artillery or missiles. After that, the Shreth'kil figured they had no choice but to engage human armed forces and destroy them before bringing in their sonic weapons."

Jim nodded. "General, we heard D.C. was one of the first places hit. Is the President okay?"

Monge exhaled slowly. "The President was evacuated to the Mount Weather bunker shortly after the invasion began. From what we understand, the Shreth'kil hit it a few hours after the President arrived. We haven't heard from him since, and have to assume . . ." He tightened his lips for a moment. "We have to assume the President is dead."

Jim froze. The words sounded surreal. The President dead? He'd never been a fan of the current occupant of the Oval Office. Still, the man was President, his Commander-in-Chief. Was he really dead?

"Oh my God." Valerie pressed a hand against her chest, her eyes wide with shock.

"Shit," Chuck said in a stunned whisper, while Doug and Williams gaped at the screen.

Jim closed his eyes and drew a deep breath, forcing himself to accept the death of the first sitting President in fifty-some years. "Is Continuity of Government in effect?"

"To an extent," Monge answered. "Right now the only communications systems we have that work are the ones the LAW brought with them, those and a few short wave radios we scrounged up. The Shreth'kil launched one hell of a cyber attack against us. Apparently they have these quantum computers. Don't even ask me to explain how exactly they work. Let's just say they make our computers look like an old Pong game. Completely took out our satellites, cell phones, internet, everything."

"Do we have a President, Sir?"

"Yes. We had to go down a few places on the succession list to get one, but as of right now, our Commander-in-Chief is Treasury Secretary Jorgensen."

Jim furrowed his brow, summoning up what he knew about the man. Since cabinet members were considered high value targets for terrorists, Delta Force received extensive backgrounds on each one.

Edward Jorgensen, 52, wife and two children. Masters in economics from Stanford, doctorate in same from Yale. Taught at Brown for ten years before becoming director of The Center for Economic Justice. Supporter of the ACLU, Amnesty International and Greenpeace. No real world experience. Probably no clue how the military works.

All in all, not the guy he wanted as President in a crisis like this.

"What are our orders, Sir?"

"This comes directly from the President. All surviving United States military personnel are to fully cooperate with the forces from the League of Alternate Worlds, and do everything in their power to resist the Shreth'kil invasion."

Jim nodded. He thanked God even a die-hard lefty like Jorgensen had the sense to realize talking and appeasement wouldn't end this war. It was either fight or end up on a Shreth'kil dinner menu.

But as to his other order, "fully cooperate with the forces from the League of Alternate Worlds . . ." He just stared at the screen and chewed on his lower lip.

"I know the LAW just showed up on our doorstep, Major," Monge said. "But the ones I've been around are good people. They genuinely want to help us, and they have a lot of experience fighting those bat-faced bastards."

"Yes, Sir," he responded in a flat tone.

"Do whatever you can in your neck of the woods to fight these things."

"You can count on me, Sir, and my family."

Monge grinned. "I have no doubt about that. One other thing. If you engage any Shreth'kil, try to take out the demon-looking ones first."

"Why them?"

"Your LAW friends didn't tell you?"

"We've been on the move quite a bit since they found us," Jim said. "I haven't had a chance to ask them why some of the Shreth'kil look different."

"It's their way of showing their status," Monge told him. "We show our rank with stripes and bars and stars, they show theirs with cosmetic surgery. The bat-looking ones are the grunts, the ones with stubby horns and beaks are NCOs, and the demon ones are the officers. Rule of thumb is, the more demonic they look, the higher up in the chain of command they are."

"Good to know, Sir. Thank you."

"Take care of yourself, Major. You and your family."

"*Hu-ah.*" Jim gave him the Army Ranger reply for "Heard, Understood, Acknowledged."

"*Hu-ah.*" Monge replied before signing off.

Jim turned around and found Kenaevya targeting him with a concerned stare.

"Problem?" he asked.

"It appeared you were rather hesitant to trust us, even though we did save you from either being killed or winding up in a Shreth'kil's stomach."

The corners of Jim's mouth twisted. "The President ordered all U.S. military personnel to cooperate with you people, and I'll obey that order."

"Cooperation is not necessarily the same as trust." A stony expression fell over the One Cent's face.

Jim's eyes flickered between the Aztec and his Amazon CO. "Put yourself in my shoes. Two days ago I'm on a hunting trip with my sister and my cousins. Suddenly the world's invaded by a bunch of monsters, and a group of people who look straight out of a *Star Wars* movie show up and say they're from alternate Earths and that they're on our side." He fixed his stare on Kenaevya. "You're in command of a special ops unit. You know trust is something that has to be earned over time."

Kenaevya said nothing. Jim felt tension knotting his muscles as the silence went on. He glanced around at the others. Chuck looked worried. Valerie shifted her weight from one leg to the other. One Cent narrowed his eyes at him. Probably concerned that a comment like that threatened unit cohesion, which in turn threatened the lives of his men. At least, he'd think that if he was worth his salt as senior NCO.

Kenaevya stepped toward him, her angular, beautiful face hardening. She stopped inches from Jim, staring down at him. He met her gaze.

Then she did something completely unexpected. She threw her head back and laughed.

Jim's face scrunched in bewilderment. Out the corner of his eye he glanced at Valerie and Williams, who exchanged confused looks with one another.

Kenaevya looked back at him, smiling wide. "I admire your honesty. Quite frankly, if you did trust us implicitly as soon as we met, I'd consider you naïve. And you do not strike me as a naïve man, Major Rhyne."

"I'm glad you understand."

Kenaevya gazed at the ground in thought for a few moments before looking back up at him. Her voice softened. "I know these past few days haven't been easy. The world as you know it has been turned upside-down. People and creatures from places you only thought existed in the realm of science fiction have appeared. No doubt you're praying that we are indeed true allies, and not here with our own agenda that will be detrimental to your Earth. I only hope that, in time, you can come to trust us as you do your brothers in Delta Force." She looked over at Valerie, Doug and Chuck. "Or your own family."

"I hope so too, Major," Jim said.

Kenaevya flashed him a smile and stuck out her hand. "Well then, ready or not, it looks like we are in this together."

Jim stared at her hand for a second before taking it. The Amazon gave him a firm handshake, firmer than some guys he knew. The smile on her face grew wider as they locked eyes with one another.

Jim couldn't help but smile back.

CHAPTER 15

"So when are we gonna stop just watching these fuckers and start blowin' them up?" Chuck groused twenty minutes after a Shreth'kil supply convoy drove past their concealed position near U.S. 60.

Major Kenaevya looked at him and sighed. "I know you want us to rid your Earth of the Shreth'kil, but a counter-attack of the magnitude necessary to accomplish that takes time and planning to achieve."

Chuck snorted. "Great. And while you plan, who knows how many people these things are gonna eat."

"Chuck, I am sorry. I understand your frustration, but -"

"Yeah, I'm frustrated. We've been with you people for, what, three days now? And all we're doing is sitting in the bushes counting how many damn trucks those monsters drive up and down the highway. How about callin' in an air strike or something? You know, do something useful."

"Believe it or not, Chuck, this is useful." Doug did little to keep the annoyance out of his voice. "Just storming in with guns blazing only works in movies. In real life, we can't go in to a major attack blind. We need an idea on how many Shreth'kil are in this part of Kentucky, where their bases are, what weapons systems they have, their supply routes. And unfortunately, gathering all that intelligence, and having others process it, takes time."

"Great. And while we're all takin' our time, the Shreth'kil will probably have eaten everyone in Kentucky."

Doug groaned and turned to Kenaevya. "You'll have to excuse my brother. He was born without much patience. Or tact. Or manners."

"Blow me." Chuck gave Doug a harsh gaze before turning away from his brother.

Jim sat about ten feet away watching the argument. He shook his head. The past two days they had been so busy moving from one place to another and observing Shreth'kil activity that Chuck and Doug didn't have much of a chance to bicker. He prayed the truce between the brothers would continue. Though it seemed apparent that had been too much to ask for.

"Man," he heard Williams mutter behind him. "Seeing that makes me glad my mom and dad decided not to have any more kids after me."

Jim gave the pilot a non-committal grunt.

Ten minutes later they moved out, heading east. The eleven men, women, and dinosaur snaked through the woods along the highway at five-yard intervals, though Jim noticed Kenaevya slowing her pace ahead of him. In a few minutes, he found the tall Israeli-Amazon beside him.

"Are they always like that?" she asked. "Your cousins, I mean."

"Unfortunately. To be honest, it's gotten worse over the past couple of years."

"Any particular reason why?"

"My family has a tradition of military service. My father was an Army Ranger, fought on Grenada and in the First Gulf War. His brother, my Uncle Phil, was a tanker. Hell, you can go back to the Civil War and find Rhynes fighting on both sides. So when Chuck decided he'd rather play baseball than go into the Armed Forces, that caused a bit of . . . consternation in the family. Especially with Doug."

"And you?" Kenaevya asked.

"I would have liked to have seen him carry on the family tradition. But Chuck's an adult, and it's his decision whether or not to serve."

"Tradition is important."

"I agree. But so's the freedom to make your own choices in life. Isn't that one of the things we fight for?"

Kenaevya let out a slow breath. Jim sensed more than saw the woman fix him with an appraising stare. "For the vast majority. For people like me, like us, we were born into this life. To serve a cause greater than ourselves, to protect those who cannot protect themselves from evil. On my Earth, it is inconceivable for someone with Amazon blood in their veins to not take up arms on behalf of their nation, or in the LAW's case, for all humanity . . . and Dinokind."

Jim gave her a sideways glance. He held his breath momentarily as he noticed the pride and strength radiating from Kenaevya's face. He even noted it in her voice. Admiration grew inside him, admiration for this woman's devotion to duty, for her sense of honor, for the confidence she had in her convictions.

His eyes remained locked on Kenaevya. She had to be one of the most interesting women he'd ever met. An actual Amazon from another Earth. He wanted to learn more about her. What had her childhood been like? What sort of traditions did Amazons have on her world? Did she enjoy hobbies outside of the warrior life? He sensed a sort of . . . playfulness? Maybe wittiness in her conversations with him. There just seemed so much more to Major Myra Kenaevya than being a LAW Recon Trooper.

Plus she was gorgeous.

Jim clenched his teeth. *Don't think that.* He didn't want to have *those* thoughts about Kenaevya. That would be a betrayal to Hannah.

The sun started coming up a couple hours later. Kenaevya called for a break, saying they would rest for four hours. Jim settled down next to a bush, dug out a blanket from his MOLLE pack and wrapped it around him. He was asleep in minutes.

He found himself standing in a church, wearing his Army Dress Blue Uniform. His eyes locked on a slender blond woman in a wedding gown slowly making her way down the aisle. Her eyes met his, and a smile spread across her face.

Jim smiled back, his heart pounding at a jackhammer pace. He was really going to do it. He was really going to marry Hannah Greer. More than a few of his friends and family thought this day would never happen. Some even told him marrying this woman would be a mistake, given all her baggage. But they never saw the inner strength that he did, her determination to conquer the demons of alcoholism once and for all.

And she had done it. Hannah was three years clean and sober. Sometimes, Jim used the strength she exhibited to beat the bottle as an inspiration to get through the toughest parts of Ranger School.

They had overcome so many obstacles together, which only made their love even stronger. How could he not want to spend the rest of his life with this woman?

She stood by his side, beaming at him. They both turned to face the minister.

"Jim. Jim."

Hannah and the church dissolved around him. His eyes flickered open. Valerie's face hovered over his.

"C'mon, big brother." She grinned at him. "Time to wake up."

Jim groaned, clenching his teeth. He didn't want to wake up. He wanted to stay in the dream, with Hannah.

With a sigh, he forced himself to rise. Some of the others had started eating breakfast. Jim dug into his MOLLE pack and pulled out a beef ravioli MRE. He began to pour water from his canteen into the pouch containing the flameless ration heater when he heard Valerie speak.

"I know you guys have better equipment than us," she said to Trooper Mackanin. "Do you also have better rations than these damn Meals Rejected by Everyone?" She held up her MRE package.

"Why don't we trade and y'all can find out for yourself."

Valerie handed over her MRE and Mackanin gave her his food package, what the LAW troopers called a Portable Rations Package, or PORPACK.

"Lao salad?" Val's brow furrowed. "Lao as in Laos?"

"The LAW is made up of a wide variety of nationalities," said Kenaevya. "So we have a more . . . international flavor with our PORPACKs."

Val bobbed her head from side-to-side. She finally opened the PORPACK and dug out a wad of chicken, onions and rice powder with her spork. She stuck it in her mouth and chewed.

"Hmm. This ain't bad."

"You can thank the Roman Empire for that," One Cent stated. "They take pride in being the best at everything, whether it is architecture or science or even making mass produced food."

"Sometimes, however, they take too much pride in the things they do," muttered Duguid.

"Well, whatever." Val took another mouthful of Lao salad. "This is still better than our MREs."

"Now you've got me curious," said Williams. "Let me try one of those PORPACKS myself."

O'Neal offered his to the pilot, who wound up with merguez, a spicy lamb sausage from Morocco. Doug traded rations with One Cent and Chuck did the same with Duguid. A brief smile flashed across Jim's lips. It was a small thing, to trade food, but he viewed such gestures as another step toward building stronger ties with their LAW allies. In their situation, the better the team chemistry, the better their chances of succeeding in their mission, and surviving it.

"Looks like it's you and me, Major." Kenaevya held out her PORPACK.

Jim looked at it, then drew his head back in surprise. "Chicago deep dish pizza? Are you kidding me?"

"As I said, we have a great variety in our rations. And what do you have?"

"Beef ravioli."

Kenaevya's face wrinkled, not that it did anything to detract from her beauty.

Stop thinking that way.

"Is it Kosher?" she asked.

"Um, I don't know. I don't think so. But I might have something in here that is." He searched his MOLLE pack until he found a spicy penne pasta MRE and figured that would suffice. Kenaevya accepted it with a thank you and a smile.

He inserted the bun-sized pizza into the heater pouch, then munched on the mini garlic breadsticks that came with it.

"I would share one of my PORPACKs," said Deathswipe. "But I doubt whether you desire uncooked gull breasts."

Williams grimaced. "You'd be right about that, but thanks anyway."

"So, um, Lieutenant Deathswipe?"

The dinosaur turned to Chuck. "Yes?"

"Um, I just wanted to know. What's your Earth like?"

"In what way?"

Chuck, who sat cross-legged on the ground, shifted a little. "Um, well, since you're, like, a dinosaur, you know, is your Earth, like, a big jungle? Do you drive cars and live in buildings and stuff?"

Deathswipe snorted and fixed his ink black eyes on Chuck. The veins in Chuck's neck stuck out, and he looked away from the dinosaur.

"How many hundreds of thousands of years has it been since your primate ancestors left their caves and built permanent dwellings for themselves? Why would you assume things to be different for my kind?"

Chuck just stared at Deathswipe, mouth agape, as if unsure how answer.

"For your information, our dwellings are larger than yours, made mostly of stones, and have pens and aviaries for our meal animals. So as you see, we ceased living in jungles long ago."

Chuck shifted uncomfortably. "Uh, right. Sorry, man."

That resulted in a prolonged growl from Deathswipe, and the stiffening of his lizard-like body. Jim also noticed O'Neal and Mackanin wince, while Duguid shook his head and muttered something under his breath the earpiece translator couldn't pick up.

"Go easy on him, Lieutenant," said Kenaevya. "I'm sure Chuck is not aware of how sensitive you are to that word."

Deathswipe turned to her. A few moments later he nodded. "Yes, Madam."

Kenaevya nodded back to her XO, then scanned the Rhyne family, Chuck in particular. "Forgive Lieutenant Deathswipe. I know many cultures use the word 'man' as a general means of addressing someone. But for the Dinos, well, so far theirs is the only Earth we've discovered where dinosaurs, not humans, evolved into the planet's dominant species."

"It is a fact most of my kind still find hard to accept." Deathswipe emitted a low growl. "Two hundred-seventy four Earths have been discovered since the founding of the League of Alternate Worlds. We expected there to be more worlds where our species evolved. Yet somehow, that is not the case."

"But Lieutenant," Mackanin chimed in. "I've told ya about the Theory of Exponential Divergence, multiple actions creating multiple Earths and so on. Just goin' on statistics alone, there have to be countless Earths where the Dinos also evolved."

"But we have not found any of those Earths, have we, Trooper?"

Mackanin frowned. "No, Sir."

Kenaevya let out a sigh. "Deathswipe is not the only one who has these issues. There are several countries and empires that exist on one Earth, but that aren't found on any other known Earth except in the pages of a history book. It can be rather shocking to realize that the nation or empire you grew up in, that has remained strong and stable for hundreds, in some cases thousands, of years, does not exist on any other Earth."

"The Major is correct." A harsh expression came over One Cent's face. "There is no other Earth where the Aztec Empire lasted beyond the Seventeenth Century, save mine. On my Earth, we controlled all of what you know as Central America, even parts of Colombia and Venezuela. When we learned of the existence of parallel worlds, it was inconceivable to us that our empire did not thrive anywhere else, that we did not defeat Cortes and his Spaniards. We were a superpower on my Earth . . . until the Shreth'kil invaded twenty years ago. What took us five centuries to build was destroyed in less than five months."

"So are the Shreth'kil still on your Earth?" asked Doug.

"No. My Earth was liberated eight years ago. But the Aztec Empire is a shadow of its former self. Some feel we can never be as great as we once were." One Cent scowled.

Silence hung over the group. Jim just stared at the One Cent, fear building up inside him.

Could that be me one day? Could the time come when the Shreth'kil had been defeated, but the United States shattered beyond repair? He didn't want to believe that. This country had been through a civil war, a horrific influenza epidemic, the Great Depression, two world wars, the insanity of the Sixties, yet it had endured. Surely America could endure an invasion of other-worldly creatures.

But the Aztecs couldn't. And how many other nations and empires met the same fate because of the Shreth'kil?

"So long as there is one Aztec in the multiverse, there will always be an Aztec Empire," Kenaevya noted. "Especially if that Aztec is you, One Cent."

One Cent simply nodded. "Thank you, Major."

Everyone went back to their meals. It took a few minutes before the small talk started up again. Jim, his family, and

Williams kept the topics harmless. Sports, TV, movies, music. He found it interesting to learn that on Mackanin's Earth, the Athletics were still in Philadelphia and the Lakers remained in Minneapolis. *Back to the Future* turned out to be a flop on Kenaevya's world, and Led Zeppelin stayed together until 1994 on O'Neal's Earth.

"So what about you, Duguid?" Val asked the French sniper. "What are some of the differences between your France and ours . . . or, other Frances?"

A dark scowl formed on Duguid's face. "It is not my France."

Valerie gave him a puzzled look. "I don't get it. I thought you were French."

"French." Duguid spit on the ground. "I am not French. I am American. Not that our esteemed Emperor, Alain the Ass, sees it that way. To him we are still citizens of the French Empire, even though we reside thousands of miles from France. Though that does not stop Alain the Ass from bleeding us dry with his outrageous taxes, or monitoring our phones and mail and i-messages without cause, or invading our homes without justification, or stationing soldiers on every street corner to harass us for their enjoyment."

"Dude, why are they so harsh on you?" asked Chuck.

"That is what happens when you lose your revolution. My America lost our war of independence more than seventy years ago, and we are still paying for that loss." Duguid snorted, then focused on Chuck. "You are fortunate that on this world you Americans won your revolution. And I would assume this world's Duke of Wellington defeated Napoleon the First at Waterloo."

"He did," Jim answered.

"Again, you are fortunate."

Valerie frowned. "I'm sorry all that happened in your America."

Duguid acknowledged her with a grunt. "Our subjugation will not last forever. When this war with the Shreth'kil is over, Independents like myself will turn our attention to the Empire, and we will finally have our freedom."

Jim digested the sniper's words. It appeared the League was not akin to the Federation in *Star Trek*, with everybody arm-in-arm and getting along. Apparently, being united against a common enemy did not mean one forgot about old enemies, or forgave them. He had a feeling if – *No if. It has to be when* – the Shreth'kil were defeated, people like Duguid would not wait long to settle scores with –

A dull hum filtered through the woods.

"Sounds like a Shreth'kil convoy," Doug said.

"Everyone move out," ordered Kenaevya.

They shoved their unfinished meals into their packs. The LAW troopers lowered the visors on their helmets and sprinted through the woods.

The group reached the highway just as the Shreth'kil convoy appeared. Six transport trucks and three armed escort vehicles, all headed east.

"Hauling supplies?" Doug asked after the convoy passed.

"I'm not sure," Kenaevya answered. "Most of Kentucky is in Shreth'kil hands. Any combat supplies they'd transport would be headed west or north, not east."

"So what's east of here?" Val asked. "Fort Knox. Maybe they're using it as a supply depot."

"No." Kenaevya shook her head. "The Shreth'kil razed Fort Knox during their initial assault. Elizabethtown is not too far from here. Many times they'll use a civilian facility like an airport or a large college campus as a supply depot. Or as . . ."

Jim tilted his head. "Or as what?"

"Or as a depot for another kind of supply."

"Like?"

She paused. "Like cattle. Human cattle."

CHAPTER 16

I can't believe she's calling this a test.

Jim held his breath and slid just a few inches along the ground, which felt damp and cold from the falling rain. Through the spaces in the dripping wet brush he saw their silhouettes in the darkness. Four Shreth'kil soldiers, sitting in a circle in a clearing, taking a break from their patrol to eat. He would have been content to leave them be. Recon meant staying out of sight and observing, not engaging the enemy. The Shreth'kil were no doubt on alert after their LAW friends wiped out the patrol that nearly got him and his family. A second lost patrol would likely mean more trouble for them.

But when this patrol landed nearby fifteen minutes ago, Kenaevya insisted they take them out and see if they carried any useful intelligence. She also wanted Jim to lead the assault with his family so, as she put it, "I can see for myself how you locals handle yourselves in combat."

It was risky, but he had to admit it would go far in building trust between his group and Kenaevya's. If they got into some serious shit, the LAW troops would want to know they could depend on Jim and his family.

He slid forward another few inches, tensing at the soft rustle of grass, leaves and branches underneath him. He was mindful of the fact Shreth'kil had better hearing than humans. Still, the steady patter of rain and their constant talking – a series of screeches and shrieks – probably disguised whatever sounds he made.

I hope.

Jim gazed at the four Shreth'kil, only twenty feet away. They continued screeching amongst themselves. His translator earpiece picked up some of their conversation.

"Why were we chosen to patrol in this miserable weather?"

"Yes. Even humans have enough sense to stay out of the rain."

"If any of us have a right to complain, I do. The last Earth I was assigned to, I was at a base in Nevada. It was nice and warm, it hardly rained, and all the humans were in pens, not running about and shooting at us."

Jim resisted the urge to shake his head. It was so unbelievable to hear the monsters bitch just like human soldiers. *We actually do have some things in common.*

He purged the thought from his mind. The Shreth'kil had invaded his Earth and were turning humans into food. Whatever the two species might have in common didn't mean shit. Only one thing mattered.

Killing all these bat-faced bastards.

All the Shreth'kil had their rifles slung over their shoulders. At least they had the sense not to put them on the wet ground and foul them up. Still, they would all need a few seconds to slide the weapons off their shoulders and have them ready to fire. Jim, meanwhile, had the SiG-Sauer 300 pistol Kenaevya loaned him in his hand.

Another slide along the ground. Another. A clump of trees blocked out the Shreth'kil. Excellent cover for when he sprang his ambush.

He lay under some brush, ignoring the rain that soaked his ACU. Slowly, he moved his right arm forward, ready to slide again.

A *splat* penetrated the noise of rain and screeching voices. Another followed, and another. Footsteps.

Shreth'kil footsteps.

Jim froze as one of the bat-like monsters rounded the tree. Dread filled him. Had it heard him? Jim slipped his finger through the trigger guard of his SiG. Would he have to take this thing out? Would it screw up his ambush?

A pair of long, hairy legs stopped less than two feet away. A chill that had nothing to do with the rain gripped him. He stared up at the Shreth'kil, ready to shoot.

Instead of looking around, the creature turned its back to him and faced the tree. It then stuck out its legs and squatted.

What the hell is it doing?

A wet, popping sound came from the Shreth'kil. Jim fought the urge to flinch when several dark objects splattered on the ground in front of him.

The thing was taking a shit.

A foul stench hovered over him, like a skunk rolling in raw sewage. It overwhelmed his nostrils and slithered down his throat. He clenched his teeth, the urge to gag building.

Deal with it. One sound and everything falls apart.

More Shreth'kil shit splattered the ground. Jim didn't think it possible, but the smell got even worse. Nausea burned his stomach and climbed into his throat.

Hold it in. Tough it out.

The Shreth'kil straightened up, emitting a sound that was a half-sigh, half-growl. It then walked back to the others.

Jim exhaled in relief, and nearly choked. This shit was almost toxic.

Two fingers tapped his leg. Kenaevya, who lay on her stomach just behind him. Three taps. That meant Team Three, Valerie and O'Neal, had sent her three clicks over the radio to let them know they were in position. A minute later Kenaevya tapped his leg twice. Team Two, Doug and Mackanin, also in position. Not long after came four taps to his leg. Team Four, Williams and One Cent.

Worry crept through his mind. After him, Doug was probably the next best qualified for a commando-style attack like this, being with the 101st Airborne. While highly trained infantrymen specializing in heliborne tactics, they couldn't be considered special ops soldiers on the level of Jim. Valerie and Williams did their fighting in the air, not on the ground. Still, they had some things going for them. Both Doug and Valerie knew how to move quietly from their years of hunting. Williams could also move stealthily when necessary thanks to his SERE training. They also had the element of surprise on their side. That should be enough to take out this Shreth'kil patrol.

I hope.

If something did go wrong, they had the LAW troopers backing each of them up. In addition, Deathswipe, Duguid and Chuck sat fifty yards away covering them with a light machine gun, sniper rifle and hunting rifle respectively.

Jim bit his lip. He'd planned this best he could in a short amount of time. He felt he had all his bases covered.

Still, so much could go wrong.

He exhaled and slid out from under the brush, careful to avoid the Shreth'kil shit. Once clear of the brush, Jim got to

his feet and tread softly up to the tree. He turned to
Kenaevya and gave her a thumbs-up. She sent five rapid
clicks over the radio, the go signal. A second later she stuck
up her right thumb.

Jim swung around the tree. He barely heard the sound of
several people crashing through the brush. Instead he
leveled his SiG at the head of the Shreth'kil sitting in front of
him. It just started to turn when he pulled the trigger twice.
Two deep thumps came from the suppressed pistol. The
Shreth'kil twisted around and fell on its side. Alarmed
shrieks rose from the remaining creatures. More gunfire
erupted around the tiny encampment. The Shreth'kil to his
left fell face first into the wet ground, shot by Doug. The
creature across from the one Jim killed grasped its throat.
He glimpsed Valerie level her pistol at the Shreth'kil's
shoulderblades, between its wings, where its body armor
didn't cover, and fire. It pitched forward and lay still.

Williams fired four shots at his Shreth'kil. It screeched,
clutched its right arm, and started to get up. Jim swung his
pistol around to get it. Williams charged forward, firing four
more shots at its head. The Shreth'kil went into a brief
spasm, then collapsed.

"We're secure," Kenaevya announced. "Go through their
packs, find their SIIDs, and give them to Mackanin. Then
hide the bodies."

Jim opened the pack belonging to the Shreth'kil he killed
and pulled out the PDA-like device, what Kenaevya called
the SIID, Shreth'kil Infantryman Information Device. He
handed it to Mackanin, then caught a glimpse of one of the
Shreth'kil ration packs lying on the ground. He leaned down
to get a better look at it.

Oh God.

Next to the pack lay a human hand, the thumb and index
finger eaten off.

His face scrunched in anger as he stared at it. Fucking
sick bastards! He wished the four dead Shreth'kil were
instead four hundred, or four hundred thousand, or four
million.

Then he thought about the hand. It looked male. Who
had it belonged to? What had he done? Did he have a

family? How much did he suffer when the Shreth'kil turned him into field rations?

"Major."

He turned to find Kenaevya holding the legs of the Shreth'kil he'd shot. "A little help here."

"Um, right." With a final scowl at the hand, he tromped over to Kenaevya. Together they hauled the body into the woods. A few yards behind them Williams and One Cent carried their dead Shreth'kil, the others following them with the last two corpses.

"If I may, Captain," One Cent said to the pilot. "You need to exercise better fire discipline. You fired eight shots, but only had three hits."

"Hey, I killed the son-of-a-bitch, didn't I?"

"True, but you wasted five rounds you may need for later. We are not able to get more ammunition whenever we want."

"Okay, point taken." Williams nodded. "Still, how about a, 'not bad for a flyboy?'"

Jim couldn't help but smile. He had to admit, Williams had a point. For a fighter jock, he gave a good accounting of himself in the ambush. But One Cent was right. Williams needed to improve his skills with a pistol.

Too bad they didn't have the time, or rounds, to spare for target practice.

A couple hundred yards from the encampment they dumped the Shreth'kil bodies under some brush. Not exactly the best hiding job, but by the time any other Shreth'kil found these bodies, they'd be long gone.

After they policed the area of their shell casings, they headed away from the ambush site. The rain kept coming down as they hiked one mile, then two. At the third mile, Kenaevya called a halt. Almost immediately, Mackanin broke out his laptop. He ran a thin cable from his computer to one of the Shreth'kil SIIDs, then started tapping on the keyboard.

"So what's he doing with those things?" Jim heard Chuck ask Lieutenant Deathswipe.

"Trooper Mackanin is downloading the information on the SIIDs."

"Cool. So we can, like, read what they got on there?"

"No. The SIIDs are encoded for Shreth'kil use. Mackanin will download any information they possess and transmit it to our battalion headquarters, and they will likely pass it on to LEDMI."

A puzzled look formed on Chuck's face. *"Led-me?"*

"League Directorate for Military Intelligence," Deathswipe answered.

Jim watched Mackanin type away on his laptop when he sensed someone approaching. He looked to his right as Kenaevya sidled up next to him, a smile on her face.

"Good work back there, Major."

"Thanks. It's not easy pulling off an ambush like that on short notice, especially when you have a couple pilots as part of your assault group."

"Nonetheless, you and the other locals performed admirably, even if Captain Williams needed a few extra rounds to take down his target." She grinned at that.

A tingle went through Jim's stomach. Even with her helmet and combat gear, Kenaevya still looked beautiful when she smiled.

A stab of guilt went through him. He clenched his teeth and pushed the thought from his mind.

She continued, "You planned this ambush, you led it, and you succeeded. As I said before, I've worked with Delta Force troopers on other Earths, and they have never disappointed me with their performance."

"Well, good to know we maintain our high standards throughout the multiverse."

"Rest assured, you do." Kenaevya paused.

Jim breathed deep, a surge of pride shooting through him.

The rain fell harder, soaking his already damp camouflage hunting jacket. Chills swept over his body. He looked around at his family. Val's teeth chattered. Chuck hugged himself, his head trembling. Jim frowned, wishing they had found some better foul weather gear back at Fort Campbell.

"So did you always wish to be part of Delta Force?" Kenaevya asked.

Jim turned to her. "Actually, no. My ultimate goal was to be an Army Ranger, like my Dad." He tightened his lips, wondering how his father and the rest of his family were doing.

Knowing Dad, he probably has them all holed up somewhere, armed to the teeth.

At least he hoped so. He didn't want to think about the alternative.

"But," he continued. "After Nine-Eleven . . . you do know about Nine-Eleven, right?"

"Yes. That happened on several other Earths, though the targets vary. World Trade Center, Empire State Building, Pentagon, White House, U.S. Capitol Building."

"Yeah. Anyway, after Nine-Eleven, I kept watching on the news how these fucksticks went around blowing up buses and nightclubs, talking about how America was weak, thinking everyone was scared of them. Well, I wanted to show those maggots that there were some people in America they needed to be scared of. And if I wanted to do that, that meant being in Delta."

"And have you been successful?"

"I've gotten my fair share of scalps," Jim answered. "A few less of those scumbags in the world thanks to me and my buddies."

Kenaevya said nothing. She straightened, shoulders set back, her gaze never wavering from him. Jim studied her expression. She seemed to be staring at him in . . . admiration? A tingle went through him. He didn't know if that was good or bad.

"Transmission complete, Major," Mackanin announced.

"Very well." She nodded to the Texan. "Let's move out."

They continued east, paralleling U.S. 60. Two more Shreth'kil convoys drove by, one headed east, the other west. By the time the sun came up, they had reached the junction of U.S. 60 and U.S. 31W. Kenaevya directed them south down 31W, toward the small city of Radcliff. The rain, thankfully, started to let up.

Two miles down the highway they spotted a large ranch house, several smaller dwellings, stables, barns, paddocks and large pastures. Most definitely a horse farm. Not that he saw a single horse there. He lowered his head, knowing what must have happened to them. Farm animals were just as much a staple of the Shreth'kil diet as humans. A shame. He liked horses. Growing up in Kentucky, he and Valerie had done their fair share of horseback riding.

"No sign of any activity," reported Duguid, who used his helmet's advanced optics to scan the farm.

Kenaevya slowly worked her jaw back and forth. "I think we can all use a break from this rain. It will also be nice to sleep someplace with a roof over our heads."

"Fine by me," said Williams. "Sleeping on the ground ain't my idea of fun."

"That's because you air force boys are spoiled," O'Neal said in a half-kidding tone.

Williams just beamed at him. "And proud of it."

Valerie chuckled softly. Williams sent a smile her way.

Jim sneered.

The group headed toward the horse farm. Just before they entered the property, Kenaevya divided them into teams to clear the buildings. Jim and Duguid were assigned to the barn. They found it devoid of people or animals. The same was true for the rest of the farm.

Once all the sweeps had been completed, Kenaevya called them to the ranch house, save for Deathswipe and O'Neal, who had the first watch. Jim entered a spacious living room with a high wooden ceiling, nice furnishings and a large gray brick fireplace.

"Oh sweet, a fireplace." Chuck walked over to it, rubbing his hands together. "Let's get this thing fired up."

"Absolutely not." One Cent turned to him. "The Shreth'kil have obviously cleared this place of all people. If we light a fire, they'll see the smoke coming from the chimney and investigate."

"Aw, for fuck's sake." Chuck slapped his hands against his sides.

"We'll get dry and warm the old fashioned way," said Kenaevya. "Ring out your clothes, then get some towels and blankets."

"We should also check for any food and water, or any other supplies we might need," Jim suggested.

Kenaevya nodded. "We will, right before we leave. For now, I want everyone to dry themselves and get some rest."

It turned out the house had four bedrooms, each with its own bathroom, another bathroom upstairs, and another downstairs. Jim went into one of the smaller bedrooms, probably a guest room, shut the door and wriggled out of his MOLLE pack. He caught sight of the bureau across the room. A framed photo sat on top of it. Nearly twenty people of all ages stood bunched together in front of the ranch house. Obviously a family photo, most likely the family that owned this farm. His jaw tightened. What happened to them? Were they alive? Had the Shreth'kil chopped them up and stuffed them into ration packs? His eyes fell on a smiling, brown-haired little boy in the photo, then on the lanky pre-teen girl next to him. Anger flared inside him. He thought about the Shreth'kil who'd been eating that hand, thought about all his butt-ugly pals.

Fucking sons-of-bitches.

Groaning, he tore himself away from the photo and headed into the darkened bathroom. By force of habit, he felt the wall for a light switch, then stopped. The Shreth'kil had knocked out all power.

He stripped himself naked, rung out all his clothes in the shower stall, then hung them on the door. On his way out he checked himself in the mirror. His brown hair sat flat and damp on his head. Stubble covered his round face. His taut frame appeared even leaner. He'd definitely dropped several pounds since the Shreth'kil invasion. How long ago was that? Almost two weeks now.

And how long before Kenaevya's LAW friends get rid of them? How many more people like that family in the photo are going to wind up Shreth'kil chow?

Jim snatched the white cotton towel hanging from the rack and wiped himself off. He walked back into the bedroom and dug through his MOLLE pack, pulling out a fresh ACU, socks and underwear. He slipped on a pair of olive drab boxers and grabbed an undershirt when the door opened. His head snapped up.

What the . . .

Kenaevya stood in the doorway, holding a couple bath towels. Jim's heartbeat picked up when he noticed what she wore. A dark green undershirt and boxers. Nothing else. His eyes roamed up her long, firm legs. The undershirt nicely hugged her torso, and her ample breasts. Her black hair was longer than he'd imagined, and had golden highlights.

"Major. I just wanted to see if you needed any fresh towels."

He barely heard her, instead focusing on the stirring below his waist. The very intense stirring that made him . . .

Oh shit.

"Um . . . uh . . ." He felt his cheeks redden as he grabbed his pants and hurriedly put them on.

Kenaevya threw her head back and laughed. Jim's face scrunched in a quizzical expression.

"Oh, quit acting so embarrassed, Major Rhyne," she said. "I've seen my fair share of naked men in my lifetime. Besides, with a body like yours, you have nothing to be embarrassed of." She tacked on a wry grin.

Jim froze, just staring at her. His cheeks probably blazed the color of a traffic light. Did Kenaevya want to . . .

What more do you need to convince you?

He swallowed. Any other guy in his position wouldn't wait another second before rushing over to this gorgeous Amazon warrior and ravaging her.

But those other guys wouldn't have an image of Hannah floating through their minds.

"Um, thanks. Um, I'm good with towels. Thanks."

"Good. That's . . . good."

An uncomfortable silence hung between them. Jim glanced at the bed next to him. His muscles tightened as images of Hannah dueled with images of him and Kenaevya rolling around naked beneath the sheets.

"Um . . ." He chewed on his lower lip, trying to think of a way to head off something he knew he'd regret. "Um, so, you know, ever since I met you, I've been curious about what Amazon Earth is like."

Kenaevya blinked, the surprise on her face evident. "Oh." The surprise turned to disappointment. She took a breath. "Well, because of the accomplishments of my sisters, dating back to the time of the Ancient Greeks, we don't experience the sort of gender issues common to most other Earths. All those with Amazon blood are expected to serve in the military, we cherish honor and strength. That's been the case for all my sisters for thousands of years. Though we did end the practice of cutting off our right breasts long ago."

Jim shook his head in astonishment. "What?"

"In ancient times, Amazons would remove their right breast so it would not interfere when using a sword in battle. I thank God we don't do that any more. I happen to like my breasts." Kenaevya stuck out her chest.

Jim couldn't help but look. Heat consumed his body.

"So, um, what else?"

Kenaevya walked over to the bed and sat down, crossing her long legs, surprisingly smooth considering all the time they've spent in the field. Had she just shaved before coming here?

"Can you be more specific?" she asked.

"Well, do you go to, I guess, any special Amazon schools?"

Kenaevya chuckled. "No. We learn Amazon traditions from our parents. We go to the same schools as everyone else."

"Really?"

"Of course. It would make no sense to keep ourselves separated from those we are pledged to protect. One misconception about us is that war is the only thing that concerns us Amazons. Untrue. When I was in high school, I participated in basketball and track and field – the discus. I even played bass guitar in a heavy metal band."

"Seriously?" Jim's eyes widened.

"Yes. Many Amazons love metal. The powerful, unrestrained beats and lyrics. It does get one's blood pumping. And what about you? Do you enjoy metal?"

"Some groups, yeah, like Iron Maiden and Metallica."

"And did you ever play an instrument."

"Actually, yeah," Jim nodded. "Clarinet, in my middle school and high school bands. But my main thing back then was, well, you may not believe this."

"Try me."

A half-smile formed on Jim's lips. "I actually did ballroom dancing throughout high school and college."

Kenaevya's jaw fell open in surprise. "Ballroom dancing? That definitely does not sound like something a member of one of your country's most elite fighting units would do."

"That's what a lot of people say. But let me tell you, a lot of women like ballroom dancing, and I got my fair share of dates because of it. And that's how I met . . ." He pressed his lips together and looked away from Kenaevya.

"Who did you meet?" she asked.

Jim's shoulders slumped. "My wife."

Surprise flared across Kenaevya's face. "You're married?"

His gaze fell to the floor. "I was."

"What happened?"

He let out a long breath before looking up at Kenaevya. He debated telling her, not just for personal reasons, but for security reasons as well. The full story would require him to divulge some very sensitive information to a person he'd known for barely two weeks.

Then again, the government he served barely existed, and the world faced a much more dire threat than religious crazies blowing themselves up.

"I told you about the War on Terror. Well, the way that war's being fought is completely fucked up. We had almost three thousand Americans killed in one day because of these bastards, yet there are people in this country who think The War is a farce, just a way for certain politicians to keep people scared to stay in office. Then we can't call the Islamic terrorists we're fighting 'Islamic terrorists' because it's not politically correct."

"That's insane." Kenaevya scowled.

"Yeah, and it gets worse. We give these murdering bastards Constitutional rights, you've got bleeding heart politicians and human rights groups who say throwing a bug in some terrorist's room to scare him or denying them sleep is torture. But when those shit-sucking dregs set fire to some contractors and hang their bodies from a bridge, or kidnap a truck driver and lop his head off on the internet, they don't say a damn thing. That's what we have to deal with in this war."

Kenaevya shook her head, looking aghast. "How do you expect to win a war when you show more concern for the enemy than your own people, or are afraid to even identify the enemy?"

"We find ways around it. That's what happened my last tour in Afghanistan."

Jim took a breath before continuing. "I was assigned to Task Force Eleven, a joint counter-terrorist operation there. Since our interrogators were handcuffed thanks to Washington, and with traitors in our own government leaking sensitive information every chance they got, we put together a black op. I mean, the blackest black op you can imagine. Nothing got written down, nothing got broadcast, absolutely no trail. We were tasked with hunting down high value terrorists, pumping them for information by any means necessary, then putting a bullet in their head and dumping them in a hole. I was on one of those missions when Hannah's father died. Heart attack."

"I'm sorry."

"Our only means of communication was this band of anti-Taliban fighters in a little village who had a radio, and we were only supposed to rendezvous with them and send a pre-arranged signal to headquarters when our mission was completed. So I had no idea Hannah's father had died. It devastated her."

Jim sighed. "When Hannah was six, her parents went through a really, really nasty divorce. And her mother was a prize. She did drugs, cheated on Hannah's father. But the court gave her custody of Hannah because she promised to get treatment." Jim's jaw clenched for a moment. "Hannah told me that she cried her eyes out when her mom dragged her out of the courtroom. Even at six she knew just how bad her mother was. She wanted to be with her father, but all he got was one weekend a month with her. Still, Hannah's mother didn't like him having any contact with her. So a few months after the divorce was finalized, she took Hannah halfway across the country, stopped going to treatment and cut off all contact with Hannah's father. The cops caught up with her a couple months later in North Carolina, in some crap apartment getting high and banging some sleazebag. All with Hannah in the next room."

The disgust on Kenaevya's face was evident. "That . . . woman has no business caring for a child."

"That was what Hannah put up with almost every day. That and . . . her mother started abusing her. The whole thing really messed her up. But her dad helped get her through it. They grew really close because of it. And when he died, Hannah . . . Hannah just didn't know what to do. And I couldn't help her because I was somewhere in the Hindu Kush tracking down a bunch of sub-human vermin. So two days after the funeral she was home and . . ." His throat constricted. Tears stung the corners of his eyes. "She was a recovering alcoholic. Hadn't touched a drink in years. So when she started again, she couldn't stop and . . . they said it was alcohol poisoning that killed her."

Kenaevya placed a hand over her heart. "Ma . . . Jim. I'm so sorry. That's horrible."

He clenched his teeth, pushing back the tears, letting the guilt and anger overcome his grief. "It's my fault."

"No, it's not." Kenaevya stood. "You were on a mission at the time."

"Yeah, and because we were incommunicado, I had no idea what she was going through. I didn't even know she died until I got back to headquarters, three weeks later! I never even got to go to her funeral!" He stalked back and forth. "I was her husband. I was supposed to comfort her, to be there for her. But where was I instead? Halfway around the world protecting people I didn't even know. Meanwhile, I couldn't save the woman I loved."

He fell silent, staring at Kenaevya, sympathy radiating from her brown eyes.

"Myra, I know . . . I know what you want to happen here. If things were different, I would love to. I think you're an incredible woman. But if we did anything . . ." He glanced at the bed. "I'd feel like I was betraying Hannah. Again."

"You did not betray your wife." Kenaevya took a step toward him. "What happened to her, it was just horrible circumstances. I'm sure you were the best husband you could be. But you had your duty -"

"Yeah, I had my duty. My duty as a husband. And I failed. I failed at that as badly as you can."

"You have to stop blaming yourself for your wife's death," Kenaevya said. "It was not your fault."

"That's what my sister keeps telling me."

"And she's right."

"No, she's not. And with all due respect, neither are you." He snatched the rest of his dry fresh clothes. "Now if you'll excuse me, I need to change and get some sleep."

Before Kenaevya could respond, he strode into the bathroom and shut the door. Just in time. The last thing he wanted was for that Amazon warrior to see a tear trickle down his cheek.

CHAPTER 17

Jim and Kenaevya kept their dealings with each other cool and professional the rest of their time at the horse farm. The next morning after breakfast, they headed out. The rain had let up when they reached the outskirts of Elizabethtown. Along the way, they spotted more convoys heading to and from the town. In addition, several Shreth'kil helicopters flew out of the town, along with a bulky, twin-prop transport aircraft that looked like a cross between a V-22 tilt-rotor and an old C-119 Flying Boxcar.

"Is there an airfield in this city?" asked Lieutenant Deathswipe.

"Yeah," Jim answered. "A little regional airport."

"Then that would make Elizabethtown a good place for a supply depot," said Kenaevya. "They can ferry supplies to Shreth'kil troops at the front quicker."

"Why not just open a transit portal to give 'em whatever they need?" asked Chuck.

"Because right now the Shreth'kil likely have this part of your country ringed with quantum jammers to interfere with the local electromagnetic field and prevent us from opening our own portals to infiltrate commando units or launch a surprise attack."

They pushed further into Elizabethtown. Another transport aircraft took off, headed east. Jim watched it, clenching his teeth. How he wished he had a Stinger missile to blow that damn thing out of the sky, to deny the Shreth'kil the food, water and ammo all armies need to keep going.

He stared at the ground, thinking about the fighting beyond Kentucky. Kenaevya's HQ had updated them on how the war was going on this Earth. Unfortunately, most of the news wasn't good. Ohio and West Virginia had fallen, with Shreth'kil forces advancing through Pennsylvania and Virginia. Heavy fighting continued in several states west of the Mississippi, especially Texas and California. Beyond the borders of the U.S., the NATO and Middle Eastern countries still put up resistance, though Kenaevya's superiors feared it wouldn't last much longer. Russia, China and India had become meat grinders, as all three countries had plenty of men to throw into the fighting, along with nuclear weapons. The Shreth'kil, however, had answered in kind, though they only used their nukes on military targets. Jim figured it wouldn't make sense for them to vaporize Moscow, Beijing or New Delhi. That would mean millions upon millions of people turned to ash or irradiated instead of winding up in Shreth'kil bellies.

The LAW had sent rapid reaction forces to help the "local" militaries, mainly in the form of carrier battle groups, marines and light infantry, or Velites as Kenaevya's bunch called them. Not enough to defeat the Shreth'kil , just enough to try and slow them down to allow a much larger LAW force time to assemble.

They couldn't assemble fast enough for Jim's taste.

The group hiked through the woods paralleling U.S. 31W. Every so often, Jim glanced over at Kenaevya. His heartbeat picked up, thinking about her clad in just her underwear, admiring her taut body and those long firm legs. Once again his imagination conjured up images of the two of them in bed, part of him wondering if he should have acted on his desires.

I can't do that. I shouldn't even be thinking that. Hannah . . .

He felt more than heard a whisper in the back of his mind telling him he had to move on.

Move on. He sneered at the phrase. To him, "move on" was another way of saying forget about Hannah, the woman he loved, the woman he married.

The woman he failed.

Biting his lip, he looked at Kenaevya again. His chest tightened. He couldn't deny he was attracted to her. Who wouldn't be? The woman had super model looks, an athletic build, the kind one would expect from a beach volleyball player. But there was much more to Kenaevya than her looks. Jim found her to be a good soldier and leader. She treated the men, and dino, under her with respect. She possessed intelligence, compassion and humor. Her Amazon heritage made her even more fascinating.

Maybe I should . . .

What about fraternization?

Jim wondered if that even applied here. Technically, he wasn't in the same unit as Kenaevya. Hell, they weren't even in the same military, or even from the same Earth. So he probably could . . .

He closed his eyes and groaned to himself. Now wasn't the time to be thinking about this stuff. He needed to keep his head on straight and focus on gathering all the intel he could on Shreth'kil activity in Kentucky.

They moved through woods, commercial centers and residential neighborhoods until they neared Elizabethtown Regional Airport. Clumps of trees stretched around the perimeter of the airport, along with a scattering of houses. The group entered one of them, a two-story dwelling – deserted, as expected – and set up an observation post. Two rooms faced the airport, an office and the bedroom.

"Oh God," Valerie muttered as she looked around the bedroom.

Jim's stomach lurched when he saw the stuffed animals on the bed, the sparkly pink cell phone on the nightstand, and the posters of afeminine-looking teen pop singers. A collage of photos hung from one of the walls, almost every picture showing a cute, smiling blond girl who couldn't be more than twelve. He clenched a fist, knowing what fate this girl and her family would suffer.

"Mackanin, I'm going to begin photographing the airport," Kenaevya told the Texan. "Establish a link with my EWABS." She used the acronym for her Enhanced Warrior Battle System suit.

Mackanin, sitting at the desk, tapped at his keyboard. "Link established."

Kenaevya, her helmet's visor down, kept her head still as her right hand hovered over the keypad attached to her left arm. She pressed a button, moved her head a couple inches to the left, and pressed the same button again.

"Pix are comin' through fine, Major," Mackanin reported.

Jim and Valerie looked over the Texan's shoulder. The screen had two small windows, each one with an image of the airport.

"A digital camera in the helmet." Val smiled and nodded. "Way cool."

Jim nodded, too. What he wouldn't give for Delta Force to have something like that.

Kenaevya continued snapping pictures for ten minutes. Jim studied each photo. The Shreth'kil had six mobile anti-aircraft systems around the airport, four with missile launchers, one with a laser, and another with a multitude of tubes.

"What's that?" he asked Mackanin. "Some kind of gun system?"

"That's one'a their Death Dealers. Our designation, not theirs. It's an electronically-fired weapon, uses the propellant of the first round to ignite all the subsequent rounds behind it, resultin' in a high rate of fire. That sucker can spit out about forty-thousand rounds a second."

"Holy shit," Valerie stammered.

Jim's eyes widened. He'd heard of such weapons on this Earth that eliminated ammunition feeds and casing ejection systems, which helped increase the rate of fire to hitherto levels. But all those systems were still in the testing stage.

The photos also showed six machine gun nests along the perimeter. A collection of airplanes, mostly small, single-engine prop jobs, were bunched together in the far corner of the airport. Moved by the Shreth'kil, no doubt, to make room for their aircraft, currently comprised of three helicopters and four medium-sized transport planes. Hippos and Taniwhas, according to Kenaevya. Apparently, the LAW took a page from NATO's book in coming up with their own names for enemy aircraft. Though while the two alliances used "H" words for helicopters, the LAW used "T" words for transport or cargo planes instead of "C" words.

They stayed in the house throughout the afternoon and into the evening. Two more Hippos and two more Taniwhas returned to the airport. An eight-vehicle convoy arrived. Dozens of Shreth'kil hurried over to it and moved pallets from the vehicles into a pair of Taniwhas, all under the watchful eye of a thickly-built soldier with a jutting beak, stubby horns, and a longer neck than his underlings.

Probably an NCO.

The Shreth'kil also had two pairs of sentries flying around the airport at all times. When night fell, two squads of Shreth'kil flew out from the airport, most likely going on patrol. Thankfully, they didn't check this home, or any of the others around the airport. They probably had no reason. To them, the people in all these houses had long since been removed.

Around 2215, Jim took a break and headed down the hall for the bathroom. He pulled down his pants and took a dump. A brief smile formed on his lips. It felt nice to finally do this on an actual, working toilet instead of in the woods. The group had discovered earlier in the day when Kenaevya tried the faucet for the kitchen sink that the Shreth'kil had turned back on the local water supply. It didn't surprise Jim too much. Those monsters needed water just as much as humans. At least it gave him and the others the chance to shave and bathe. He'd been in the Army long enough to know that simply feeling clean, which most civilians took for granted, could do wonders to lift a person's spirits, if only for a brief time.

After he finished, he washed his hands and exited the bathroom. That's when he noticed a figure sitting in the darkened hallway, propped up against the wall and eating a candy bar. It took a moment for Jim to recognize him.

"Hey, Chuck."

His cousin stared up at him and nodded. "Hey." The word was muffled by the wad of candy in his mouth.

"How're you holding up?" Jim asked.

Chuck snorted and resumed chewing. After he swallowed, he answered. "I'm friggin' bored. Just sittin' in this damn house lookin' at a damn airport."

"This is our job, Chuck. Learning everything we can about this airport so the LAW has an easier time taking it out. Trust me, in this line of work, boring is good. You don't want things to get exciting."

Chuck's head snapped up. He stared at him with wide eyes, face tightening. A twitch formed on Chuck's right cheek.

Jim's brow furrowed. "You okay?"

Chuck just stared at him in silence. His shoulders slumped and he looked away.

"Chuck?"

No response.

"Chuck," Jim said in a much firmer voice. "If something's bothering you, I need to know now."

His cousin exhaled loudly through his nose. "How do you do it?"

"Do what?"

"You know. You and Val and Doug. Heck, even Captain Williams. You got bullets flying all around you and shit blowing up, and . . . and you hold it together. I mean, how do you do it?"

Jim shrugged. "We just do. That's what we're trained for."

"That's it? I mean, how can you not be scared?"

"You don't think I'm scared? Or that Valerie and your brother and Captain Williams aren't scared? Anyone who says they're not scared when there are bullets flying all around them is a damn liar."

"Well you guys didn't look scared back at the church, or in the woods after we got shot down. And me, I . . . I . . . I looked like a chickenshit." Chuck's voice quivered. He turned away from Jim, who crouched down next to him.

"I didn't want . . . I mean, I'm a Rhyne. You think it would be in my blood to just fight when the shit went down. But all those bullets, and those monsters, and . . . Shit, man. I'm just nineteen. I don't wanna die. And it's like if I move, I'm gonna get hit, and . . . when you told me to throw that grenade and I . . . I fucked up, man. I fucked up and I nearly got all of us killed!" Chuck trembled. "I'm sorry, man. I'm sorry."

Jim said nothing, just watched as his cousin bit his lip. Even in the darkness, he could see the moisture welling up in Chuck's eyes.

"Chuck." He grasped his cousin's shoulder. "If I was your coach, I'd probably give you some kind of motivational spiel to get you out of this funk. But right here, right now, I don't have that luxury. We've got an important job to do, and I need everyone to have their head in the game. If it were up to me, I'd send you home, because what we're doing is no place for an untrained civilian. But I can't do that. For better or worse, you're with us, and we have to depend on you, just like me and Val and Doug have to depend on each other, and on Major Kenaevya and Captain Williams and

One Cent and all the others. You know what happens in baseball when the pitcher doesn't back up the third baseman on a throw from the outfield, right?"

"Yeah. If the ball gets past him, a run scores."

"Right. Your entire team could lose the game, all because one man did not do his job. But in baseball, you can just learn from your mistake and come back the next game. That doesn't happen in this line of work. You mess up here, people die. And in this case, those people might be your family. If we ever get into another situation where the bullets are flying and we need your help, think about what will happen if you let fear rule you. Think about how you might wind up seeing Valerie lying dead on the ground, covered in blood, ripped apart by bullets and shrapnel. Or think about the same thing happening to your brother." Jim paused, his chest tightening. "Believe me, it's hell living with the knowledge that someone died because you let them down."

Chuck didn't say anything. But a sobering look came over his face. His shoulders rose as he drew a slow breath. "Yeah. Um, yeah. I'll do my best, man."

The corners of Jim's mouth curled. Doing your best was fine for your high school football team. Not in special operations. But given Chuck's psyche, that answer would have to suffice. For now.

"Good man." He patted Chuck on the shoulder and rose.

"Thanks, Jim. I appreciate the advice. I wish . . . I wish Doug would talk to me like you did, instead of just ridin' my ass all the time."

"Go easy on Doug. Believe it or not, the guy just wants what's best for you."

Chuck scoffed. "Yeah. More like what he thinks is best for me."

Jim started to respond, but held his tongue. He knew this was one argument he couldn't win right now.

Their surveillance of Elizabethtown Regional Airport continued through the night and well into morning. They got a rough head count of the Shreth'kil, somewhere between 400 to 500. A trio of Shreth'kil poked around one of the mobile surface-to-air missile, or SAM, launchers, likely doing some kind of maintenance. Was it a chronic problem, or something easily fixed? Jim hoped for the latter. It could mean the difference between success and failure when the LAW attacked this base.

Whenever the hell that happened.

Three more supply convoys arrived at the airport, their cargo loaded onto Hippos or Taniwhas, which flew off to God only knew where. They also noted that each convoy had traveled south on 31W going into the airport, then left the opposite way.

"Wherever that supply base is, it can't be too far from here," O'Neal stated after the last convoy drove out of sight.

"I agree." Kenaevya took the four steps needed to cross from the window to desk where Mackanin sat. "Bring up a map for Elizabethtown. Let's see where the Shreth'kil might set up a supply base."

"Unfortunately, we weren't able ta get ourselves a map of this Earth's Elizabethtown. Best I can do is pull up maps of Elizabethtowns from Earths similar to this one."

Mackanin tapped a few keys. Within moments thirty small windows appeared on the screen, each displaying a map. A couple more taps on the keyboard, and orange circles sprouted on the maps.

"Alrighty." Mackanin's finger hovered over the screen. "Now twenty-six of these maps show a shopping mall about four miles from here along Highway Thirty-One West."

"You mean Towne Mall?" Valerie looked over Mackanin's shoulder. "I had a friend in high school who had relatives here in E-town. She said as far as malls go, that place was tiny."

"Perhaps," said Kenaevya. "But it still might be enough to suit the Shreth'kil's purposes. Given the size of this town, its airport and the aircraft they're using, I'd say this place is set up to re-supply infantry units." She turned back to Mackanin. "Anything else?"

"Well, twenty-four of these maps show a high school just a few miles north of the mall. Keen Johnson High School, John Hardin High School or Samuel Haycroft High School, dependin' on which Earth you're all on."

"A high school? For a supply base?" Val scrunched up her face.

"The Shreth'kil have done it on other Earths," O'Neal told her. "Think of all the classrooms, the gymnasium, the auditorium. You take out all the students and teachers and you've got plenty of storage space."

"Either one of them would be a good choice," Jim said. "Close to the airport, cuts down on travel time, reduces the risk of ambush."

"I agree." Kenaevya nodded. "We'll stay here through the afternoon, continue gathering intelligence on the airport, then head out for the mall and the high school."

The hours passed slowly as they kept track of changes in the guard shift, the flight patterns of the sentries over the airport, which Shreth'kil seemed to be in positions of authority. They also watched a battle drill early in the afternoon, and took careful note of the Shreth'kil's deployment, strategy and reaction times.

As dusk set in, Jim and the others scavenged the house for anything useful. Food was top priority, and they took every canned good, box of cereal, and package of cookies, crackers and candy they could stuff in their packs. Other items they took included blankets, extra clothing, towels, toiletries, matches, a flashlight, and a pair of handguns Jim figured the former owners, unfortunately, would no longer need. After refilling their canteens and camel packs, the group slipped out of the house. They gave the airport a wide berth before heading back toward the highway. It was already dark by the time they reached the Towne Mall.

Several cars, trucks and SUVs sat in the parking lot. Jim figured they had been there since the beginning of the Shreth'kil invasion. The mall itself was dark, with no sign of Shreth'kil activity.

They pressed on, heading north toward the high school. A couple times they stopped and hid when they spotted a Shreth'kil patrol flying overhead. Luckily they remained unseen.

At around 2300 hours, they arrived at the high school, John Hardin High School according to the marquee near the main entrance. At first sight, Jim's face twisted in incredulity, taken aback by the school's unusual design. It looked like a jumble of buildings, some beige in color, others reddish-brown. Some had slanted roofs, others were more oval-shaped. One area of the school had a white tower sprouting up.

There were other features, ones the architects of this school couldn't possibly have imagined. Like the machine gun nests on the roofs, or the mobile SAM launcher, or the concertina wire surrounding the campus.

All of it belonged to the Shreth'kil.

"I believe this is a sign we've found their supply base, wouldn't you say?" O'Neal said with a half-smirk.

Kenaevya assigned Mackanin to set up a command post in the nearby woods, with Williams and Chuck acting as guards. The rest she divided into groups of two to watch the school from all sides.

"Major Rhyne, you're with me," she told him.

Jim felt the veins in his neck stick out. After what happened two days ago, he didn't know if being so close to Kenaevya would be a good thing or a bad thing.

We're both professionals. We don't have time to think about . . . that right now.

He and Kenaevya made their way along the treeline, stopping when they reached the rear of the high school. Stretched out before them was the football field, and in the middle of it sat a huge dome-shaped tent.

"What do you suppose they're using that for?" Jim asked.

"Could be any number of things. Storing supplies, mess hall, command center."

"Mm." He frowned. "Guess there's only one thing to do. Sit and watch, and hope that after a while we get a better idea."

Kenaevya softly chuckled. "Such is the adventurous life of a Recon Trooper."

Jim turned to her, smiling briefly. He really liked her sense of humor, along with . . .

Mission. Focus on the mission.

An hour passed. The only activity around the tent was the two sentries walking their circuits. A machine gun nest had been placed on top of the press box, the two Shreth'kil manning it chatting between themselves more than keeping an eye out for any threats.

Something moved near the school. Jim pressed the scope he'd detached from his hunting rifle to his eye. A door at the rear of the school had opened. A Shreth'kil with a small beak and little stubby horns – probably a junior NCO – loped down the walkway, entered the football field and walked up to the tent. He went inside, then exited a minute later and returned to the school.

"Wonder what that was about?" Jim whispered.

Kenaevya shook her head. "I have no idea."

About ten minutes went by before the door opened again. Two Shreth'kil soldiers emerged, clutching their rifles. They took a few steps down the walkway, stopped and stood opposite of one another, then screeched at the door and gestured emphatically.

What Jim saw next made his chest tighten.

A man stepped out of the door, bearded, a bit on the chubby side, and from his scrunched up posture, terrified. The Shreth'kil soldiers shrieked louder at him. The man trembled and shuffled along the walkway. Another man followed, then another, then a woman, then another man, then two women. The procession grew in size to twenty-five, men and women anywhere from teenagers to the elderly. Most of the women, and quite a few of the men, openly wept. More Shreth'kil guards appeared, marching the humans toward the tent.

"Oh God," Kenaevya gasped.

"What?"

"I think I know what that tent is for." Jim swore he heard her swallow before she continued. "It's a processing tent."

"Processing tent? What does . . ." He cut himself off, a sick feeling slithering through his stomach. He looked back at the tent, and watched the humans enter one by one. Dread swelled inside him, causing him to shiver. He didn't need to ask Kenaevya what she meant by processing. He knew.

Forcing his hands not to shake, he lifted the scope to his eye. A heavyset teenage girl stopped near the Shreth'kil at the tent entrance, clasping her hands together, looking as though she was begging. The Shreth'kil let out a loud shriek and snapped its right hand toward the tent. The girl sobbed and went inside.

A middle-aged man with a huge paunch entered the tent next, followed by a rather pudgy woman. In fact, all the people in line looked well-fed.

Just like chickens and turkeys. Fatten 'em up before . . .

The breath caught in Jim's throat. He leaned forward, clutching the scope tighter.

No. No friggin' way!

A plump, dark-haired woman shuffled toward the tent, head down, convulsing with sobs.

Jim recognized her. She'd been part of Reverend Crawford's congregation. Her husband had been the guy from Hopkinsville who told them that demons had attacked the city and carried people away.

His heart raced. Could any more people from the congregation be here? That woman's husband and young daughter? The skinny teenager who told them what he'd seen on the internet?

Little Amanda?

Soon all twenty-five people were inside. Tension clutched every muscle in Jim's body. Sobs filtered out of the tent, along with a few desperate pleas.

An electronic whirring came from the tent. Jim clenched his teeth. The sound reminded him of . . .

Oh God.

The sobs grew louder. The whirring died down. Seconds later fearful cries erupted. "No! No, please! Please! No!"

A woman. Was it the plump woman from Reverend Crawford's congregation? Jim lowered the scope, his hand shaking. He laid on his stomach, eyes locked on the tent, every fearful cry from the woman tearing at his soul.

Why am I just sitting here? You're a soldier. You took an oath to protect these people.

Logic and training punched through his emotions. Rushing the tent, guns blazing, would just get him killed, compromise the mission, and do nothing to save those people.

The whirring started again. Jim jerked as a scream of sheer agony pierced the air.

Other screams went up, screams of terror, louder than before. Every few minutes one of those screams would change from terror to agony. Anger, helplessness and loathing latched on to Jim's soul. Tears welled up in his eyes with every anguished cry. He made a fist and pounded the ground.

"Jim." Kenaevya placed a gentle hand on his shoulder. "I'm so sorry, but there's nothing we can do to help them."

Another tortured cry came from the tent.

"Bullshit."

"What?" Kenaevya asked.

Jim looked to her. "There is something we can do. I bet they have a lot more people in there, waiting their turn to wind up on some fucking Shreth'kil's plate. Well that's not gonna happen."

"What are you talking about?"

Jim's face tightened into a mask of determination. "I've had it with just sitting around and watching. It's time we do something, like bust every single prisoner out of that school."

CHAPTER 18

"Jim, I sympathize with you. I truly do. But what you desire is simply not possible."

"I don't want to hear that, Myra." Jim's face stiffened as he stared at Kenaevya. The two were in the office of an abandoned house two miles from the Shreth'kil supply base at John Hardin High School. "The only thing I want to hear is how you and your LAW friends are going to help me rescue the people being held at that school."

"You saw how the Shreth'kil have fortified that school. They must have anywhere from two hundred to three hundred soldiers there. How many are we? Eleven. That number goes down to seven when you count those of us with special operations training. Any rescue we attempt would end in disaster for us."

"Well here's an idea. Have Mackanin dial-up your superiors on whichever Earth they're on and have them send us reinforcements."

"Given how deep we are in Shreth'kil territory, and with this entire region under a quantum jammer umbrella, my superiors may consider such a rescue too risky."

"Too risky?" Jim flung his arms out to his side. "Everything we do in this line of work is risky."

"True. And an operation like this would risk our mission in Kentucky, which, in case you have forgotten, is to gather as much intelligence as possible on Shreth'kil activity to aid our forces when they arrive to liberate your Earth."

Jim stood, arms akimbo, and fixed Kenaevya with a hard stare. "You felt it was worth the risk to expose you and your troopers to save us from the Shreth'kil."

Kenaevya bit her lip. "That was different. We faced only a squad of Shreth'kil, in an isolated forest. And we felt our mission would benefit by having a few locals with us. So yes, at that time, we felt it worth the risk. But what you're asking here, to attack a fixed, heavily defended installation, the risk is too great."

"So that's it then? We just leave the rest of those people there?" Images of little Amanda formed in his head. His fury burned. "You know what's going to happen to them.

Are you telling me you're okay with that?"

"Of course I'm not okay with it!" Kenaevya snapped, her face contorting in anger. "Do you think I didn't feel anything when I watched those people being marched into that tent, and heard their screams? Do you think I didn't hate myself for not being able to do anything to help them?"

"Then do something to help the rest of them."

"And if we do, then what? Let us say there are two hundred people being held at that school. Perhaps we're lucky enough to save over half of them. A hundred or so lives saved. But that means we would also have to leave this area, with our mission not complete. The information we fail to gather might jeopardize future LAW operations in Kentucky, perhaps all of these United States. In saving a hundred people, hundreds of thousands of others, perhaps millions of others, may die."

"You're talking hypothetical. I'm talking about a certainty. The certainty that if we do nothing, however many people the Shreth'kil have at that school will die."

"We're both in the same line of work," Kenaevya said. "You know as well as I do how critical good intelligence is to the success of any operation. Our mission here is important for the coming LAW counter-attack. I cannot fault your desire to save those people, but you must think of the bigger picture, and not let your emotions get the better of you."

"Well maybe it's time my emotions *did* get the better of me. Maybe I'm sick and tired of sitting behind bushes just watching those ugly fuckers while they chop up people and stuff 'em into Shreth'kil MREs. And maybe you'd feel different if it were people from your Earth they were doing this to."

Kenaevya's lips parted, as if she was about to reply. Instead, she shut her mouth tight and just stared at him. She clenched a fist. For a moment, Jim wondered if she'd hit him.

She didn't. Her shoulders sagged a bit, and her gaze fell to the carpet.

Jim raised an eyebrow. What the heck was going on with her? Kenaevya looked almost . . . melancholy. Not the sort of reaction he'd expect from an Amazon warrior like her.

Guilt surged through him. Had his last comment struck a nerve with her?

Kenaevya looked back up at him and swallowed. "I'm sorry, Jim. I truly am. I wish . . . I wish I could help."

She started for the door.

"Myra, wait." He reached out and grasped her wrist. She stopped and turned to him. He felt her tense, but she made no move to pull away.

He stared down at his fingers around Kenaevya's wrist. *I know she has feelings for me. Maybe I can use that to my advantage.*

Jim fought to keep his face from twisting in disgust. He genuinely liked Kenaevya. To manipulate her emotions for his own benefit was not something a real man would do.

What's more important here, Jim? Your sense of honor or the lives of a bunch of innocent people?

He bit his lip, craned his neck, and stared Kenaevya in her liquid dark eyes. He drew a breath. No. Emotional manipulation wouldn't do it here. Yelling at her wouldn't work. He needed to approach this from a practical, military standpoint.

"Myra." He softened his voice. "Think about it this way. It's not just about saving those people. It's about disrupting the Shreth'kil supply line. You said that base most likely resupplies infantry units. I don't care how advanced they are. If they don't have ammo and food and water, then they don't fight. Their advance through Pennsylvania and Virginia slows down, and that buys us more time for those LAW reinforcements to assemble and help us. Plus . . ." Jim chewed on the inside of his cheek. What he was about to say was maybe more of an emotional argument than a practical argument, but dammit, the people fighting this war weren't robots. They had emotions, and they had to be taken into account.

"You heard the reports from your HQ," he continued. "We're getting our asses kicked out there. Even with your rapid deployment forces helping us, all we're able to do is slow down the Shreth'kil, not stop them. My people need to know the Shreth'kil can be defeated. They need a victory. Maybe in the scheme of things, it's a minor victory, but it's still a victory."

Kenaevya's eyes flickered toward the wall, a thoughtful look on her face. Jim suddenly realized he still held her wrist. He gave it a gentle squeeze.

Several long seconds of silence passed. He didn't let go of Kenaevya's wrist. He continued staring at her, trying to read her expression, wondering what thoughts were going through her head.

"I was married once as well."

Jim's face scrunched in puzzlement. What had prompted her to admit that?

Slowly, she rotated her head toward him. "His name was Paul Harroman, an Englishman from an Earth where the British Empire still exists. He was a captain in an L-A-W armored regiment. We had a son, David. Two years ago, I was on a mission to Earth E-W-4-3." She closed her eyes and shook her head. "That world was in chaos. India and Pakistan devastated each other in a nuclear war, and that seemed to prompt everyone else who had atomic weapons to launch them at each other. Iran and Israel, North and South Korea, Egypt and Libya. America, Russia and China were all on the brink of launching their own missiles. And somehow, we had to try and get all the nations of that world to cooperate and fight the Shreth'kil. Even with an invasion by a race of human-eating creatures, the mistrust between so many countries could not be overcome. The LAW ended up doing the bulk of the fighting on that world. Meanwhile, Paul was on leave, and decided to take David to see the Grand Canyon on Earth C-W-2-7 for his fifth birthday."

The breath caught in Jim's throat as Kenaevya slid her hand up and intertwined her fingers with his. She continued. "The Shreth'kil launched a surprise attack on Arizona. They sent sweeper units through the Grand Canyon and . . . they took my husband and son."

The revelation sent a shudder through Jim. He squeezed Kenaevya's hand. Her jaw quivered for a moment, then stopped. It seemed as though she was doing her damnedest not to cry.

"Myra, I'm so sorry."

She gave him a stiff nod. "I was enraged when I found out. I wanted to go to whatever Earth the Shreth'kil took them to and save them, and then I wanted to slay every last

one of those monsters. But no one knew which Earth Paul
and David and the other people had been taken. There was .
. . there was nothing I could do. For the first time in my life
I felt helpless. For a long time I felt like I failed them."

"You didn't fail them. There was nothing you could have
done. You were on a . . . on a mission." His voice trailed
off. *Oh my God.* He couldn't believe he said that. That's
what Kenaevya had told him about Hannah's death. That's
what Valerie had told him. And now . . .

"It's not an easy thing, Jim," Kenaevya said. "To forgive
yourself for something like that. But eventually you do.
Eventually you succumb to logic, and you admit to yourself
there was nothing you could have done, and allow yourself
to live."

"Yeah, I've had people tell me that before. But for me,
phrases like 'move on' and 'live again' feel like ways to say
'forget about your dead wife.'"

"No. You will never forget Hannah, just like I will never
forget my husband and my little boy. But wallowing in guilt
and grief and misery will not bring them back, and it won't
help us in our lives, especially when we both have a
purpose."

"Which is?"

"To protect people." Kenaevya bit her lip. "Those
people still held captive in the school, they depend on people
like you and me to keep them safe. If we don't do
everything in our power to do that, then what good are we?"

"Then you'll help me?"

"Yes." Kenaevya nodded. "You are right. We should
save those people. All the better, too, if in the process we
can prevent more supplies from reaching the front lines and
stall the Shreth'kil advance through your eastern states."

She took hold of both Jim's hands. "You have my word,
I will do everything I can to convince my superiors to
approve this rescue mission."

"Thank you." Hope swelled inside him. He locked gazes
with Kenaevya, who smiled at him. His respect for this
woman increased a hundred-fold. So did his sympathy for
her. All this time, he never realized that she had experienced
the same sort of loss he had, perhaps an even worse one as
she also lost a son along with a spouse. Yet since the first

night they met, she never showed a hint of that pain. He wondered how much strength, how much trust, it took for her to cast aside her Amazon pride and open up herself to him.

Probably the same amount it took for him to tell her about Hannah.

They continued staring at one another, still holding hands. His heartbeat picked up. Suddenly he found himself closing the distance between them.

They kissed. Gentle at first. Soon their mouths opened wider. Kenaevya clamped a hand on his shoulder, her fingers pressing down until it hurt. Fire shot through his body as he ran a hand through her hair. She pressed her body against his and let out a small . . . snarl? Did she just snarl?

Surprise and excitement surged through him as Kenaevya buried her face in his neck, first kissing, then biting. Jim returned the favor, and gave a startled gasp when Kenaevya's hands clenched his ass and squeezed tight.

Their mouths separated, and they both drew deep breaths.

"Well that was . . . intense," Jim said.

"And enjoyable." She gave him a sensual smile. "But, we have more important things to do right now."

"Yeah, you're right."

They released each other. Jim followed Kenaevya out of the office and into the upstairs hallway. The smile refused to leave his face. He figured being an Amazon, Kenaevya would be fierce in battle. Apparently, that ferocity carried over to more . . . intimate matters. If a first kiss with an Amazon was like that, he could only imagine what the sex must be like.

Hannah. What would she think?

Now the smile faded. He slowed his pace as they reached the stairway. The guilt returned. My God, he just kissed another woman, wanted to have sex with her. How could he do that?

He then thought about what Kenaevya had said, how you never forget a loved one who's gone, and how you must allow yourself to live.

And love someone else?

Jim grunted and shook his head. Dammit, this was not the time to be thinking about stuff like that. Not when they were in the middle of Shreth'kil-occupied Kentucky, and trying to convince Kenaevya's superiors to rescue a bunch of prisoners.

They descended the stairs to the living room, where the rest of the group relaxed.

"Mackanin. I need you to contact headquarters." Kenaevya waved for the Texan to come to her.

"Yes, Madam." He sprang to his feet, grabbed his laptop and followed her and Jim back to the upstairs office. After he set up the computer on the desk, he tapped a couple keys. Within seconds the face of a thin woman with black skin appeared on the screen.

"Identify," she ordered.

Mackanin replied. "Alpha Alpha Seven One Sigma Five Six Sigma."

The woman looked down for a few moments. "Authenticated. What is your message?" Jim noted the woman's accent. African.

"Standby for Major Kenaevya." Mackanin looked up at her.

"Thank you, Mackanin. You're dismissed."

"Yes, Madam."

Once he left the room, Kenaevya sat at the desk and said to the African woman, "This is Major Kenaevya, requesting to speak with Legatus Durnfeldt."

"Yes, Madam. Standby."

The screen went blank. Jim dwelled on the rank Kenaevya used for this Durnfeldt person. Legatus. That was a rank from the days of the Roman Empire, the equivalent of a general.

The screen flickered back on. This time a stony-faced man with close-cropped blond hair appeared.

"Legatus." Kenaevya sat straighter in her chair while Jim looked over her shoulder.

"Major." Legatus Durnfeldt nodded. "You wish to speak to me." The man's accent was definitely German.

"Correct, Sir. There has been a new development in our mission."

"What sort of development?"

Kenaevya spent the next few minutes informing Durnfeldt about the Shreth'kil supply base in Elizabethtown, and the people being held captive at John Hardin High School.

"Major Rhyne and I discussed the possibility of a rescue mission for the prisoners at the school."

"Rescue mission?"

Jim tried to keep from frowning at the doubtful tone in Durnfeldt's voice.

The Legatus took a breath before continuing. "You do understand, Major, that your mission is one of intelligence gathering, not active combat."

"Yes, Sir."

"And you are aware that you would need reinforcements for such an operation to succeed. Reinforcements that we cannot transit directly to your region. They would have to transit to a place outside the Shreth'kil's quantum jammer field and fly several hundred miles to reach Elizabethtown. In addition, a mission like this would mean we would have to extricate you and your squad from Kentucky, and with the Shreth'kil undoubtedly increasing security after such an attack, it would make it next to impossible for us to insert another recon unit into that area."

"I understand, Sir, and I, too, have considered all those possibilities. But attacking that supply base could help slow down the Shreth'kil advance through Pennsylvania and Virginia. In addition, the rescue of so many prisoners could provide a morale boost to the locals still fighting the Shreth'kil. You know as well as I do that, even with our rapid deployment forces, the fighting does not go well for our side on any front. The people on this Earth need a victory, they need hope."

This time, Jim couldn't keep the smile off his face. *Go, Myra.* He did manage to restrain himself from putting a hand on her shoulder.

Durnfeldt said nothing. He just folded his hands and stared directly ahead. Jim could sense the wheels turning inside the guy's head, weighing the pros and cons. The tension increased with each passing, silent second.

C'mon, buddy. Say yes. Say yes.

"Major." Legatus Durnfeldt finally spoke.

"Yes, Sir."

"You are aware that I am loathe to let politics influence my decisions in field operations."

Kenaevya tilted her head. "Sir?"

"Some of Earth A-A-7-1's leaders," Durnfeldt used the LAW designation for this Earth, "have expressed dissatisfaction in our efforts to rescue those captured by the Shreth'kil. The President of that Earth's America has been one of the most vocal. In fact, we have received more than a few reports of dissension, even outright brawling, between local forces and ours, the locals accusing us of allowing their people to be turned into food for the Shreth'kil. I do not need to tell you how important it is to have a unified front against the Shreth'kil, especially after our experience on Earth E-W-4-3."

"No, Sir. You do not."

"I will be sacrificing an intelligence asset, but the trade-off may be more cooperation from the locals of that Earth. Very well, Major. I approve your request for a rescue mission."

"Thank you, Sir."

"Thank you, Sir," Jim repeated, forcing himself not to pump his fist in triumph.

Durnfeldt nodded. "Transmit all the intelligence you have gathered on the supply base and the airfield to me. I shall begin assembling all the assets you will need."

Kenaevya tapped a few keys on the laptop. "All data on Elizabethtown should be coming through now."

Durnfeldt looked off-screen. "Data received. I shall contact you as soon as all assets are ready."

"Acknowledged."

"Stay safe, Major."

The screen went dark.

Jim smiled and grasped both of Kenaevya's shoulders. "You did it."

She patted his left hand. "I think we can attribute this more to luck than my negotiating skills. Either way, we succeeded."

Jim bent down and kissed the top of Kenaevya's head. He rested his cheek in her thick black hair and closed his eyes. His thoughts drifted to the prisoners at John Hardin High School.

We're coming, folks. We're coming.

CHAPTER 19

"Five, four, three, two, one. Ciccaba's established orbit 40,000 feet above the high school," Mackanin reported, staring into the screen of his laptop.

Jim and the others gathered in the basement, gazing at the overhead image of John Hardin High School, courtesy of a UR-42 Ciccaba, the LAW version of a Predator drone. The unmanned aircraft had been launched from one of the B-146 Crusader bombers the LAW had based at Narsarsuaq Airport in Greenland to support their rescue mission. He watched the drone cycle through its sensors, including thermal and magnetic imaging, which allowed them to see inside the school. The thermal picked up numerous pulsating red and orange blobs gathered in one section of the school.

"Schematic overlay," Kenaevya ordered.

Mackanin tapped a few keys and inserted the blueprints for the school within the image from the Ciccaba.

"Looks like that's the gymnasium there," he stated.

Valerie leaned closer. "How many people are in there?"

Mackanin's fingers danced over the keyboard. Small circles appeared around the individual blobs. An instant later a number flashed in the screen's upper right-hand corner. 316.

Deathswipe hissed. "We will need many aircraft to evacuate such a large number of prisoners."

"And us," Williams added. "I don't know about you, but I don't plan on sticking around here after kicking over this hornet's nest."

"Using aircraft will be too risky," Kenaevya said. "We will likely need to destroy the quantum jammer for this area."

"Which will not be easy, either," Duguid pointed out. "Given how the Shreth'kil defend them."

"I know. But I imagine that is an option headquarters will more readily accept than putting so many aircraft and pilots at risk."

"Hey." Williams tilted his head. He leaned forward and pointed at the screen. "What the heck are those two doing?"

Jim focused on the southeast corner of the gymnasium,

where two shimmering, human-shaped blobs appeared to be undulating. He noted the steady rhythm, back and forth, back and forth. What could they . . .

"It appears they are having sex." One Cent grunted, a sneer marring his face.

"No way!" Chuck gaped, then barked out a laugh. "Damn! Locked up by the Shreth'kil and they still manage to sneak off and get some."

Jim tensed, watching the reactions of the Recon Troopers. All of them turned to Chuck, unsmiling. Both Duguid and One Cent shook their heads. A low growl came from Deathswipe's throat. Kenaevya narrowed her eyes at Chuck, then drew a slow breath. "This is not something to celebrate. Most likely those people are breeders."

"What'd ya mean, breeders?" A quizzical look came over Chuck's face.

"Standard doctrine for Shreth'kil prisoners. They will designate girls and woman from about fifteen years of age to their early thirties and force them to be impregnated by male prisoners."

"You mean they . . . they eat the babies?" Valerie's voice trailed off.

"No." Kenaevya's lips tightened. "When the babies are born, the Shreth'kil take them to facilities on other Earths."

"Facilities," Duguid snorted. "They are cattle pens, for people. The babies are stuck in there and fed until they grow up big and fat for those monsters."

Valerie placed a hand over her chest. The veins in her neck stuck out. "So no one . . . no one raises them? No parents or anything?"

Kenaevya sighed and shook her head. "The children are fed by machines. They have no one to nurture them. They basically become nothing more than animals."

Her gaze fell to the floor. She clenched her fists. Jim stopped himself from going over and wrapping his arms around her. The setting wasn't appropriate for that. Still his heart went out to Kenaevya. He'd bet anything she was thinking about her son. His stomach turned into a cold ball as he wondered whether little David suffered such a fate.

He looked back at the computer in time to see the couple climax. Anger burned through his soul. He didn't think he could hate the Shreth'kil any more than he already did, but after this . . .

Scowling, his eyes darted around the screen. Some of the classrooms had small groups of orange and blue blobs. Shreth'kil. Most likely asleep, since he learned from Mackanin that their body temperature dropped to match their environment when they slept, just like many species of bats. He imagined walking in with his M-4 and shooting them all in the head. No. Shooting was too quick. He wanted them to suffer.

Too bad the Army didn't use flamethrowers anymore.

For the next two days, the LAW maintained constant Ciccaba coverage of not only John Hardin High School, but the regional airport, and the rest of Elizabethtown and the surrounding area. Mackanin used all the images obtained by the drone to create a 3-D model of the small city, which floated above the upturned screen of his laptop.

"Now is that cool or what?" Williams grinned at Valerie.

"No 'or what' about it. That is seriously cool."

The two grinned at one another for longer than Jim cared for.

Mackanin expanded or contracted certain sections of the model at Kenaevya's direction as they laid out their plan. The school's main building had six machine gun nests, with a seventh atop the football field's press box. They would have to be taken out for any rescue mission to succeed. Another machine gun nest had been set up at the school's main entrance. In all, 255 Shreth'kil had been identified. One Ciccaba's cameras even picked up the one who appeared to be the base commander, given his long neck, curved horns, and lizard-like tail. Mackanin officially designated him Demon Alpha. Appropriate enough, Jim thought, considering the monster's appearance and actions.

I guess that guy from Reverend Crawford's congregation wasn't that far off when he called these things demons.

Mackanin's computer also collected images of all the Shreth'kil the Ciccabas photographed and listed them in probable order of rank. So far they had identified eight "officers," ten "senior NCOs" and numerous junior NCOs and enlisted soldiers. Kenaevya made them all memorize the features of the officers and senior NCOs. They would be among their priority targets.

They also learned the rotation of the Shreth'kil guards. Taking them out would be difficult since they usually flew instead of walked. Jim figured that would be a job best handled by snipers like Duguid.

Another worry was reinforcements from Elizabethtown Regional Airport. It would only take a few minutes for Shreth'kil soldiers to fly from there to the high school once the assault went down. They also had to consider the Shreth'kil supplies stored at the high school. Magnetic imaging scans indicated where they kept their ammo, food and all the other essentials for the average Shreth'kil infantryman. They would need explosives to destroy them.

Jim mulled over the information. While 255 Shreth'kil seemed like a lot, he figured if they were like the typical support unit in any army, most of them wouldn't have much combat experience. Hell, many of them may not have even fired a rifle since whatever passed for Shreth'kil basic training. A company-sized force of special ops soldiers like himself and Kenaevya's bunch, with the proper support, could pull off this mission.

Kenaevya had Mackanin sent off the information to their superiors. Until they heard back from them, all they could do was continue their surveillance of the high school.

A day passed. The number of prisoners decreased by twenty as a Ciccaba showed them being taken to the processing tent. Jim looked away from the computer screen. *I'm sorry.* Twenty more people he couldn't save. He tried to quell his anger and frustration by reminding himself things were progressing with the rescue mission. Unfortunately, not fast enough for those twenty people.

At 1935 hours, Mackanin received a message on his computer from 95th Recon Battalion HQ. They were to meet the LAW rescue force at the horse farm outside Elizabethtown tomorrow at 1630. After getting a few hours of sleep, the group set out well before dawn. They avoided a couple Shreth'kil patrols, and arrived at the rendezvous point with an hour-and-a-half to spare. Kenaevya positioned everyone at various locations around the farm to keep watch for any Shreth'kil, and any sign of the rescue unit.

At 1628 hours, Deathswipe, who stared at the pasture from the kitchen window, announced, "They are here."

Jim walked to the screen door leading to the back porch, accompanied by Valerie and Williams. He looked out at the pasture and furrowed his brow.

"You sure, Lieutenant?" he asked the dinosaur. "All I see is a lot of grass and empty space."

"Wait, look. There." Valerie pointed to the sky.

He followed his sister's extended finger. He still saw nothing save for blue sky and white clouds. What the hell was . . .

Then he noticed something shimmer, something big. He opened the door and stepped out onto the porch, Val and Williams right behind him. The object hovered above the pasture, emitting a deep fluttering sound. He squinted and leaned forward. A shape took form, bulky with a tail that sloped up and wings above the fuselage.

"Is that an Osprey?" He wondered aloud, referring to the tilt-rotor aircraft used by the U.S. Marine Corps.

"The outline looks right," said Williams. "Except ours don't have that electro-chromic skin."

Jim just nodded, watching the Osprey, which used the same *Predator*-style camouflage as the Recon Troopers' EWABS armor, set down. A minute later another Osprey, its fuselage also projecting an image of the sky, landed.

"Let's go." Kenaevya led the group out the back door, leaving Duguid, O'Neal and Doug to guard their rear.

"I don't believe it." Val shook her head, staring at the still disguised tilt-rotors.

Kenaevya turned to her. "What? You've seen our electro-chromic camouflage before."

"No, not that. Just . . . you guys are so advanced, I didn't think you'd be using something like a V-22 Osprey."

"There are Americas in the multiverse that still use B-52s, Hueys and F-4 Phantoms even though they are fifty, and in some cases sixty, years old. They are still good and effective aircraft. That's how the LAW feels about the Osprey, the Blackhawk and the C-130 Hercules."

The rear ramps of the Ospreys lowered. Jim halted for a moment when he spotted the people and equipment inside.

With the electro-chromic camouflage, it almost looked as though they floated above the ground.

The LAW troopers in the first Osprey walked forward, led by a Japanese man who couldn't be more than five-five, but had a stern, unsmiling face and dark, intense eyes.

"Major Akageri." Kenaevya greeted him with a slight bow.

"Major Kenaevya." The Japanese trooper returned the bow. "It is good to see you again. Per Legatus Durnfeldt's orders, I place myself and my troopers at your command."

"Thank you, Major."

Akageri bowed, then spun around to the other troopers. "Get everything unloaded! Hurry! We cannot afford to linger here."

That's when Jim noticed what Akageri carried on his back. A sword! An actual samurai sword.

"Yo." Chuck sidled up to Deathswipe. "What up with the sword?"

"Major Akageri comes from an Earth where the Japanese Empire was victorious in World War Two. Their officers still carry swords into battle."

Jim gazed into the first Osprey, counting at least twenty LAW troopers, including Akageri. He peeked inside the second aircraft and found roughly the same number of troopers in there. Face scrunched, he turned to the sky, expecting more Ospreys to appear.

None did.

"This is it?" he walked up to Major Akageri as he exited the Osprey. "Forty soldiers?"

Akageri stopped and regarded him with annoyance. "Who are you?"

"Hayata." Kenaevya stepped over to them. "This is Major Jim Rhyne, United States Army Delta Force. A local. He's the one who recommended the rescue mission at Hardin High School."

Hayata Akageri just stared at him, then grunted. "Forty soldiers added to your force is sufficient for this rescue."

"You gotta be kidding. There's over two hundred-fifty Shreth'kil at that school. We need at least a full company for this assault."

"I wouldn't worry too much, Major." A tall man with tan skin and a huge grin approached him. "Captain Ed Vasquez. I'm Major Akageri's XO." He used the acronym for Executive Officer. "Used to be with the U.S. Army Rangers on my Earth before I joined the LAW."

Jim shook Vasquez's hand, adding a, "Hu-aah," then wondered if the Rangers on that Earth used the term.

"Hu-aah. Always nice to see some things stay the same from Earth to Earth. Anyway, like I said, don't worry, Major. We've got some serious force multipliers with us."

As if on cue, four tracked constructs rolled down the ramp. Each one looked like a robotic arm attached to a flat platform. Jim's eyes widened when he noticed what those arms carried.

"Holy shit, look at those things!" Chuck gaped.

"Grizzlies. Robotic weapons platforms," Vasquez explained.

Jim nodded, staring at the robots. One of them carried a pair of .50 caliber machine guns. The second Grizzly had a minigun. The third bore two light machine guns, similar to Deathswipe's, and a grenade launcher. The last Grizzly carried two anti-tank rockets and a light machine gun.

Jim whistled in amazement. "Yeah, we should have plenty of firepower for this."

He also learned Akageri's platoon, or contubernium in the LAW vernacular, had brought six airborne robotic weapons platforms called Firebrands and Pilums, which resembled radio-controlled helicopters and airplanes. These "toys," however, carried .50 caliber guns and grenade launchers.

The contubernium also consisted of a heavy weapons squad with two mortar crews, two anti-tank rocket launchers and two shoulder-launched SAMs, eight demolitions experts, six field medics and two snipers. They also had four Pack Mule robot platforms to carry their heavier gear.

"We also have some extra IA-15 assault rifles and body armor for you and the other locals," Vasquez explained to Jim as they set off toward Elizabethtown. "Along with some of our combat goggles and comm units. You're gonna love 'em. Advanced optics, range finder, laser targeting, you can access our video and communications feeds, call up maps, identify Shreth'kil vehicles and equipment. They told me this is a pretty tech-savvy Earth, so you should have no trouble using this stuff."

"Thanks, Captain." Jim nodded to him. He instantly took a liking to Vasquez. The guy had a friendly demeanor, seemed eager to help, and didn't talk down to people. All in all, the perfect person to interact with indigenous forces.

And this time, indigenous means us.

When night set in, the newly enlarged group spent more time hiding than moving, as the Shreth'kil were more active. Again, they avoided all enemy patrols and returned to Elizabethtown early the next afternoon. Kenaevya led them to a block of interconnected red brick, one-story houses four miles from the high school that would serve as their staging area. The marquee on the front lawn read BRIGHT SKY ASSISTED LIVING HOME. Several troopers, Jim included, tried unsuccessfully to stifle coughs as they walked through the hallways. The odor of rotten food and human waste hung in the air, along with a tinge of that antiseptic smell common to places like this. He clenched his teeth as he stared in every room he walked by, taking note of the empty beds, wondering about the men and women who once occupied them. Had the Shreth'kil taken them to process into food? He thought about some of his prior visits to places like this to see older relatives in their final days, and remembered the shape they and the other residents had been in. Would the Shreth'kil want to eat elderly people who, in many cases, had withered away, their bodies ravaged by one disease or another? Did they just shoot them all and dump them somewhere?

They set up their command center in the facility's storm cellar. Once Mackanin called up the holographic display of John Hardin High School, Major Akageri went over the plan put together back at 95th Recon Battalion HQ, codenamed Operation: Robber Baron, with Kenaevya adding her own tweaks here and there. Jim also learned the LAW had committed several other assets to this mission besides Akageri's Recon Troopers. The B-146s from Greenland would participate. Along with launching a Ciccaba for overhead imagery, an AEWM-192 Mystic electronic warfare missile would orbit Elizabethtown, jamming Shreth'kil communications, computers and sensors. A salvo of

AAWP-59 Rapiers, large cruise missiles that, in addition to a warhead, carried several small missiles and smart bombs, would take out the regional airport. Jim hoped the Shreth'kil there would be so busy with that mess they wouldn't be able to send reinforcements to the high school.

Farther away from Elizabethtown, a LAW carrier battle group would transit into the Gulf of Mexico. From there, the carrier *Catherine the Great* would launch UF-25 Skyshark unmanned attack jets, while the cruiser *Manuel L. Quezon* and the missile sub *Vendetta* fired Minotaur cruise missiles to take out the quantum jammer for this area, located just outside Louisville. Once that was destroyed, they would move the prisoners to the designated transit zone, or TZ, a small wooded area behind a residential neighborhood less than a mile from the school. Then they would step through the portal and wind up safe and sound at a LAW base in Reykjavik, part of the Scandinavian Empire on Earth V-E-2-8.

Jim digested everything. It seemed like a sound plan.

So long as everything worked.

Worry clawed at the back of his mind. This mission had so many elements to it. What if the Skysharks and Minotaurs couldn't get through the Shreth'kil air defenses and take out the quantum jammer? What if the Rapier attack on the airport was defeated and the Shreth'kil sent reinforcements to the school? What if they couldn't take out the machine gun nests? What if one or more of the Grizzlies or the Firebrands or the Pilums failed? No matter how advanced the LAW was, machines were machines, and sometimes they just didn't work as advertised, usually at the worst possible moment.

Please not another Operation: Eagle Claw. Jim couldn't help but think of the failed Iranian hostage rescue mission in 1980. All Delta Force operators had that incident drilled into their heads as an example of how overcomplication and micromanagement can doom an operation. In Iran, it resulted in the collision of a helicopter and a C-130, the deaths of eight Americans, and the end of the mission before Delta got anywhere near Tehran.

Right now, however, it was the only plan they had. They would just have to make sure it worked. The lives of nearly 300 people depended on it.

"Before this plan is executed," Akageri stated, "I wish to take my soldiers to the target area and have them see it with their own eyes. There is only so much one can determine about terrain features from a drone."

"You read my mind, Hayata." Kenaevya flashed him a brief smile. "That will be the only way to determine the best positions for our snipers, grenadiers, mortars and command post, along with plotting our egress route to the transit point."

With their group now at 57 members, Kenaevya decided to have them reconnoiter the high school in three sections of 19 soldiers each. Doing it with everyone at one time would just increase their risk of detection.

Kenaevya led the first section herself, with Jim, Doug, Mackanin, Duguid and 14 of Akageri's troopers accompanying her. They crawled on the ground, ducked behind trees and buildings, and marked down what they thought would be the best positions for their fire support personnel.

The sun had nearly disappeared beneath the horizon as Jim, Kenaevya and Doug crawled to a clump of bushes, discussing the possibility of using it for one of the mortar positions.

"I'd put it here," Doug said. "There's good concealment and a good view of the front of the school."

"I agree." Kenaevya nodded. "Though these bushes won't do much to stop Shreth'kil bullets. The crew would only be able to fire a few rounds before having to move to a -
"

"Hey!" Jim spoke in a loud whisper. "We got a convoy coming."

The trio watched as three Shreth'kil supply trucks and two guard vehicles rolled to a halt in front of the school. Seconds later the doors of the main entrance flew open. A dozen Shreth'kil, rifles at the ready, lined the walkway leading to the vehicles. Jim also noticed two of the rooftop machine guns angled down to cover the grounds.

"What the heck's going on?" Doug asked.

Jim opened his mouth to answer, "I don't know," but froze in shock. He just gaped at the three figures that suddenly strutted out of the school. He blinked a few times, hardly believing what he saw.

Three young Hispanic men stood inside the Shreth'kil gauntlet, none of them afraid. In fact, from their body language, they acted like they belonged among them. The first guy, who had a husky build, a goatee, and wore a blue basketball jersey that, unbelievably, looked brand new, grinned as he gazed upon the newly arrived vehicles. The two behind him, both lean and roughly high school age, also smiled and shook their heads. All three sported tattoos on their arms and necks.

Gangbangers, Jim assumed. They had to be.

But what the hell are they up to? Why –

That's when he received his second shock. Two Shreth'kil exited the school and walked up to the gangbangers. One was of the Mothman variety and carried a small computer. The other resembled the Jersey Devil, and Jim recognized him.

Demon Alpha, the CO of this base.

The big gangbanger said something to Demon Alpha Jim couldn't make out. The Shreth'kil commander then let out a series of screeches, and an electronic voice blared from the computer of his subordinate.

"Yes. You can have reward when food unloaded."

The three gangbangers howled with delight, then hurried back into the school. A few minutes later a line of prisoners shuffled out the doors.

"C'mon, bitches!" shouted the big gangbanger, pushing a hefty middle-aged man. "Get all this shit inside! Move it!"

The prisoners hauled cardboard boxes out of two of the supply trucks and took them into the school. Jim zoomed in with his new LAW-issued combat goggles to check out the contents and reported his findings to Kenaevya and Doug.

"Let's see, we got cereal, candy bars, snack cakes, cookies, chips, lots of canned stuff like pasta and soup and fruit."

"I guess now we know why most of those prisoners look overweight," Doug said. "Most of the food they're giving them is high calorie, high fat."

"It's the same principle we apply to cows and chickens and other such animals." Kenaevya bit her lip before continuing. "Fatten them up before taking them to the slaughter."

Jim bit back boiling rage as he watched the prisoners carrying food back into the school, the three gangbangers constantly yelling and pushing and hitting them.

"What the hell is up with those guys?" Doug scowled. "Why are the Shreth'kil letting them act that way?"

Jim's face twisted in anger. "Kapos."

"What?" Doug shot him a quizzical look.

"So you had them on this Earth, too." Kenaevya sighed and lowered her eyes.

Doug turned to Kenaevya, then back to Jim. "What the hell's a kapo?"

"The concentration camps in World War Two." He glanced over at Kenaevya and noticed her body tense. *I guess that happened on her Earth, too.*

He continued. "The kapos were Jewish prisoners who helped the Nazis keep the other Jewish prisoners in line. They were pretty vicious and brutal bastards."

Doug's mouth hung open. Slowly, he shook his head. "You gotta be kidding. I can't believe any Jew would help the Nazis back then."

"We Jews are like any other people. There are good ones, and there are bad ones. And the bad ones, like the kapos, would make a deal with the devil to save their own skin. Just like those three are doing." Kenaevya jerked her head toward the gangbangers.

Ten minutes later, all the food had been unloaded.

"That's it, boss," the big gangbanger said to Demon Alpha, then grinned and rubbed his hands together. "So is it reward time?"

"Yes," the translation computer blared. "Go get reward." Demon Alpha waved two Shreth'kil soldiers over to the last supply truck. They swung open the doors, waving their arms and shrieking, "Out! Out!"

Jim's chest tightened when he saw a trembling brunette climb out of the back. Another girl followed, and another, and another. Before long, a dozen young girls, none of whom looked older than eighteen, stood in a little clump, some of them crying, all of them absolutely terrified.

"Line up, bitches!" yelled the big gangbanger. "Line the fuck up! Right here! I fucking said line up." He punched a petite blonde who moved too slow for his liking. She dropped to the ground, crying and clutching her cheek.

"Yo, get the fuck up, bitch!" One of the lean gangbangers yanked her to her feet. She cried even louder.

Jim gritted his teeth, his finger caressing the trigger of his IA-15.

You can't do anything.

His head trembled with fury. He was sick and tired of not being able to help anyone, of watching people be taken away by the Shreth'kil, listening to them scream as they were chopped to pieces. And now he had to sit back and watch these girls . . .

He closed his eyes and felt tears well up. *You won't help them by getting you and Doug and Myra killed and screwing up the mission.*

God forgive me.

Jim opened his eyes and saw the big gangbanger – *Fatfuck. That's your name now* – walk up and down the line of girls. Suddenly he stopped in front of one with short blonde hair and an athletic build. She may have been a cheerleader. She also couldn't be older than sixteen.

His blood froze when Fatfuck nodded and leered. He grabbed her by the back of the neck and pulled her to the truck.

"No. No, please!" the girl cried. "Please!"

"Shut up, bitch!" Fatfuck punched her in the gut, causing her to double over. "Next time you open that mouth, my dick better be in it!"

He picked up the girl and threw her in the back of the truck, then climbed in.

A heavy silence hung in the air. Jim couldn't move a muscle. Nausea filled his stomach. How the hell could he just sit here and let this happen?

He jerked when a feminine scream erupted from the truck. The remaining two gangbangers cheered.

"Yeah, give it to her good, Mo'Dog!"

"Yeah, *esse!* Tear up that pussy!"

The other eleven girls sobbed as the screams continued.

A few minutes later Fatfuck, a.k.a. Mo'Dog, climbed out of the truck, wearing a triumphant smile. He high-fived his scumbag buddies, then turned to the line of young girls.

"Who's next?"

Jim held his rifle in a death grip, glaring at the gangbangers.

You shitsucking maggots just signed your death warrants.

CHAPTER 20

Anger festered inside Jim as he sat cross-legged on the floor, stripping down his LAW-issued IA-15 assault rifle and putting it back together. He gritted his teeth, trying to focus, to familiarize himself with his new weapon. Instead, the screams echoed through his mind, the screams of that teenage girl Fatfuck raped yesterday. Raped her while he just watched.

Don't fight angry. You fight angry, you make mistakes, then you and your friends die.

He exhaled loudly, trying to get control of his anger, mold it into something useful. Something like determination. Determination to free all the prisoners and get them safely to the LAW base on Scandinavian Empire Earth. That had to be his priority. Vengeance had to be pushed way down to the bottom of the list.

He finished putting the IA-15 back together, finally feeling comfortable with it. Just to be sure, he broke it down and put it back together five more times. Then he got up and wandered the halls of the retirement home. He greeted every new LAW trooper he passed, making a point to chat with them. In a few hours, they'd be going into battle, and he'd like to know a little about the men and women he might have to depend on to keep his ass in one piece.

Many of his conversations were enjoyable, and sometimes fascinating. Centurion Hafaz hailed from an Earth where his native Iran had become the biggest democracy in the Middle East, and had seriously entertained trying out for archery in the Olympics before joining the LAW. Trooper Escomay was an honest-to-God Spartan, as that nation had taken the place of Greece of his Earth. Centurion Wierzbowski had been a paramedic in Chicago before joining the LAW, and was rendered speechless when Jim informed her that the Cubs had not won twenty-one world championships here as they had on her Earth.

"Hell, they haven't won one since before World War One," he added.

He continued through the hallways until he heard a familiar voice from one of the rooms. "Working with these things makes me feel like I'm reliving my childhood."

It was Valerie.

Jim walked up to the room and looked in. His sister and Captain Williams knelt on the floor, checking over the weapons systems for one of the Firebrands and one of the Pilums. Their primary job during the battle would be to reload the guns and grenade launchers for the small aerial combat drones.

"So you weren't into Barbies growing up?" asked Williams.

"Barbies." Valerie snorted. "You can only dress up that damn doll so many times before you get bored. Give me a radio-controlled helicopter, let me buzz all the kids and dogs and cats in my neighborhood, and I was one happy girl."

"We would've got along great. I used to build my own model rockets when I was a kid. I could've tried to use 'em to shoot down your helicopters."

"Ha! You'd never get close to me."

"If the Shreth'kil could do it, so could I."

Valerie laughed and playfully slapped Williams on the shoulder. He chuckled, too.

Jim scowled and walked away. *Damn Romeo.*

Three doors down, he saw Doug sitting in a chair, tapping the keypad that operated his combat goggles.

"You got the hang of those things yet?" Jim asked as he walked into the room.

Doug pulled the goggles up and over his LAW-issued helmet. "I should. I've been working with this thing for the past three hours, trying to familiarize myself with everything it can do. The last thing I want to do is press a wrong button in the middle of a firefight and get myself or someone else killed."

Jim grinned briefly. Say what you would about his cousin, the man was meticulous.

"I have to say," Doug continued. "I'm glad we're finally going to do something besides sit around and watch the damn Shreth'kil do whatever the hell they want. I mean, I know the importance of recon, but in the Hundred-First, we're trained to engage the enemy, not watch them run supplies to their soldiers or turn people into stew." He sighed and shook his head. "It must take a special kind of personality to deal with that."

"Trust me, it's not easy. It makes me sick having to hide in the bushes and watch stuff like what happened yesterday."

Doug grunted, the twisted look on his face indicating he hated having to watch those young girls being raped by those maggots instead of helping them.

"You managed, though," Jim said. "You've done good during this whole thing."

"Thanks, Jim."

"Don't mention it. Heck, maybe once the LAW helps us take back our Earth, you can put in for Ranger School. We're probably gonna need a lot more of those guys."

"Maybe I will. What can I say? Recon's not my specialty, but I recognized the importance of what we were doing, did what needed to be done, and didn't whine about it like some people."

Jim frowned. Naturally, Doug had to get a pot shot in at Chuck.

Several seconds of silence passed between them. Doug turned away, biting his lower lip. "He shouldn't be on this mission. Chuck, I mean."

"I know who you're talking about, and I agree. A mission like this is difficult enough for trained soldiers like us, nevermind a nineteen-year-old civilian. But what are we supposed to do? We can't just leave him here, not when we're all supposed to exfiltrate through that transit portal."

Doug stared at the floor, not answering.

"Look, we've got Chuck on the simplest duty possible, guarding the command post. And Valerie and Williams will both be with him. He'll be fine."

"Yeah. Until the bullets start flying."

The corners of Jim's mouth curled. "I talked to him about that, told him what's at stake if he doesn't fight. He listened. He'll do fine when things get hairy."

Doug snorted. "You really believe that?"

"Yeah, I do. It might help if you told him that, too."

"What, some kind of locker room-type speech, like Denzel Washington in *Remember the Titans?* This is combat, not a football game."

"I know, and normally I wouldn't suggest something like that. But we're only hours away from executing a very risky and very complex rescue operation. So if some kind of Denzel Washington-type speech does the job, I'm all for it. And it'll mean a lot more if it comes from you, his own brother."

Doug exhaled slowly. "I don't know. To be honest, if I start telling him how he needs to act, he'll just get defensive and it'll blow up into an argument. That's how it always works."

Jim opened his mouth, about to tell Doug it was time for that to change. But he stopped himself. The problems between Doug and Chuck had been going on for the past couple of years. This wasn't some movie or TV show. It would not be resolved by a conversation that lasted a few minutes. Those two would end up arguing, and this close to the mission, he needed both brothers to have their heads in the game, not steaming over their latest verbal bout.

Better to keep them apart, for now.

He let Doug get back to working with his combat goggles, shaking his head as he entered the hallway.

Are those two ever gonna get this resolved? Sometimes the whole situation was hard for him to comprehend. Lord knew he and Valerie had had their issues with one another over the years, but they always worked them out, or at least came to tolerate one another's decisions. He couldn't imagine being so pissed off at his sister that he couldn't stand to be in the same room with her.

"This is Kenaevya," her voice burst from his earpiece. "Everybody have something to eat now. Final mission briefing is in thirty minutes."

Jim headed back to the basement and grabbed one of the PORPACKs he got from Mackanin out of his MOLLE pack. It was labeled, "The All-American Meal," and contained two hot dogs, mustard, ketchup and relish packets, potato chips, baked beans, an apple pie flavored energy bar, and the most interesting feature, beer-flavored powdered drink mix. Non-Alcoholic, of course.

He headed back upstairs, making for the building's communal dining hall. That's when Valerie exited from the room to his left and nearly bumped into him.

"Whoa! Sorry there, big brother. Didn't see you."

"That's okay."

"So, off to our last meal." She smiled and held up her PORPACK, General Tso's Chicken with rice. "Well, let me rephrase that. Our last meal before the mission."

"Well, Myra did sound the dinner bell, didn't she?"

"Oh." Val nodded slowly. "So it's Myra now."

"What's that supposed to mean?"

"C'mon, Jim. Don't play innocent with me. I know you two have something going on."

He opened his mouth to deny it, but couldn't give voice to the lie. How the hell could Valerie know about him and Kenaevya? He hadn't told anybody what happened between them at the house near the high school.

"How?" was the only word he managed to mutter.

"Please, I'm your sister. I can tell when you have the hots for a woman. There've been a few times I caught you looking at Major Kenaevya. The last time I saw you stare at a woman like that was . . . well, was Hannah."

His eyes flickered in all directions, except his sister's. "Do you think it's too soon for . . . that?"

"You're the only one who can answer that, Jim. But if it helps, I do approve."

"Thanks." He smiled at her and gently grasped her shoulder. "That means a lot. Just . . . just keep it to yourself. Hell, what we're doing is against regs."

"Not really, when you think about it. We're not part of the LAW Armed Forces, and we weren't technically assigned to Major Kenaevya's unit. We're just tagging along with them. So if you and her want to . . . um, be together, then I think it's perfectly legal."

"Maybe. Still, keep it on the down low. I don't want to risk any problems because of fraternization with the commanding officer."

"No worries. My lips are sealed," Valerie said. "Besides, fraternization isn't as big a deal in the LAW as it is in our military."

"When did you find that out?"

"Major Kenaevya told me."

"When?"

A wry grin formed on Valerie's face. "After you two almost got it on back at the horse farm."

Jim's eyes widened. "What? You were . . . what the hell?"

"Oh relax. Women always talk to each other about their guys, even Amazon women. She was concerned about you, so we talked. I even did you a solid, told her about some of your other combat missions, at least the ones I know about. You should have seen her reaction. I think war stories are as much an aphrodisiac to Amazons as chocolate and flowers are to regular women like me. So you see, I didn't tell any embarrassing stories about you. If anything, I made you more irresistible to her."

Jim couldn't help but laugh. "Thanks, Val."

"Hey, anything for my big brother. Now bring it in."

He hugged her. When they released, he fixed her with an appraising stare. "So your idea about fraternization, are you applying it to a certain flyboy?"

Valerie's jaw fell open. She stayed that way for several seconds, then burst out laughing. "I knew it! I knew sooner or later you'd say something about me and Dan."

"Dan? So you do have something going on with him?"

"And why would you think that?"

"Because I've seen you two together, being friendly. *Very* friendly."

"And you, of course, have to play the overprotective big brother, don't you?"

"Hell yes. C'mon, Val. The guy's a player. He dishes out all these smooth lines, gets what he wants out of a woman, and moves on to his next conquest. Trust me, I know the type."

"So do I. That type's been after me since high school." She softened her voice. "Look, for your peace of mind, absolutely nothing is going on between me and Captain Williams."

"Really?"

"Yes, really. Jeez, you almost sound disappointed. Look, like I said, I know the type. Yes, Dan is a cool guy, and smart and charming, but I know better than to get involved with a ladies man like him."

"Then how come you don't stop him from flirting with you."

"Because we women like it when men flirt with us, even if we know nothing will ever come out of it."

Jim rolled his eyes.

Valerie chuckled. "Yeah, I know. We women are complicated. Now c'mon, let's eat."

They joined the rest of the group in the communal dining hall and wolfed down their meals. A half-hour later, they assembled in the basement, where Mackanin's computer projected a floating 3-D image of John Hardin High School and the surrounding area. It still made Jim uncomfortable knowing this mission would be done in the middle of the afternoon. In all his years in the Rangers and Delta Force, missions like this usually took place under cover of night.

At least, that's how it happened with a human enemy.

The Shreth'kil, however, were less active during the day, and between the hours of one to four p.m., those that remained awake would not perform efficiently, as their body's natural inclination would be to sleep.

Kenaevya went over the plan, again and again, then she had each member of the rescue team run down their duties, again and again, making sure everything was burned into their brains. She also threw out numerous scenarios. What would they do if one or more of the drones failed? What if reinforcements arrived from the airport? What if the Shreth'kil found their command post and destroyed it? She did not throw out what they would do if the drones and missiles from the *Catherine the Great* battle group failed to take out the quantum jammer. Without a transit portal to evacuate through, they were all screwed.

Even as Jim visualized the rescue plan, worry still clawed at the back of his mind. Operations like this usually required a lot more preparation time. He wished they could build a mock-up of the school and run through the operation over and over. He wished they had time to better familiarize themselves with their LAW-issued weapons and gear. He wished he could get to know the new LAW troopers better.

Unfortunately, they didn't have the time to do any of that. All he could do was memorize the plan, and pray they could cope with any complication that arose, which for an operation like this, was inevitable.

They just started going over the plan again when a steady beeping came from Mackanin's computer. The 3-D image of John Hardin High School vanished, replaced by a needle-like aircraft with delta wings. Underneath the B-146 Crusader bomber floated a series of words and numbers. FLASH 7749 MAUMTURK.

Jim held his breath, his eyes transfixed on the code. An anxious feeling coursed through his body.

Kenaevya's slow breath could be heard by everyone in the basement. Jim's gaze shifted to her as she moved her head left and right, taking in the rescue team.

"All right. That's the code we've been waiting for. The bombers have taken off from Greenland. Operation: Robber Baron is officially under way. Move out."

CHAPTER 21

Jim had been in special ops long enough to know one thing. Complications always cropped up in every mission. The intel weenies overlooked something, some hi-tech gadget crapped out, the elements or terrain delayed their progress to the target area. Whatever the case, something would happen to make an already difficult mission even harder.

The first something happened when the rescue team was within a mile of John Hardin High School.

"Major," Mackanin reported to Kenaevya. "The Ciccaba just picked up a Shreth'kil mechanized infantry force in Big Spring, twelve miles west of us."

"How big?"

Mackanin glanced at his laptop's screen. "From the look of 'em, I'd say about a company-sized force."

"Twelve miles." Jim grunted and looked at Kenaevya. "Doesn't matter if that Mystic missile of yours jams all the Shreth'kil's radios. As soon as they see drones over the airport and smoke coming from the high school, they're going to know something's up and head here."

"Mm. The last thing we need is to have to fight APCs." She turned to Mackanin. "Contact the Crusaders. Tell them to retask some of their missiles to take out that mech company."

"Yes, Madam."

Half-a-mile from the high school, they were delayed for about fifteen minutes waiting for a Shreth'kil patrol to pass by. When they finally made it, they crept and crawled to their assigned positions. Mackanin, along with Valerie, Chuck, Williams and the two drone operators, set up the command post behind the dumpster of a convenience store less than a quarter-mile away.

That's when they learned of another problem.

"Message from *Catherine the Great,*" said Mackanin. "Her battle group's under attack by Shreth'kil aircraft."

Dread coiled around Jim's insides.

"Are they able to launch their strike against the quantum jammer?" Kenaevya asked.

"The Skysharks have taken off, but the Shreth'kil have already shot down three of 'em. Escort destroyer *Rochambeau* reports heavy damage, and so does . . ."

"So does what?"

Mackanin sighed over the comm system. "So does cruiser *Quezon.*"

Jim's jaw clenched. *Dammit, no!* The *Quezon* was tasked with launching cruise missiles at the quantum jammer. Without that ship, did they even have a chance of overwhelming the air defenses around it?

He couldn't help but think of Operation: Eagle Claw again.

"What about the sub?" Kenaevya asked.

"*Vendetta's* launchin' its missiles. The carrier's AF-75 Threshers and the escort ships are trying to hold off the Shreth'kil aircraft to give the missiles and drones a chance to reach the coast."

"What if they cannot?" This from Major Akageri. "What if they are all destroyed? If that quantum jammer remains operational, there is no way for this mission to succeed."

A long pause. A cold, invisible hand clutched Jim's stomach as he looked to the high school. He thought of the prisoners inside, thought about the fate that awaited them if they failed.

We can't be this close and just scrub the whole mission.

He nearly jerked in surprise when he heard Kenaevya's voice in his earpiece. "We must have faith that the navy will do its job. We proceed as planned."

Jim closed his eyes and smiled briefly. *Thank you, Myra.*

One after another, troopers reported that they were in position and awaiting the go signal. Jim glanced at a small computer-generated window to his left, displaying missile tracks from the lead B-146 Crusader and linked to his combat goggles by Mackanin's laptop. The multiple green lines steadily approached an animated white line. Beneath it a digital clock counted down 8:42 . . . 8:41 . . . 8:40. Once those tracks crossed the white line, five miles from Elizabethtown Airport, their attack would begin.

Jim scanned the school. The Shreth'kil manning the machine gun nests either talked amongst themselves or looked as though they tried their best to not fall asleep. He also spotted four airborne sentries, then looked at his watch. By his guess, they would be an hour-and-a-half into their shift. Like any sentry, human or not, they'd be bored out of their mind and probably thinking of either getting something to eat or going to sleep instead of watching out for any threats. Only a handful of Shreth'kil went into and out of the school, doing whatever duty they needed to do to help support the troops at the front. A few of them carried sidearms, and most didn't even bother to wear body armor. Why should they? They were support troops, and to them, Kentucky had been secured. They probably didn't expect an attack on their base.

Your mistake, and it's gonna be a fatal one.

He did worry that the attack on the *Catherine the Great* battle group would force Demon Alpha to put the base on full alert. A few times he held his breath and waited for alarms to go off and Shreth'kil to rush out of the school armed to the teeth.

It didn't happen. Had they not received word of the battle in the Gulf of Mexico? Then again, that was roughly 700 miles south of here. If Demon Alpha did know about it, he may have thought it was too far away to affect them.

Another fatal mistake.

Jim took deep breaths, trying to keep his heartbeat steady, as he checked the missile tracks. 2:15 from crossing the "Go Line." 2:14 . . . 2:13 . . . 2:12.

He mentally ran down his tasks for the mission.

1:55 . . . 1:54 . . . 1:53.

He looked over at Kenaevya, who squatted with her back to him. *Be careful.* He closed his eyes and pushed down all the feelings he had for her.

1:00 . . . :59 . . . :58 . . . :57.

Jim gripped his rifle tighter, expecting another piece of bad news to pop up at the last second and force them to abort the mission. But his comm system remained silent. His eyes slewed over to the window with the missile tracks. The green lines nearly touched the white line.

:05 . . . :04 . . . :03 . . . :02 . . . :01.

Red words flashed in his goggles. EXECUTE. EXECUTE. EXECUTE.

"Execute order received," a Brazilian accented voice burst from his earpiece. Senior Trooper Macceo, who commanded the aerial drones. "Launching Firebrands. Launching Pilums."

Jim tensed, his eyes darting from the school to the sky, waiting to hear the buzz of the little helicopter-like Firebrands overhead.

He heard no buzz. He did pick up a slight flutter over the gentle breeze. *Damn, those things are quiet.*

A Shreth'kil in one of the rooftop machine gun nests straightened up. It held a hand over its dark goggles and gazed to the west, in the direction the Firebrands would be coming from.

Oh crap. They –

Several cracks split the air. A cloud of red exploded from the Shreth'kil as it tumbled backwards. Its partner grabbed the machine gun and tried to swing it around. A three-round burst from the Firebrand's .50 caliber gun blew its head off.

A dull thump came from another Firebrand as it soared into view. Its grenade struck another machine gun nest. The blast sent one torn up Shreth'kil tumbling off the roof. Shrieks of alarm went up from the surviving monsters. Another machine gun nest blew apart.

The two Shreth'kil in the machine gun nest near the school's entrance looked to the sky, pointing to the Firebrands diving at the roof. Before they could do anything, a white contrail tore through the air and slammed into them. Sandbags, machine gun and Shreth'kil all vanished in an orange flash. Seconds later, another LAW Carl Gustaf 20 anti-tank rocket struck the mobile SAM. Jim and the other troopers around him turned away as the very air shook from the explosion. Sharp zips passed over their heads. Shrapnel.

He whipped his head around, checking the roof. Tracers from one of the rooftop machine guns cut through the air. Two bright yellow streaks connected with a Firebrand. The little helicopter twisted around, then fireballed.

"Shit," Jim cursed under his breath. His grip on his IA-15 tightened as he watched the remaining two Firebrands circle the roof, praying neither one got shot down.

Movement to his left. One of the Shreth'kil on the ground collapsed, a spray of blood flying from its head. Moments later a second monster met the same fate. Duguid and the other snipers had begun taking out any Shreth'kil caught in the open.

Sharp whistles split the air. Seconds later a string of explosions went off nearby. Mortar rounds fell on the concertina wire, creating gaps in the sharp, metallic barrier.

A brief orange flash erupted on the roof. Four machine guns down, two to go.

C'mon, c'mon. He grinded his teeth together as he watched a Firebrand skim the roof and launch a grenade. A fifth machine gun nest exploded.

A string of tracers streaked from the last machine gun. The Firebrand banked to the right, barely avoiding them. The little helicopter cut left, then right. Another line of tracers flew by it. A puff of smoke erupted from a tube on the Firebrand's right wing stub. The explosion blew off several roof tiles six feet away from the machine gun nest.

Dammit, c'mon!

The Shreth'kil gunners fired another burst at the Firebrand, missing it.

They never saw the other Firebrand racing up behind them. It fired two bursts from its .50 caliber guns. Both Shreth'kil flailed and collapsed.

"All machine guns neutralized," Mackanin announced. "Repeat, all machine guns neutralized."

"GO! GO! GO!" Kenaevya shouted.

She sprang to her feet and sprinted forward, O'Neal a few steps behind her, followed by Centurion Hafaz, then Jim. In all, thirteen men and women ran in a staggered line, weapons up.

Jim checked his field of fire for any threat, peering past the twisted, burning remains of the mobile SAM. Black smoke billowed from the wreckage, smoke that carried the stench of burnt metal, rubber and flesh. He ignored it. He'd smelled it many times before. The only thing that mattered was being alert for any Shreth'kil.

Look up. Look up, he had to remind himself. His eyes flickered to the sky. A contrail arced over the school and raced toward one of the airborne sentries. A LAW IMPM-35

Pike shoulder-launched SAM, tuned to the Shreth'kil's distinct body heat. The missile connected with the creature and exploded. Flaming body parts spiraled through the air.

Jim returned his gaze groundside. No Shreth'kil in sight. He resisted the urge to check behind him. Other troopers were responsible for covering that area. He had to trust in them, even though he'd only known most of the people in his assault group for a couple of days.

Deep thumps echoed around the school. It had to be One Cent and the other grenadiers pumping anti-personnel rounds through the windows of the rooms where the Shreth'kil slept.

They crossed the driveway and ran onto the sidewalk. The front door had to be just –

A door twenty feet away opened. A Shreth'kil hurried out, pistol in hand, swinging its head left and right.

Jim squeezed the trigger. Three 8mm rounds ripped into the Shreth'kil's chest. It fell against the doorway and crumpled to the ground. Jim's gaze fixed on the monster, his finger still around the trigger in case he needed to fire another burst to finish it off.

He didn't.

Kenaevya's rifle barked three times. Glass shattered. The assault group rushed through the front door and into the hallway. The layout of the school appeared in Jim's mind. He mentally marked down how many yards they had left before reaching the gymnasium.

They turned one corner, then another. His goggles automatically went into night vision mode to compensate for the darkened hallways. Lockers and hand-made cardboard posters flashed by as they moved deeper into the school. More muffled thumps reverberated through the hallways. More grenades taking out large groups of Shreth'kil in their makeshift quarters.

A door flew open to his left. He glanced down the hall as smoke wafted out of a classroom, followed by one Shreth'kil carrying another one, clearly wounded.

Both monsters were less than three feet from Kenaevya.

Fear turned Jim's body cold. *Myra.*

That fear vanished when Kenaevya squeezed off three bursts from point blank range. Both Shreth'kil fell backwards. She then rushed into the room, O'Neal on her heels. The rest of the group came to a halt as quick bursts of gunfire came from the room. Just as quickly as they went in, Kenaevya and O'Neal exited the classroom.

"GO! GO! GO!" shouted the Israeli-Amazon.

They hurried down the hallways, past the cafeteria. Not far now until they reached the gymnasium.

One of the troopers toward the rear opened fire. Jim quickly glanced to his right. Far down the hall two Shreth'kil lay dead, one of them a Jersey Devil-type. Not Demon Alpha. One of his junior officers.

When they reached the corner of the hallway, Kenaevya's right fist went up. *Halt!* She poked her rifle around the corner. A window opened in the left corner of Jim's goggles. A video feed from Kenaevya's rifle scope/camera showed two Shreth'kil standing in front of the double doors leading to the gymnasium, their rifles up, ready for action.

Kenaevya grabbed a flash-bang grenade from her belt, pulled the pin, and chucked it around the corner. Two surprised shrieks went up.

A thunderclap shook the air. It was followed by tortured screeches.

Kenaevya rushed around the corner. Two bursts erupted from her IA-15 rifle. Jim soon rounded the corner and spotted two dead Shreth'kil by the door.

After slapping a fresh clip into her rifle, Kenaevya edged up to the door. She stood on the left side, with O'Neal on the right. She turned to the rest of the group and held up her fingers.

Three . . . Two . . . One. Kenaevya pointed at the door. She and O'Neal shoved them open. The assault group rushed inside.

"EVERYBODY DOWN!! EVERYBODY DOWN!!"

Panicked screams erupted throughout the gymnasium. The group split up. One to the left, one to the right. One to the left, one to the right, and so on. Jim's eyes and rifle swept the folded up bleachers and the high ceiling, scanning for any sign of Shreth'kil.

"CLEAR!!" someone hollered.

"CLEAR . . . CLEAR . . . CLEAR!!"

"CLEAR!!" Jim shouted just as the second assault group, led by Major Akageri, stormed through the gymnasium's rear entrance.

Jim looked around. People crowded the hardwood from one end of the gym to the other, all lying down, many of them trembling or crying, or both.

"I'm an American soldier!" he hollered. "We're getting you all out of here!"

Several heads lifted up to him. He noticed disbelief on a majority of faces. Several seconds passed before he watched their eyes widen. A few people jumped to their feet.

"Thank you. Oh, thank you."

"Bless you."

Others just cried tears of joy. Jim scanned the prisoners, hoping to find anyone he recognized from Reverend Crawford's congregation.

His stomach turned into a lead ball when he saw a group of young girls huddled together near the sidelines, many with haunted looks on their faces. A tremor went through his body as he identified each and every one of them. They were among the group of girls who'd been raped by Fatfuck and his two maggot buddies. He even recognized the blonde cheerleader-looking girl, the first victim of the kapos. A lump formed in his throat as his gaze remained locked on the girl, who hugged her legs to her chest, a vacant look in her eyes.

I'm sorry. I'm so sorry.

"Man, am I glad to see you, Holmes."

Jim swung around. Anger flared inside him when he saw the large young man standing a few feet away.

It was Fatfuck.

Jim glared at him, his shoulders slowly rising and falling with each breath. Just behind Fatfuck he spotted the big gangbanger's two scumbag buddies, both smiling.

"Man, we thought we was dead," said the taller of the two subordinates.

"Yeah." Fatfuck nodded. "These things, man, they like, eat people. Good thing you guys showed up here."

Jim's face tightened with rage. His head shook. Was this shitface serious? Did he think he could stand there and play innocent like that?

He glanced over at the cheerleader, who hugged herself tighter. A short black girl next to her put her arms around the other girl's shoulders as she sobbed.

He turned back to Fatfuck, who gave him a friendly smile.

Taking a loud breath, Jim raised his rifle and pulled the trigger. Screams rippled through the gymnasium as a gusher of blood and brains burst from Fatfuck's head.

"Shit!" the tall gangbanger cried out as his boss fell backwards, blood spilling out of what remained of his skull and covering a large bulldog painted on the hardwood.

"What the fuck, man?" hollered the other gangbanger, who sported a goatee. "You fucking crazy? What'd you do that for?"

"Kill 'em!" shouted a paunchy middle-age man. "Kill 'em both!"

"They work for those monsters!" A full-figured brunette pointed at them. "They've been beating us and raping us ever since we got here!"

More of the prisoners shouted their desire to see both gangbangers killed.

"They're lying, man!" Goatee yelled. "We didn't do none of that!"

"Bullshit!" A hefty man in his early forties jumped to his feet. "You raped my wife, you son-of-a-bitch!"

The man charged Goatee and tackled him. The gangbanger managed to stay on his feet and pounded his attacker on the back.

Jim hurried forward and spun around his rifle. He slammed the butt into Goatee's back. He gasped and sank to his knees.

Three more prisoners advanced on the tall gangbanger. The guy backed away and pulled something out of his pocket.

"Back the fuck off!" He held out a shank. "Back off or I'll cut all you's!"

Jim started to bring up his rifle when he noticed Major Akageri coming up behind the gangbanger. The Japanese warrior quietly drew his sword and calmly walked closer to the gangbanger, whose attention was completely on the prisoners who wanted to get him.

"You! Scum!" Akageri barked.

The tall gangbanger started to turn.

Akageri's sword flashed around. Several people screamed as the gangbanger's head bounced across the hardwood. A few prisoners desperately scrambled out of the way to keep from being hit by the head. Blood spurted from the severed neck of the gangbanger's body. It quivered, then toppled over. Jim caught Akageri's gaze. The man simply nodded at him.

Meanwhile, the forty-something guy kicked Goatee in the ribs, twice. "Yeah! Cut off his fucking head, too!"

"No!" screamed the black girl comforting the cheerleader. "Cut off his fucking balls!"

"Wait!"

A sudden silence fell over the gymnasium as Kenaevya strode over to them. Goatee gasped for breath as he tried to push himself to his feet. She just stared down at him, not saying a word.

In an instant, she bared her teeth. Her right foot came up, and came down on Goatee's knee. Jim flinched at the sickening *crack* that drilled into his ears.

Goatee howled, rolling from side to side as he clutched his knee. Tears streamed from his eyes.

"Kill him, dammit!" demanded Forty-Something.

"We won't kill him," Kenaevya said calmly.

"Why not?" shouted the black girl. "Those mother fuckers raped us."

Kenaevya held up a hand. "We will not kill him. But the Shreth'kil . . ." A wicked smile crossed her lips. "After we all leave this place, and he's the only one here, how do you think they'll react? Do you think they'll forgive him for allowing all of you to escape?"

Goatee's eyes blazed with fear. "No. No, man! You can't! They'll . . . they'll . . ."

"Yes! They'll turn you into food!"

Goatee trembled, and tried unsuccessfully to choke off a sob. "Please don't! I'm sorry, man. Okay? I'm sorry! I didn't have a choice."

"Yes you did. You could have shown a minimum of honor and bravery and not betray your own kind to those monsters."

Kenaevya turned her back to him and looked around at the assault group. "Check the prisoners. See if there are any seriously wounded."

Jim and the others went around the gymnasium, tuning out Goatee's pathetic cries. With over 300 prisoners, all they could do was give cursory exams to them. If any had serious injuries, O'Neal, Centurion Wierzbowski or the other medics in the assault group would be called in. For several girls and women, most of their wounds were of the emotional kind, and would likely require some sort of therapy.

On the plus side, they all looked better fed than most prisoners of war throughout history. Of course, the Shreth'kil would want their human cattle to have as much meat on them as possible before . . .

Jim halted when he came upon a skinny teenager with a black eye and a swollen lip. Bruises covered his acne-scarred face.

"Kid." He bent down next to him. "Hey, kid. You remember me?"

The teen looked up at him. His good eye registered surprise. "You're . . . You're that Army guy who was at our church."

"Yeah, that's right." Jim nodded, remembering how the teen told him about the attacks on New York, Chicago and Norfolk. "I never got your name."

"Travis. Travis Wolcott."

"Good to see you again, Travis." He winced as he looked over the boy's injuries. He had no doubt who gave him those beatings. The poor kid seemed to have the look that attracted bullies, and Fatfuck and his two butt-buddies certainly qualified as bullies. "Is anyone else from your church here?"

"Yeah. Yeah, a bunch of us. The Demons took us all here after they knocked us out. They've been giving us a lot of eat, but just to fatten us up because . . ." Travis' jaw tightened. He shivered.

"I know, kid." Jim grasped his shoulder. "But that's not gonna happen to you. We're gonna get you out of here."

"Th-Thank you." Moisture glistened in Travis' eyes. "Thank you."

"How many others from your church are here?"

"Maybe . . . maybe fifteen, twenty. The others, the Demons took 'em and they never came back. The Reverend, he . . . he was one of them."

Jim closed his eyes and lowered his head. Reverend Crawford was a heavyset man. The Shreth'kil certainly wouldn't have waited long before taking someone like that away for processing.

"At the church, there was a little girl. Amanda. She was the first person there we met. Is she . . . is she here?"

"Yeah. She's over there." He pointed to Jim's left. "With her mother."

He turned. Tears stung the corners of his eyes as he saw a little brown-haired girl being held by a young blonde woman. He closed his eyes. *Thank you, God. Thank you.*

Jim patted Travis on the arm. "Don't worry, kid. We're gonna get you fixed up when we get you out of here."

Travis nodded and thanked him again before Jim headed over to Amanda and her mother. He clenched his teeth, trying not to shed any tears, trying to keep it together.

"Hey, Amanda."

She looked up at him, as did her mother.

"Major Rhyne." She smiled at him, a smile that nearly overwhelmed his heart. He smiled back, noting how both mother and daughter had put on several pounds since the last time he'd seen them.

"Thank you." The mother got to her feet. Jim grimaced, noticing the woman's torn and stained dress, and the bruises on her once pretty face. He thought back to how Amanda's mother looked when he saw her at the church. The gangbangers would definitely have targeted her.

"Thank you. God bless you." The mother hugged him.

"It's okay. You and Amanda are gonna be fine." He looked around. "Where's your husband?"

The mother looked at him. Her jaw trembled. A sob escaped her throat.

Jim bit his lip and closed his eyes. *Dammit.*

He tried to push the news aside. The time to mourn would come later.

"Are you gonna take us home now?" Amanda looked up at him.

Jim placed a gentle hand on top of her head. "No, honey. But we are taking you, and your mother, and all these people someplace where you'll be safe."

So long as the LAW navy destroyed that quantum jammer.

CHAPTER 22

The medics applied splints to those prisoners with broken limbs as quickly as possible. Once they finished, Jim and the others herded them out of the gymnasium through the rear exit. He lingered near the rear, constantly checking the other doors in case any Shreth'kil entered. Many of the prisoners trembled or cried at the constant sound of gunfire filtering in from the outside.

"Most of that is from our guys," Jim tried to reassure them. "Keep moving. Keep moving."

"Where are we going?" a short, gray-haired woman asked Centurion Hafaz.

"We're taking you somewhere safe. Please keep moving."

The woman's eyes widened. "What did you say? What language is that?"

Jim groaned. Without the sort of translation earpieces he had, none of the prisoners would know what the non-English speaking LAW members were saying.

"Um . . . Safe. You . . . safe," Hafaz struggled in English.

"Holy crap!" said a portly man next to her. "He sounds like Arab. What the hell's an Arab doing here?"

"Yeah, and that guy with the sword looks Japanese," said another man. "What the fuck's goin' on?"

A few other prisoners started voicing their dismay, while Hafaz tried to move them along with the few English words he knew.

Shit, we don't have time for this. Jim hurried over to Hafaz. "Keep moving, people! We gotta get out of here now!"

"Why are we working with them?" the portly man jabbed a finger toward Hafaz.

Jim bit down on the inside of his cheek. What would they think if he told them the truth about soldiers from other Earths? Would they panic even more?

"This is a multi-national team we put together for this mission. All the countries of the world are working together to fight the Shreth'kil. And if you don't want to be captured by them again, you have to get moving."

Whatever worries they had about Hafaz seemed to dissolve with that last statement. The prisoners started moving forward again.

Jim breathed a sigh of relief, then turned to Hafaz. "Sorry about that."

"Don't worry, Captain. I've received similar reactions on Earths that have experienced Nine-Eleven or the Miami Dirty Bomb Attack."

Soon the last of the prisoners filed out of the gymnasium. Jim checked over his shoulder and saw the sole surviving gangbanger, still clutching his shattered knee. Tears streamed down his cheeks.

"Please," he begged. "Please don't leave me here. Please don't let 'em eat me."

Jim scowled, remembering the girls this piece of shit and his buddies raped.

"Fuck you."

He ignored the gangbanger's cries as he exited the gymnasium.

A deep roar caught his attention. The Grizzly with the minigun opened up on a group of Shreth'kil coming out the rear of the school. Tracers tore into the winged monsters, clouds of red bursting from them.

Another group of Shreth'kil appeared on the roof. Jim held his breath for a moment when he recognized one of them.

It was Demon Alpha.

The monsters sent a barrage of rifle fire down at the Grizzly. The combat robot raised its minigun. Sparks burst around its metal hide. A couple of small, firecracker-like explosions erupted from the ammunition drum. Jim clenched his teeth, hoping it would fire.

Hoping . . . hoping . . .

"Grizzly Three is disabled," announced Centurion Tarcius, a citizen of the Byzantine Empire who controlled the ground drones. "Repeat, Grizzly Three is disabled."

Three of the Shreth'kil around Demon Alpha raised their rifles over their heads and shrieked in triumph.

None of them saw a Firebrand swoop down and pop a grenade. An orange and black flash went off near the Shreth'kil. Two of them fell backwards onto Demon Alpha and tumbled out of sight. Two other Shreth'kil flailed and collapsed. The last, whose body had probably been shielded from shrapnel by his comrades, turned and spread his wings, trying to take off.

A .50 caliber burst from the Firebrand cut him down.

Jim and the other commandos led the prisoners along the football field and past the processing tent. The bodies of several Shreth'kil lay sprawled in front of the entrance. Deathswipe was assigned to cover this area. He probably took them out with his machine gun.

Jim looked back at the prisoners. They continued moving, but worry crept through him as he noted each and every one that passed by him. The majority of the people they rescued were middle-aged or senior citizens, and many of them not in the best of shape. Some looked like they had been overweight even before they got here. Others probably became that way since their capture. Many of the older people moved slowly. Painstakingly slow. They only had less than a mile to go to get to the TZ. Jim wondered how long it would take to get them all there, if it would give the Shreth'kil time to bring in reinforcements.

He scanned the south and saw plumes of smoke rising from the direction of Elizabethtown Regional Airport. It looked like the Rapier missiles were doing their job there. He hoped they gave that Shreth'kil mech company the same kind of punishment.

"Grandpa?" a young, female voice shouted further up the line. "Grandpa? Grandpa!"

Several prisoners staggered to a halt. Jim jogged toward the commotion. He saw an overweight, balding man fall on his side. A plump teenage brunette stood over him and screamed in fright.

Jim slung his rifle over his shoulder and rushed toward them.

"Make way! Make way!" Wierzbowski shouted. She dropped to her knees and felt the man's neck.

"No pulse." She looked at the man's face. His lips had a bluish tint, and his skin was ghostly pale. "I think he had a heart attack."

The granddaughter cried hysterically. "Do something! Help him!" Another prisoner, a middle-aged woman, came over and hugged the sobbing girl.

Wierzbowski looked up at Jim. "Start CPR. I'm gonna get the defibrillator."

He straddled the man and clasped one hand over the other. Just as he was about to begin chest compressions, he noticed several prisoners standing around him.

"Hafaz! Keep everyone moving!"

"Yes, Sir." The Iranian trooper shouted and waved everyone forward. They obeyed, except for the crying granddaughter and the woman hugging her. Jim decided to make them an exception as he pushed down on the old man's chest.

Wierzbowski soon had the defibrillator set up. "Move!"

Jim got away from the man as Wierzbowski used a pair of medical scissors to cut open the man's shirt, then attached the pads to his bare chest.

"Clear!"

A short *thump* came from the machine. The man jerked, but didn't move again.

"Nothing. Hitting him again."

"Grandpa!" the granddaughter shouted. "Grandpa, please!"

Jim bit his lower lip, praying as Wierzbowski shocked him again. *C'mon, buddy. You can't pack it in now.*

Wierzbowski still didn't get a heartbeat. She zapped him a third time with the same result. She sighed and lowered her head. A few seconds passed before Wierzbowski looked up at the granddaughter. "I'm sorry. He's gone."

"No! No! Try again! Try again, please!" The girl tore away from the woman holding her and fell to her knees. "Grandpa! Grandpa, no!"

Jim looked away, the veins in his neck sticking out. He couldn't imagine fate being any crueler. The guy had just been saved from being turned into Shreth'kil chow, only to die barely five minutes later from a heart attack.

He stared back at the granddaughter, who was still crying. It didn't feel right to interrupt her mourning, but given the situation . . .

"Honey," he touched the granddaughter's shoulder. "Honey, I'm sorry. We can't stick around here. We have to go."

"No. No." She shook her head.

Jim sighed and started to get to his feet. "I know it's hard, but we have to go."

"No!" She cried harder.

"Here, I'll take her," said the middle-age woman. She bent down and gently lifted the granddaughter to her feet. "C'mon, Vikki. Your grandfather wouldn't want you to stay here and get captured by those monsters again. C'mon."

The middle-age woman put an arm around the weeping Vikki and led her away.

Wierzbowski packed up her defibrillator and took a last look at the dead grandfather.

"Shit." She snorted, got to her feet and marched off.

Jim frowned and looked down at the man. "Don't worry. We'll get your granddaughter out of here alive."

Sucking down a deep breath, he jogged after the rest of the group.

They led the prisoners through the parking lot. The sound of gunfire tapered off. It appeared what feeble resistance the Shreth'kil put up had crumbled. Thank God. The group now entered an open field. No cover, unless you counted some knee-high weeds. Plus many of the elderly and obese prisoners had to stop and rest. Jim grimaced as he looked to the houses in the distance. They had over a half-mile to go. He prayed whatever Shreth'kil remained at the high school were too demoralized to want to pursue them. If those monsters caught them in the open, it would be a massacre.

"Let's go! Keep moving! You gotta keep moving!"

Other troopers joined Jim in urging the prisoners forward.

"Mackanin," he heard Kenaevya's voice over the comm. "Are we going to see a transit portal soon?"

"Data link with *Catherine the Great* shows the Skysharks and Minotaurs are havin' a tough time gettin' through that anti-air screen in Louisville."

Jim picked up a groan coming from Kenaevya.

"That's not all," Mackanin added.

"Don't tell me there's more bad news."

"'Fraid so. Looks like that mech company managed to shoot down the Rapiers attacking it. The Ciccaba's tracking six armored vehicles headed our way. But that's not the worst of it. Their infantry's dismounted. We've got over sixty airborne Shreth'kil inbound. They'll probably reach us in six, seven minutes tops."

Jim clenched his jaw. He looked to the houses, then back at the prisoners. No way would they make it there before the Shreth'kil reinforcements arrived, not at the rate they were going.

"Roger that," Kenaevya said. "Lieutenant Carpenter. Status."

"We're going through the school now, Madam," replied the English-accented voice of the leader of the demolitions section. "We still have a few more rooms where we need to set our charges."

"Are all charges in place at the performing arts center?" The Shreth'kil had turned that building into their main storehouse on the campus.

"Yes, Madam."

"Good. Forget about the other rooms. We have enemy inbound. Make for the TZ immediately."

"Yes, Madam."

"Mackanin," Kenaevya called out.

"Here."

"Casualty report."

"One KIA for us, from the boom boys' section."

A cold ball of lead formed in Jim's stomach. Mackanin meant the demolitions section, the section Doug was assigned to guard.

"It's Second Centurion de la Rieva."

Jim breathed a sigh of relief. His cousin was still alive. A flicker of guilt followed his relief. Surely there would be people to mourn de la Rieva back on his native Earth.

"Two more of our people suffered NLT injuries." Jim guessed Mackanin meant non-life threatening injuries. "The medics also report one hostage dead."

"Roger that," Kenaevya responded. "Attention all fire support personnel. Disengage from your current positions and head for the TZ. Macceo. Put all remaining Firebrands and Pilums on autonomous mode and have them intercept the incoming Shreth'kil. Tarcius. Autonomous mode for remaining Grizzlies. Have them cover our escape. Then all command post personnel head for the TZ."

A chorus of, "Yes, Madams," rang out over the comm network.

Jim and the others tried to keep the prisoners moving as quickly as possible. Still stragglers held up their progress. He scanned the sky, expecting to see the Shreth'kil infantry appear any second.

EWABS-clad troopers darted across the football field. He recognized Duguid with his long-barreled sniper rifle, followed a few moments later by One Cent. The Aztec paused by the entrance to the processing tent and looked in. Apparently not finding anyone in there, he backed up, fired three grenades into it, then hurried off. Seconds later three deep thumps came from inside the tent. Flames began to spread over the canvas.

Doug and the LAW boom boys rushed out of the school. One of them ran over to the damaged Grizzly and laid a demo charge on it before rejoining the others.

Jim stared down the line of prisoners, spotting Amanda's mother, who gripped the little girl's hand. He then gazed past them to the houses around the TZ, praying the portal would appear.

It didn't.

C'mon, you fucking squids. Do your fucking job.

"Major."

He turned to find Duguid running up to him.

"Has the navy destroyed the quantum jammer?"

Jim frowned. "I wish."

Duguid growled. "Damn them to hell. We're going to become lunch for the Shreth'kil because of them."

"Just keep praying your navy puts one of those missiles on target."

Duguid gave him a doubtful look.

"Yeah, I know. Pray real hard."

Several muffled thumps carried through the air. Jim turned back to the high school and saw smoke pouring from several windows. Another column of smoke rose from the performing arts center. Jim smiled as he heard pops and cracks coming from both buildings. Secondary explosions from ammunition cooking off.

Let's see how well you shitsuckers fight without bullets and rockets.

An ear-piercing scream erupted behind him. He spun around, rifle at the ready. The blond cheerleader stared past him, eyes blazing with terror. She hugged the black girl next to her and kept screaming. Fear flashed across the faces of several other prisoners around them. A few pointed and screamed.

Jim whipped around and saw the reason for everyone's screams. He closed his eyes and moaned. *Aw shit.*

Lieutenant Deathswipe hurried toward them, his gait reminding Jim of the way an ostrich runs. He never even thought about how the prisoners would react to the sight of the Dino.

"Shit! It's a fucking dinosaur!" blurted one of the prisoners.

"Kill it!" another prisoner, this one female, hollered. "Kill it before it eats us!"

A sound like a bubbling pot of water came from Deathswipe's throat. "Yes, I am a dinosaur. No, I will not eat you. Now if you are all done screaming, get moving. We need to get out of here."

More screams came from the prisoners. The cheerleader hugged her companion tighter. "I wanna go home. I wanna go home."

Deathswipe lowered his head and snorted. Jim groaned. Without the translator earpieces, all the prisoners heard were Deathswipe's aggravated growls and hisses.

"Knock it off!" Jim shouted. "Everyone quiet down! Lieutenant Deathswipe is not going to hurt you. He's on our side."

"What's going on?" a short woman in her mid-thirties demanded. "Where are all these monsters coming from?"

"Ma'am, you'll have to trust me. All of you will have to trust me. Lieutenant Deathswipe is a friend. Now look, we have got Shreth'kil reinforcements headed our way, so you've gotta move. Now!"

The prisoners started forward again, giving Deathswipe fearful and mistrustful looks. The Dino stared at the prisoners, then looked back at Duguid. "Perhaps I should have suggested to Major Kenaevya that she tell the prisoners they'd be meeting a dinosaur. Then we could have avoided all this . . . drama."

"Yes, Sir." Duguid nodded.

Jim caught the sound of high-pitched buzzes overhead. He looked up and saw the model airplane-like Pilums soar toward the high school. They were soon joined by the remaining Firebrands. Jim held his breath when he spotted dozens of dark forms in the distance.

Shreth'kil.

"C'mon, people! We gotta move!"

Several of the prisoners turned their heads skyward. The sight of so many Shreth'kil apparently spurred them to move faster.

Jim scanned the area. Worry festered when he saw no sign of Valerie or Chuck. They had a bit further to travel than the rest. He should be seeing them any time.

Any time.

C'mon, guys. Get here.

Gunfire erupted in the sky. Jim watched the Pilums and Firebrands barrel straight at the Shreth'kil. Three of the monsters spiraled toward the ground. Tracers flashed across the sky from Shreth'kil assault rifles. A Pilum exploded into a cloud of metal splinters. Two small orange and black clouds burst amongst the Shreth'kil. Grenades. Three more of them tumbled out of the sky.

Another Pilum exploded. Another Shreth'kil went down. One of the Firebrands that Jim assumed was out of ammunition tilted over and cut into a Shreth'kil's wing with its rotors. The monster flailed and dropped toward the ground. The Firebrand shuddered just as another Shreth'kil blew it apart with its assault rifle.

The remaining Pilum dove on the monsters, shooting down two. It banked away, then came around for another strafing run. Two lines of tracers intersected with the little airplane, shattering the left wing. The Pilum corkscrewed into the ground and exploded.

The last Firebrand launched a grenade. Two more Shreth'kil went down. It fired a .50 caliber burst, missing.

A second burst killed another Shreth'kil. Yellow laser-like tracers connected with the Firebrand, ripping it apart.

And there goes our aerial support. Dread filled Jim as the swarm of Shreth'kil turned and dove right for them. Two orange flashes appeared among the monsters, followed by contrails.

"GEDDOWN!!! EVERYBODY DOWN!!!" He threw himself on the ground, as did Deathswipe, Duguid and Hafaz. Jim looked behind him. All the prisoners dropped flat on their stomachs.

The contrails drew closer, closer. A chilling whistle drilled into Jim's ears. His heart raced. *Please miss. Please miss.*

The rockets streaked over them. Jim breathed a sigh of relief.

Both rockets exploded directly over a group of prisoners.

"No!" Jim's body went cold as he watched several people writhing on the ground, bleeding from shrapnel wounds. He counted seven bodies that didn't move.

"Medic! Medic!" One of Akageri's troopers hollered as he rushed over to the wounded.

Jim whipped his head toward the approaching Shreth'kil. His body quaked with rage. Two of the monsters raised their arms, ready to chuck grenades.

"Kill the fuckers!" He got to one knee and opened fire. Deathswipe, Duguid and Hafaz joined him. Their tracers tore across the sky and into the Shreth'kil ranks. The creatures with the grenades spasmed and fell. The grenades burst a good sixty yards away from them. Four more Shreth'kil dropped to the ground before the rest pulled up and retreated. Duguid leveled his sniper rifle. One second passed. Two. He then pulled the trigger. A Shreth'kil jerked, then went limp and dropped to the ground.

Jim looked behind him. Wierzbowski and another medic treated the wounded, while one of the troopers urged the other prisoners forward.

A group of six Shreth'kil wheeled around and flew overhead. Jim estimated their altitude at five hundred feet. He and the others fired, but their rounds came nowhere close to hitting them. The Shreth'kil, meanwhile, fired straight down. Jim clenched his teeth when he heard the dull thuds of bullets striking flesh. Two small round objects fell from the sky. Grenades. One landed twenty feet from any person and exploded harmlessly. The second bounced on the ground . . . two feet from Centurion Wierzbowski and the woman she was treating.

"Wierzbow-"

The grenade exploded. Wierzbowski twisted around, a geyser of blood shooting out her neck. Her patient spasmed, then didn't move again.

Jim closed his eyes tight. A day ago he'd been talking to the medic about the Chicago Cubs of his Earth and her Earth. Now she . . .

More bullets thudded into the ground near him. Thankfully none of them struck flesh. Another grenade detonated further up the line.

Two people screamed. The cheerleader and her friend. Jim's chest tightened when he saw both girls scramble to their feet and run away.

"No! Get back here!"

Both girls continued to run in a blind panic.

"Shit! Duguid, with me! Deathswipe, Hafaz! Covering fire!"

Jim and Duguid got to their feet and ran after the girls. Deathswipe's machine gun and Hafaz's rifle opened up as he watched the girls dart toward a red and white wooden house. His legs pumped furiously, trying to catch up. Every few seconds his eyes darted around, staying alert for any Shreth'kil coming their way.

None did. For the moment.

The girls disappeared around the side of the house. Jim's lungs burned as he and Duguid raced past a tree with a tire swing hanging from a branch. They rounded the house and spotted both girls near the front steps, panting. He and Duguid pulled up a few feet from them

"You two!" Jim took a couple steps toward them, taking deep breaths. "We need to stick together if we're gonna get out of this alive!"

Both girls sobbed, the cheerleader muttering. "I don't wanna die. I don't wanna die!"

"You're not gonna die if you stay with us. We're the only way you two are gonna get -"

The cheerleader's eyes widened. She unleashed a terrified scream.

Jim turned just as he heard a whoosh. A large, dark form dropped behind Duguid.

"Duguid! Behind you!"

The French sniper whirled around. A taloned hand whipped across Duguid's throat. Blood flew through the air and spattered against the side of the house. Duguid trembled. He dropped his rifle, then collapsed onto the ground.

Both girls screamed as Jim locked eyes with the bloodied, battered creature before him. He clenched his teeth when he recognized it.

It was Demon Alpha.

CHAPTER 23

Jim brought up his rifle. Demon Alpha reached out, grabbed the barrel, and yanked. Jim stumbled forward and squeezed the trigger. Several rounds streaked past the demonic-looking Shreth'kil before it tore the rifle from his hands. The IA-15 spiraled through the air and landed a good fifteen feet away.

Jim twisted to face Demon Alpha and drove his left fist into its side. The creature barely staggered. It swept up its hand. Jim's throat tightened when he felt the talons strike his torso.

But they didn't penetrate his skin thanks to his LAW-issued body armor.

He rammed his forearm into the base of Demon Alpha's throat. It backed away, hacking. Jim moved in, turned on his heel and lashed out with a sidekick. He nailed Demon Alpha in the gut. It grunted and bent over slightly.

Jim went for his pistol. Just as it cleared the holster, Demon Alpha leaped at him. The air exploded from his lungs as the creature tackled him. Both of them tumbled to the ground. The pistol fell from Jim's grasp. He sucked in a ragged breath. Demon Alpha pushed itself up, a scowl twisting its ugly face. The two locked eyes, intense green orbs meeting blood red ones.

Jim landed two quick punches to the side of Demon Alpha's head. It looked stunned. Jim scrambled away, reaching out for his fallen Beretta. He snatched it up and rolled on his back.

Demon Alpha was already on its feet. Jim leveled his pistol at it.

A clawed foot swept through the air. A sledgehammer blow struck Jim's forearm. Something cracked as razor sharp talons pierced his skin. He cried out, dropping his pistol. His arm burned and throbbed as he grasped it. Sticky wet blood flowed through his fingers. He tried to make a fist with his right hand. A white hot blade of pain tore through his forearm.

His arm was definitely broken.

Demon Alpha reached down, grabbed his collar and yanked him to his feet. Jim chopped the creature's wrist. It grunted and slackened its hold. He heard a ripping sound from his uniform as he struggled to break free.

Demon Alpha rammed a knee into Jim's gut. He wheezed and doubled over. Searing pain twisted his insides and Demon Alpha sent another knee into his gut. It let go over his collar. Jim hugged his midsection and fell to his knees. He opened his mouth to breathe, but couldn't suck in any air. An invisible vise crushed his torso.

Fight the pain. Fight the pain or you're dead. He forced himself to draw a breath. It felt like his stomach was about to explode. He definitely had a couple broken ribs. More than a couple, probably.

Something moved toward him. He looked up. Demon Alpha growled and drew back its right foot.

Fight the pain!

Jim clenched his teeth. He fell on his side, bolts of fire shooting through his body. He tried to ignore it as he swung out his legs. His right foot hooked around Demon Alpha's left ankle. With a grunt, he pulled it forward. The creature shrieked and toppled onto its back.

Jim crawled forward, reaching for his knife. He bared his teeth, barely containing a cry of agony as pain crushed his right arm. Again he tried to make a fist. This time he did cry out.

Demon Alpha sat up, flashing its sharp teeth like a predator.

His right arm useless, Jim pulled out his knife with his left hand. Pushing the pain aside, he lunged toward Demon Alpha. The blade came down on the lower part of its wing.

Demon Alpha wailed. Jim pulled out the knife and stabbed the wing again, and again, and again. The creature thrashed about, trying to push itself away. Jim let out a primal scream and kept plunging the knife into its wing. Demon Alpha swung at him, missing. Jim stabbed the wing again. He raised his knife again. Demon Alpha took another swing at him. Talons dug into the back of Jim's head and down his neck. He grunted and turned away, pressing his left hand against the wound, still clutching his knife. He felt

a trickle of blood instead of a gusher. Demon Alpha
apparently just grazed him.

The creature pushed itself to its feet. It shrieked and
kicked Jim in the stomach. He cried out, fire tearing through
his ribcage.

Fight! Fight!

Demon Alpha reared back for another kick. Jim swung
his knife in front of him. The swing was not the smoothest
in the world, since he was a righty and not a lefty. Still it
made Demon Alpha back off. Grunting, Jim rose to his feet,
holding his knife in front of him. Demon Alpha stood about
seven feet away, growling, flaps of skin and membrane on its
wing fluttering in the breeze. They circled one another, Jim
looking for an opening to attack. He found none. Demon
Alpha held out its arms, talons out, almost inviting him to
charge.

Pain bore deep into his ribs. Jim winced, trying to ignore
it. He needed to end this fight quick. Easier said than done.
Demon Alpha's talons were just as effective a weapon as his
knife. The same with the curved horns on its head.

It also didn't help that Demon Alpha was a good foot-
and-a-half taller than him.

He edged closer, eyes locked on the creature, scanning for
any opening, no matter how small. Every breath set his ribs
on fire. He fought through the pain, like he'd learned to do
at Ranger School and Delta Force training. Only the fight
mattered. Only winning mattered.

Demon Alpha tensed, bending its knees. Jim came
forward, knife extended.

With an unholy screech, Demon Alpha jumped off the
ground, wings flapping, arms extended. Jim held his breath
when he saw its talons aimed right at his head.

He threw himself to the side at the last moment. Demon
Alpha's shredded left wing swatted him on the back. He
glanced up and saw the creature tilting to the left before it
skidded across the ground.

Probably tough to fly with just one good wing.

Jim pushed himself up on all fours, his gut throbbing. He
looked to the left. His entire body stiffened when he saw the
creature rise to its feet and rush toward him. He got to his
knees and made a desperate swing with his knife. He

missed. Demon Alpha shrieked and kicked him in the side. Jim cried out and fell. He gripped his knife so tight his hand shook.

Fight! Fight! The voice tried to scream through the torrent of pain that enveloped his mind and body.

Demon Alpha stood over him. Was it actually smiling? Did it think it had won?

You don't win shit till I'm dead.

Groaning, Jim pushed himself up.

A chilling, devilish laugh came from Demon Alpha's throat. It reached down.

A sharp *crack* blotted out the laughter. Demon Alpha's right shoulder exploded in a spray of blood and flesh. It jerked backwards and wailed. It spun around, clutching what remained of its shoulder.

Jim heard another *crack*. Again Demon Alpha jerked, blood cascading from its right side. Its entire body trembled. Then for a second, it stood still.

That's when a third *crack* split the air. Half of Demon Alpha's face blew apart, blood shooting through the air. It went rigid and fell backwards, hitting the ground with a thud barely two feet from Jim. He just stared at it, breathing and grimacing. Who the hell had shot that thing? He pushed himself to a sitting position and scanned the area. A familiar figure stood on the lawn of the neighboring house, lowering an IA-15 rifle with smoke wafting from the stubby barrel.

A smile spread across his face as Chuck hurried over to him. He noticed other people behind him. Valerie, with the cheerleader and her friend in tow. Had they run away during his fight with Demon Alpha? Behind them came Mackanin, Williams, and the drone operators, Senior Trooper Macceo and Centurion Tarcius.

"Jim!" Chuck reached him first and helped him to his feet. "Jim. Holy shit, man, you okay?"

"Do I look okay?" He tacked on a grin.

"I saw that Shreth'kil fighting you and, I mean I had a shot and . . ."

"You did good." He clasped Chuck on the shoulder. "You saved my life. Thanks."

The smile that Chuck wore threatened to consume his face.

"Jim!" Val ran full speed at him and flung her arms around him.

He barely contained a roar of pain.

"Jim?" A look of distress fell over his sister's face. "What's wrong? Oh my God, look at all this blood. Your arm."

"I'm fine, Val. Well, I'm alive, anyway."

"We have to get you to a medic."

"Right now we just need to worry about linking back up with everyone else without having the Shreth'kil shoot us, then we can worry about a medic."

Valerie nodded. Her eyes drifted past him, then her jaw dropped. "Oh my God. Duguid?"

Jim frowned and lowered his eyes for a moment. "Demon Alpha got him."

"Aw shit, man." Chuck looked to the dead LAW Recon Trooper, shaking his head.

"Nothing we can do for him. Let's get back with others." He stared hard at the two teenage girls. "You two, if you want to get out of here alive, don't run away again. Got it?"

Both girls nodded.

Jim picked up his rifle and slung it over his shoulder. It wouldn't do him much good with a broken right arm, and trying to fire an assault rifle with any accuracy one-handed was a bunch of Hollywood bullshit. He then retrieved his pistol, the weapon feeling unnatural in his left hand. He doubted he could fire it as effectively, but it was better than nothing.

"We better get a move on," Mackanin said. "Our feed from the Ciccaba shows that Shreth'kil mechanized company's 'bout two miles from here."

"What about the quantum jammer?" Jim asked.

Mackanin bit his lip for a moment. "Still active. One of the Skysharks looked like it had a bead on it, but it got nailed with a SAM."

"When are you going to have some good news to report?" Williams remarked.

"It better be soon, otherwise the Shreth'kil's next barbecue is going to feature us." Jim saw the two teens quake at his gallows humor. He groaned, then said. "C'mon."

The group got to the edge of the house when Jim signaled for them to stop. He peered around the corner at a two-story light brown house whose front yard had been designated as the TZ. Tracers from the LAW troopers inside and the Shreth'kil outside streaked back and forth. In yards and on the street he saw prisoners huddled behind vehicles and trees.

"Kenaevya, it's Jim. Do you read?"

"Loud and clear." He heard crackles over the earpiece when Kenaevya responded, most likely gunfire. "Where are you and Duguid?"

"Duguid's dead. I linked up with the command post personnel, all accounted for. We also retrieved the two female prisoners that ran away."

"Good work. Where are you now?"

"Behind the red and white house about a hundred-fifty yards from the TZ."

"Acknowledged." A burst of gunfire could be heard from Kenaevya's end. "The Grizzlies are making for our position. When they open up on the Shreth'kil, make for the TZ."

"Roger." He turned to Tarcius. "What's the status on the Grizzlies?"

The Byzantine trooper checked his computer. "Grizzlies One and Two are five hundred yards from the Shreth'kil's rear and closing.

Jim grunted in acknowledgment, staring out at the suburban battlefield. All the Shreth'kil seemed to be concentrating on the TZ. A few flew over the house, trying to get at the freed prisoners. The LAW troopers still outside either shot them down or drove them off.

He looked across the field leading back to the school, trying to catch sight of the Grizzlies. He couldn't see them. *C'mon, c'mon. Where are you?*

He spotted some weeds flailing, then a glint of metal. He grinned as the Grizzlies rolled through the field toward the Shreth'kil. So far it didn't look like they had seen the robots.

Wrong! Three of the airborne monsters dove on the Grizzlies, firing their rifles. The Grizzly with the two .50 cals elevated them. A deep thumping sound erupted from both barrels. Tracers ripped through the three Shreth'kil. They spasmed and dropped to the ground.

The second Grizzly pumped out one grenade after another. Geysers of smoke and dirt went up throughout the Shreth'kil lines. More machine gun fire tore into the monsters.

"GO! GO! GO!"

Jim broke from cover, running toward the TZ. He glanced behind him. Everyone was with him, even the teenage girls, who were both being prodded along by Val.

They were within fifty feet of the TZ when Mackanin hollered, "Down!"

Jim threw himself to the ground, the impact sending jolts of pain through his body. He grimaced and looked around. A line of bullets chewed up the ground ten feet away. He gazed up and saw two Shreth'kil diving toward them. He rolled on his back, raised his pistol and fire two shots. Both missed. He doubted either round came close to the Shreth'kil. He fired again, missing.

More gunfire erupted around him. He spotted Chuck, Williams and Mackanin firing their rifles from their backs. One of the Shreth'kil twisted and dropped to the ground. The other followed a couple seconds later.

Jim scanned the sky around them. Clear.

"C'mon! Everyone up! Go! Go!"

They dashed toward the brown house. Jim stopped just behind the garage, noticing the door open and several prisoners lying on the floor. He waved everyone forward. Val and the teens darted by. Next came Chuck, then Tarcius, then Mackanin. Both Williams and Macceo were just a few feet away, their feet pounding hard.

Williams stumbled, then stomped around, swatting at his body. Macceo also did the same.

"Williams! Macceo! C'mon! What wrong?"

Williams stared at him, eyes wide, face covered in sweat. Jim started toward him, then stopped. He swore there was some kind of faint glow around the pilot.

Smoke rose from Williams' uniform. Suddenly he burst into flames. Jim gasped, then turned to Macceo when he screamed. He, too, was on fire.

"Dan!" Valerie stared at the burning men, mouth agape in shock and horror.

Chills covered Jim's body as Williams and Macceo, completely engulfed in flames, screamed and flailed. The urge to run over to them pulled at him. He resisted. There was nothing he could do for those poor guys.

How the hell . . . what could do that?

He peered around the garage as Williams collapsed. The sickening stench of burnt flesh drifted through the air. Jim clenched his teeth, trying not to vomit. He swallowed when he saw them. Six Shreth'kil armored vehicles. The lead one had what seemed to be a spotlight which glowed brightly.

Oh my God. They used a laser to turn Williams and Macceo into human matchsticks.

A contrail shot across the field and struck the laser vehicle. A fireball split it in two.

Too late. He looked back at Williams and Macceo, throat tightened. Both men lay unmoving on the ground, flames covering every inch of their bodies.

The anti-tank Grizzly barreled toward the enemy mech company, firing another missile. A second armored vehicle exploded.

Unfortunately, that had been the Grizzly's last missile.

Jim watched a Shreth'kil in the cupola of another armored vehicle swing around a large caliber machine gun and open fire. Sparks flashed across the Grizzly. Moments later smoke poured from the robot.

He turned and hurried to the front porch, stopping when he came upon Val and the teens. The younger girls sobbed uncontrollably, their eyes fixed on the burning forms of Williams and Macceo. Val also stared transfixed at them, moisture welling up in her eyes. Jim clenched his jaw, looking from his sister to Williams. A sense of disbelief came over him. How many weeks had Williams been with them? As much as he hated the way he hit on Valerie, the fighter jock was a part of their group, always ready with some sarcastic quip. Now . . . shit, he was dead.

"Val. Val!" He put a hand on her shoulder. "C'mon."

She stared up at him, looking like she might say no. But she nodded, wiped her eyes, and herded the two girls toward the porch. There in the doorway stood Kenaevya and Doug. They moved aside to let the girls through.

"You okay?" Doug grabbed Chuck's arm.

Chuck stared at him, appearing shocked that his brother had asked the question. Then he nodded. "Yeah. Fine."

"You're not." Kenaevya's eyes flickered to the bleeding wounds on Jim's arm and neck. "Go see one of the medics."

"Forget it. You're gonna need every gun you've got to hold off those ugly fucks until that quantum jammer's destroyed."

Kenaevya opened her mouth to say something when Mackanin cut her off. "He may be right, Major. The Ciccaba just picked up a swarm of Shreth'kil coming from Elizabethtown Airport. Contubernium-strength."

A grim expression formed on Kenaevya's face as she stared at him. "While you were gone, we saw some Shreth'kil fly off in the direction of the airport. Looks like they brought back reinforcements."

Jim's stomach fell into a black hole. So now thirty to forty more Shreth'kil were on their way to join the thirty or forty Shreth'kil already here, plus four armored fighting vehicles. His chest tightened, thinking of Williams and Duguid and Wierzbowski, thinking of how that damn quantum jammer was still operational.

He stopped comparing this mission to the disaster of Operation: Eagle Claw. The main reason, most of the men involved in that got out alive.

CHAPTER 24

"Make way! Make way!"

Jim took a step back as a stocky, round-faced young man barreled through the door and dashed across the lawn, carrying a tubular Carl Gustaf 20. It was Senior Trooper Decker, an American and one of the two LAW anti-tank personnel. He took cover behind a car parked on the street, hefted his rocket launcher and fired. Jim watched the projectile soar toward the Shreth'kil armored column. He clenched his jaw as it climbed higher and higher. Crap, it was going to miss.

Suddenly the missile arced over and barreled straight down at one of the Shreth'kil infantry fighting vehicles. It smashed through the top of the turret. A gusher of flame tore the vehicle in half.

Three down, three to go.

Tracers shot out of the twin-barrel turrets of the remaining three Shreth'kil vehicles. Jim dove inside the house. Valerie, Doug, Chuck, Kenaevya and Mackanin all hit the floor of the foyer as loud thumps echoed around them. Chunks of wood and plaster rained down on them as the large caliber rounds ripped through the house. Heart pounding, Jim glanced into the living room. The glass of all the windows had either been broken or shot out. A handful of LAW troopers lay on the floor, avoiding the incoming rounds.

The pounding stopped.

"C'mon!" Kenaevya ordered. "Stay down!"

They crawled out of the foyer and toward the rear of the house. More Shreth'kil rounds smashed through the house. A framed photo on the wall above Jim exploded, showering him with shards of glass and plaster. From somewhere nearby he heard a strangled gasp. He grimaced. Someone didn't get out of the way of one of those rounds.

The roar of gunfire filled his ears as they reached the kitchen. LAW troopers fired out windows. Through the shattered sliding glass doors, Jim spotted Deathswipe crouched behind some overturned patio furniture blazing away with his IMG-30 machine gun.

"Major Kenaevya!" O'Neal's voice burst over the comm system.

"Go!"

"We have multiple casualties upstairs. We need medics and reinforcements up here."

"Acknowledged. Centurion Sook. Upstairs. Tend to the wounded."

"Yes, Madam," the Korean medic radioed back.

"Myra!" Jim shouted to her over the gunfire. "We'll go up and keep laying down fire."

She gazed at his bloody right arm. "You're not much good with a rifle right now."

"I can still fire a pistol."

Kenaevya flashed him a smile. She pulled out her SiG-Sauer 300 and handed it to him, along with two 10-round clips. "Be careful."

"You too." He nodded to her, then looked to Valerie, Doug, Chuck and Mackanin. "All right, let's go! And stay low!"

Jim sprang to his feet, bent over, and raced toward the stairs. He flinched as a round cracked nearby. More thumps of large caliber shells rattled the house. None struck near them.

They rushed up the stairs and into the hallway. He directed Doug and Val into a bedroom and Chuck into the bathroom. At the end of the hallway he saw Senior Trooper Ponjedi, who carried the other Carl Gustaf 20. The Indian aimed the launcher out the window, fired, then ducked down, with Captain Vasquez next to him. Seconds later, he peered over the window sill and pumped his fist. "I got it!"

Relief flashed through Jim. Another Shreth'kil infantry fighting vehicle destroyed.

He and Mackanin headed into what appeared to be an entertainment room where O'Neal was firing out a window. A flat screen TV rested against the wall, shattered by bullets. A plastic cabinet containing DVDs and Blue Rays had also been shredded by gunfire.

Jim moved toward the window when he noticed a body on the floor. A large pool of blood drenched the carpet, flowing from the trooper's torn throat. His stomach turned to lead when he recognized the face of the dead man, his wide eyes aimed at the ceiling.

It was Hafaz.

Jim grinded his teeth together, trying to push the young Iranian's death out of his mind. There was no time to mourn now.

He headed over to the window. In the distance he saw a swarm of dots headed toward them. The Shreth'kil reinforcements from the airport. Other Shreth'kil flew overhead or took cover on the ground, raking the house with rifle and machine gun fire. Jim drew a bead on one flying Shreth'kil and fired his Beretta pistol. He ran through the entire magazine before scoring hits on the monster's leg and wing. He scowled as he shoved the empty handgun into its holster and pulled out the SiG-Sauer 300. Shooting with his left hand had made his accuracy worth shit, and they were getting to the point where they needed to make every shot count.

The big LAW handgun boomed and bucked in his hand. Miss. He aimed at another flying Shreth'kil and fired. Miss!

Mackanin stuck his rifle through the window and fired. Bullets tore through a Shreth'kil's wing. It flailed and crashed into the ground. The Texan then ducked and yanked out his rifle's spent clip.

"Mack, any news on the jammer?" Jim fired two more rounds, both missing.

"I'm monitoring it through my helmet. Still no joy."

"Shit!" Jim fired two more rounds that missed.

The house shuddered again from the impact of large caliber rounds.

"Somebody take out those last two IFVs!" Kenaevya shouted over the comm. "Now!"

More big rounds ripped through the house, including two that punched holes through the walls of the entertainment room. Jim and the two Recon Troopers hit the floor.

"Decker! Ponjedi! Kill those damn IFVs!"

"Trooper Decker is dead," reported Major Akageri from outside.

"They got Ponjedi, too," radioed Captain Vasquez. "Don't worry. I got his CG-20."

Jim emptied his SiG at the Shreth'kil, striking one in its body armor. O'Neal fired burst after burst at a group of monsters advancing toward the house, cutting down two. A contrail rose into the sky, followed by another. Pike anti-air missiles. Both connected with two Shreth'kil, blowing them apart.

"Yeah!" Mackanin hollered, swinging his head to first O'Neal, then Jim. "One'a the Skysharks broke through anti-air defenses!"

The Texan tapped a couple keys on his arm pad. A window popped up in Jim's goggles as he reloaded his SiG-Sauer 300. A shaky image appeared with trees and fields whipping past. Obviously a view from the Skyshark's camera. The image suddenly became jumbled. Jim caught glimpses of ground and sky, then some streaks of light zipping past. Anti-aircraft fire.

C'mon, c'mon, c'mon! He mentally cheered before turning and firing three rounds out the window. One airborne Shreth'kil jerked and tumbled to the ground.

"I got a lock!" announced Vasquez. "Taking the shot!"

Jim heard the thump and whoosh of the Carl Gustaf 20 from down the hall. He then glanced at the feed from the Skyshark. Directly in front of it sat a large square-shaped object with three cone-like antennas jutting out of the top.

The quantum jammer.

Bullets slapped against the outside wall. O'Neal and Mackanin poked their rifles out the window and blazed away. Jim joined them, firing four rounds at the airborne Shreth'kil. No hits this time, dammit. He ducked back down and checked the Skyshark's progress.

The quantum jammer drew closer. Any second he expected to see a missile or bomb emerge.

"Direct hit!" Vasquez shouted. "Scratch another IFV."

Jim's heart pounded furiously. They'd destroyed all but one of the Shreth'kil infantry fighting vehicles. Now the Skyshark had to –

The feed shook violently.

"What the hell!?" he blurted.

"Dammit!" Mackanin scowled. "It musta got hit by something."

Tension coiled around Jim's muscles. This couldn't happen. Not when they were so close.

The image stabilized. He let out a long sigh of relief. The Skyshark had survived.

The worry returned when it wobbled again. Up and down, left and right, fighting to stay in the air. The quantum jammer loomed large ahead of it. Jim waited, praying for the thing to launch its payload. Nothing.

"I got the last IFV," radioed Vasquez. "Gonna . . . oh shit! They're right in -"

Shreth'kil screeches filtered through the comm, followed by bursts of gunfire. Both sounds also could be heard from down the hall.

Jim rushed for the door and looked down the hallway. Captain Vasquez lay on his back, unmoving. A Shreth'kil slithered through the window, with a second waiting just outside.

"Shit!" Jim ducked back inside, staring down at his SiG. He didn't like the odds of taking on two Shreth'kil soldiers with a single pistol he had to fire left-handed.

Wait a minute. He dropped into a crouch, laid down his pistol, and rummaged through his gear. It didn't take long to find a flash-bang grenade.

He peered round the door frame. The two Shreth'kil advanced toward the hallway.

Gripping the grenade in his left hand, he slid the index finger of his right hand through the pin. Holding his breath, he yanked up, grimacing as jolts of pain blazed through his arm.

"Fire in the hole!" Without looking around the corner, Jim flung the grenade down the hall. He turned away, opened his mouth and covered his ears.

A thunderclap and brief quake shook the house. Agonized shrieking followed. Jim snatched his Sig-Sauer and dashed into the hallway. Both Shreth'kil thrashed about on the floor. He went over to the first one and fired two bullets into its head. He jumped over the body of the dead Shreth'kil and shot the other one in the head. Spotting the Carl Gustaf 20 lying beside Vasquez, Jim rushed over and picked it up.

"Dammit." He scowled when he saw two bullet holes in the launcher, including one that had torn apart the electronic sights.

"This is Rhyne," he radioed. "Two Shreth'kil just breached upstairs. I took out both of them. Vasquez's CG-20 is wrecked."

"Anti-air contingent. Can you use your Pikes on that IFV?" asked Kenaevya.

"Negative," responded one of them. "All Pikes expended."

Jim bit his lip, checking the Skyshark feed. He expected to see the screen darken, the drone having crashed.

Instead his hope sparked as the Skyshark pressed on, the quantum jammer getting closer, closer. The drone still didn't fire. Maybe it couldn't. Instead it looked like whoever piloted it was going to do a kamikaze run on the jammer.

The Skyshark sank to the left, then righted itself. More tracers shot by. It shuddered. Jim held his breath. *C'mon, just a little further. You can do it.*

The Skyshark veered wide right, the jammer disappearing from the screen.

"No, dammit. No!"

The jammer appeared again, almost filling the screen. The Skyshark shuddered. Jim clenched his teeth.

A dark mass filled the screen. Suddenly there was a bright white flash. Then static.

"YEAH!!" Jim heard Mackanin's shout from down the hall. "They got it! The jammer's down, the jammer's down!"

"What's the portal status?" Kenaevya radioed.

Jim returned to the room to find Mackanin hunched over his computer, with O'Neal firing out the window.

"Transit portal forming right across the street from us."

"All right, One Cent," said Kenaevya. "Take Section Beta and get the prisoners through the portal. Everyone else, stay behind and cover their escape."

"Roger that," Jim radioed back, then hollered. "Check out time, people! Everyone downstairs! Let's go! Let's go!"

He watched Mackanin, O'Neal, Doug, Val and Chuck dart into the hallway and pound down the stairs before following them. Kenaevya crouched by the front door, waving troopers and prisoners outside. Jim slowed up, his eyes fixed on the sight across the street. A yellow, pulsating circle of light just touched the ground.

So that's what one of those portals look like.

His fascination ended when a line of tracers streaked by the house, ripping into trees and parked cars. The top half of a LAW trooper exploded in a cloud of blood and gore.

"Shit!" Jim turned to Kenaevya, grimacing when he noticed the bloody gash on her forehead. "We're never gonna make it to the portal with that IFV out there."

"But how the hell do we take it out?" Doug asked. "All our anti-tank missiles are gone."

"Then we just get creative," said a British-accented voice.

Jim looked past Kenaevya and saw a stout, dark-haired LAW trooper. Lieutenant Carpenter, the CO of the demolitions squad.

"If I can get close enough, I can lob this at that bugger." He held a demo charge in front of him. "It'll penetrate its armor, no problem."

"That's pretty risky, Lieutenant," noted Kenaevya.

"Yes it is, Madam. But do you have a better suggestion?"

"Unfortunately I don't." She turned to Jim and the others. "I want you five to cover him. I'll have the mortars and grenadiers lay down smoke rounds. That should give you cover, and maybe allow us to get some prisoners through the portal."

"You got it." Jim nodded, then looked at Kenaevya. She kept her mouth clamped shut, but her eyes relayed her message. *Be careful.*

He flashed her a smile, reloaded his SiG-Sauer 300, then peered out the door. Kenaevya ordered the mortar crews and grenadiers to fire smoke rounds. Thirty seconds later, dark clouds floated in front of the Shreth'kil IFV.

"Go! Go! Go!"

Jim slipped out the door and hurried across the lawn. His eyes swept the neighborhood at ground level, then skyward. Two Shreth'kil spotted them and brought up their stubby rifles. Jim raised his pistol and fired. From behind him, his sister, cousins and Mackanin also opened up. One of the Shreth'kil twitched and dropped out of the sky. The other kept firing. Bullets zipped around them and smacked into the ground. They continued firing until the Shreth'kil whipped around in mid-air and spiraled toward the ground.

Jim led them behind a tall oak tree. Through a break in the smoke they saw the Shreth'kil IFV continuing forward. He turned to Carpenter. "Looks about sixty yards away."

Carpenter nodded, then pressed a couple buttons on the demo pack. A red digital display read 30 seconds.

"You sure that's enough time?" Jim asked.

"Don't worry, Sir. I'm plenty fast. I can get away before this thing goes off."

Carpenter edged out from behind the tree, getting into a quasi-sprinter's crouch.

"Carpenter. Get behind the damn tree," Jim ordered.

"I want to make sure I get a good head start. Soon as that thing comes through the smoke I'll -"

"Heads up!" Chuck raised his rifle and fired.

Jim's head snapped up. A Shreth'kil dove at them, rifle blazing. Little geysers of dirt sprouted near them.

"Carpenter!" He dropped his pistol and grabbed the back of the Brit's uniform, grunting as he yanked him back. White hot knives dug into his ribs. Carpenter's head snapped back. Blood spurted from his shoulder. More blood covered Carpenter's face, pouring out the large hole under his left eye.

"Dammit!" He slammed his left fist into the ground as Chuck and the others continued firing. When they stopped, Jim peered around the tree. The Shreth'kil hit the ground and lay there like a lump.

He also saw the IFV just twenty yards away.

Biting his lip, Jim looked back at Carpenter's body, then at the demo pack beside him.

"Mack! How do you activate this thing?"

"Jim, you can't -"

He waved his sister quiet as Mackanin knelt over the demo pack. "That button right there activates the timer. And that one turns on the magnetic clamp. Ya definitely want that on when you chuck it."

"Got it." Jim picked up the demo pack.

"C'mon, Jim," Doug said. "You've got a bad arm and -"

"And I'm the ranking officer here, so I assume the risk. Now when that thing comes through the smoke, I want you all to lob flash-bangs at it."

Doug's face scrunched in bewilderment. "What good will those do against an armored vehicle?"

"Viewing ports. The Shreth'kil have to look out them. It'll distract 'em." He checked around the tree. The IFV rolled through the clouds.

"Throw the flash-bangs! Now!"

Valerie, Doug and Chuck yanked out the grenades, pulled the pins, and threw them at the advancing infantry fighting vehicle. Three mini thunderclaps merged into one as they went off.

Jim pushed both buttons and took off running, counting down the seconds in his head. His chest tightened when he saw the IFV veer to the right, away from him.

25 . . . 24 . . . 23.

He pumped his legs, ignoring the burning in his ribs. Was he getting closer?

20 . . . 19 . . . 18.

The IFV jerked to the left. He was about ten yards away.

15 . . . 14 . . . 13.

The IFV continued to wheel left, the turret, and its twin cannons, turning his way.

10 . . . 9 . . . 8.

Less than five yards away. Jim reared back and flung the demo pack. It stuck to the turret with a loud *thunk*.

He turned and ran.

5 . . . 4 . . . 3.

Jim dove. His ribs exploded in pain when he hit the ground.

2 . . . 1.

A roar split the air. Shrapnel zipped over him. He counted to five, then rolled onto his back.

Flames consumed the shattered turret of the IFV.

Jim pushed himself to his feet and rushed back toward the tree. Doug and the others fired into the sky. Jim clenched his jaw, wondering if a Shreth'kil bullet would strike him down.

None did. He dove behind the tree and looked at the others.

"Holy shit, man!" Chuck gawked at him, clearly impressed. "That was insane."

"Yeah, tell me about it."

"All right, big brother, you had your John Wayne moment," said Valerie. "Now can we go?"

"You kiddin'? I've been wanting to get the hell out of here for the last half-hour. C'mon."

They hurried away from the tree and back to the portal, taking sporadic shots at the Shreth'kil. Prisoners, many streaming out of other houses where they had taken cover, hurried through the portal while other LAW troopers laid down covering fire.

Jim spotted Kenaevya and Deathswipe crouched behind a pick-up truck pockmarked with bullet holes.

"Impressive, Major," Kenaevya smiled at him as Deathswipe's machine gun chattered away.

"Don't expect me to make a habit of it."

They continued firing, driving off Shreth'kil soldiers. Jim glanced over his shoulder, watching the prisoners go through the portal. A few stopped hesitantly near it, their expressions ranging from wary to scared. Part of him couldn't blame them. He doubted any of the prisoners knew the true origin of their LAW rescuers.

Thankfully, all the flying lead was enough to conquer their fears and make them enter the portal.

A couple minutes later, Major Akageri came over to them. "All prisoners are through the portal."

"Good," said Kenaevya. "Start withdrawing our forces."

In twos and threes, the surviving LAW troopers dashed through the transit portal. Jim and the others stayed behind the pick-up to provide covering fire. Once his SiG-Sauer ran dry, Valerie handed him her P230 pistol. He was down to one round when Kenaevya turned to him.

"Your turn to go. Deathswipe, Akageri and I will cover you."

Jim almost opened his mouth to argue, not wanting to leave without her. But she was in charge. Reluctantly, he nodded.

"C'mon!" He waved his family and Mackanin toward the portal. They got up and started running.

A flurry of bullets smacked into the asphalt. Jim turned and swallowed a breath. Chuck stumbled as Deathswipe cut loose with his machine gun. Two Shreth'kil tumbled out of the sky.

"Chuck!"

He recovered and kept running, giving him a thumbs-up.

Jim's gaze then fell on Kenaevya. *She'll be all right. She'll be all right.*

They neared the portal. Jim tensed. What would going through it be like?

Don't hesitate. Don't hesitate.

He closed his eyes and ran into the light.

A warm feeling surrounded him. All the hairs on his body stood on end.

His boots clanged on something metal.

Jim opened his eyes, which grew wide when he observed his surroundings. A huge underground cavern stretched out before him, large enough to hold something, say, the size of New Orleans Superdome, with room to spare. He then looked down and saw he stood on a metal platform with two large glowing pylons on either side. A column of LAW personnel ushered the prisoners through a door on the left side of the cavern. Joining them were several stretcher parties for the wounded.

He also noticed a pair of squat vehicles ringing the platform, with troopers manning pintel-mounted machine guns and grenade launchers. An entire platoon – contubernium - of troopers stood around the vehicles, weapons at the ready. Probably in case some Shreth'kil decided to come through the portal.

"Keep moving!" A trooper with a Spanish accent waved them forward. "Keep moving!"

Jim and the others hurried down the ramp. Once they were past the security forces, he turned back to the portal. Worry crawled through his chest and into his stomach. He waited for Kenaevya to come through.

Waited . . . waited.

C'mon. It's your turn now. C'mon.

No one came through the portal.

Tremors gripped his legs. *Dammit, Myra. Don't do this to me. I can't do this again.*

A hand gently grasped his shoulder. He turned to find Valerie next to him, worry etched in her face.

Jim turned back to the portal. *Please . . .*

One figure came through, the unmistakable form of Deathswipe. Seconds later a second figure emerged. Short and male. Akageri. Jim swallowed.

Kenaevya ran through the portal. Jim released a breath he didn't know he held. He stepped forward, wanting to run over and hug her.

"Shut it down!" Kenaevya hollered, waving her hand down. "Shut it down!"

Within moments, the portal shimmered and vanished.

"We did it." Val threw her arms around Jim's shoulders. He wanted to smile, but all the energy, all the adrenaline, drained from his body.

Kenaevya walked over to him. Relief flowed through him. It now dawned on Jim that he and his family actually stood on a whole other world. He wished he had the energy and the mindset to truly appreciate that.

Kenaevya stopped less than a foot from him, her eyes gazing down at his bloody, throbbing right arm. "So, do you think you can see a medic now?"

Jim chuckled. "I think that'd be a good idea."

Kenaevya smiled and placed a hand on his back, leading him to the exit. Valerie and Doug followed. He glanced over at Chuck. "Coming, Chuck?"

His cousin just stood there.

"Chuck?" Jim's brow furrowed. Chuck stood his ground. Was it him, or did his cousin look pale.

"Chuck?"

Chuck swayed a little. "Jim. I . . . I don't feel so good."

His eyes rolled back in his head. Chuck fell face first on the floor.

"Chuck!" Valerie shouted, as did Jim and Doug.

They rushed over to him. That's when Jim noticed the blood soaking the back of Chuck's pants.

CHAPTER 25

Jim lay in the hospital bed, staring up at the ceiling. He should be feeling relief that they made it through the portal onto Scandinavian Empire Earth, that most of the prisoners they freed in Elizabethtown had survived. Instead worry consumed him. Worry for Chuck. He still couldn't believe it. A ricochet from a Shreth'kil bullet had struck him above the right buttock, a few centimeters below his LAW body armor, and tore through his guts.

Please, God. Let him be all right.

He looked down at the cast on his arm, thinking back to the treatment he'd received an hour ago. The doctor, who hailed from a China still ruled by the Ming Dynasty, injected him with a calcium-based formula that would mend his broken bones in about four days. He also stuck bandages on his cuts that contained chemicals which not only killed any infection, but helped the wounds heal quicker. He used those things to keep a positive attitude about Chuck. With this sort of advanced medical technology, his cousin's chances of surviving should be good.

He hoped.

Jim pushed his head deeper into the pillow. His eyelids grew heavy. Sleep beckoned him. He fought it, wanting to stay awake in case Val or Doug came in with news about Chuck.

He scanned the bland white room again, which was designated for NLT injury patients. Three other men shared the room with him. A LAW trooper with a burned hand and two of the freed prisoners, both of whom had bruising and broken bones, likely from beatings by the kapos. All three slept.

"So do you feel up to having visitors?"

Jim turned to the doorway. His heartbeat picked up when he saw Kenaevya standing there, smiling at him. She sported one of those special chemical bandages on her forehead.

"How's your head?"

"It's fine. I've had worse."

Kenaevya sat on the edge of his bed and rested a hand on Jim's leg. Every muscle in his body tensed. Whatever tiredness he had vanished.

"How are you doing?" she asked.

"Fine now." He glanced at Kenaevya's hand. She caught his gaze, shot him a wry grin, and moved her fingers slowly up his thigh. Jim squeezed the edge of his bed with his good hand. "Where's a privacy curtain when you need one?"

"Don't worry. This room's only temporary." The smile suddenly faded from her face. "Any word on Chuck?"

"No." Jim shook his head. "Still in surgery last time I heard. Val and Doug are keeping watch. When they find out something, they'll let me know."

"Good."

Silence fell over them. Jim looked away from Kenaevya for a few seconds. Drawing a breath, he turned back to her. "How many?"

She seemed confused by the question for a moment. Then a look of understanding settled on her face. "We saved two hundred eighty-seven prisoners out of three hundred and eight. Considering everything that happened, it's a miracle we didn't lose more."

"What about for us?"

Kenaevya's jaw stiffened for a few moments. "Twenty-five troopers dead, and many more wounded."

A sinking feeling took hold of Jim's stomach. He had to force his mouth open to ask the next question. "What about the battle group? It sounded like they got nailed bad by the Shreth'kil."

"We lost the *Quezon*. The destroyer *Rochambeau* took heavy damage, but made it back. *Catherine the Great* lost ten of her aircraft."

Jim closed his eyes and sighed. My God, so many dead. All on a mission that he pushed for.

"They died doing their duty," Kenaevya said.

"Yeah," Jim muttered. He thought of all the letters he'd written to the families of soldiers who died under his command, how he used that word "duty" to try to bring some meaning to their sacrifice. He wondered if that would really comfort those who would never see their sons and daughters and mothers and fathers and husbands and wives again.

Kenaevya stroked his cheek. "I haven't received all the figures yet, but it appears Shreth'kil casualties in Elizabethtown are in the hundreds. It's no longer serviceable as a supply base. That will help our forces Pennsylvania and Virginia."

He just nodded, trying to take comfort in that. How many people had they saved in those states because Shreth'kil infantry didn't have enough ammo and food to advance? Maybe the attack on Elizabethtown would allow their side time to strengthen their defenses, or plan a counter-attack.

It was worth it. It had to be worth it.

Jim stared back at Kenaevya, then reached over and gripped her hand, giving it a gentle kiss. He continued holding her hand against his lips, relishing how it felt, and grateful that he hadn't lost her.

Hannah. An image of her smiling at him formed in his mind's eye. He remembered her telling him, on the second anniversary of her last drink, that she regretted all the days she wasted being depressed during her bout of alcoholism, how no one should have to live like that.

How many days had he felt hopeless since Hannah's death? Would she want him to go through the rest of his life feeling that way?

The answer was no. She'd want him to be happy, he was sure of that.

And he knew he'd be happy with this Israeli-Amazon warrior from another Earth.

Jim took hold of Kenaevya's arm and pulled her down until their lips met. She kissed him fiercely, running her hand up and down his chest. Holy shit, was she going to take him right here in his hospital bed, with three other patients in the room?

Their lips separated. Jim drew a quick breath, ready for more.

That's when he noticed Valerie out the corner of his eye. "Val!" He sat up.

Kenaevya pushed herself off the bed and turned to her. "Valerie. Any word on your cousin?"

She didn't answer. Her jaw trembled. Jim noticed how puffy and red her eyes were.

No. He swallowed. *Please God, no.*

"The . . . the doctors said there was too much damage."
She hiccuped, trying to stifle a sob. "He lost a lot of blood
and . . . he's dead." Her voice cracked. "Chuck's dead."

Jim went numb. The words echoed in his brain, but he
didn't want to believe them.

Chuck . . . dead?

His throat clenched. A heavy feeling formed in his chest.
He waited for Valerie to say she had made a mistake, that
Chuck was actually alive. But reality overrode his hope.

Valerie sobbed, tears running down her cheeks. She
walked over to him on shaky legs. Jim hugged her with his
good arm as she cried into his shoulder.

Kenaevya bit her lower lip, placed a comforting hand on
Valerie's back, then walked out of the room, probably
figuring this was time for family.

Valerie continued to cry. Tears welled up in Jim's eyes,
but he managed to keep them in check. He thought back to
the house in Elizabethtown, where he had argued with
Kenaevya to free the prisoners at John Hardin High School.
He remembered his determination going into that argument,
how there was no way he would give up until Kenaevya
agreed with him.

Now his stubbornness had cost him his cousin.

***

Jim stood on the little hill overlooking Reykjavik's
Faxafloi Bay. His eyes swept over the cityscape with its
blend of modern office buildings and bunched-together
houses with slanted colorful roofs. Beyond it was the snow-
capped Esja mountain range. He switched his gaze to the
harbor of the Prince Olafur LAW Armed Forces Base. A
row of knife-shaped ships, many with angular, shark fin-like
superstructures, lay at anchor.

Viracocha. Emperor-class aircraft carrier. Air wing of
ninety.

Abigail Adams. Churchill-class cruiser. Sixteen vertical-
launch silos.

Leviathan and *Kapoonis.* Kraken-class littoral combat
ships. Multi-role vessels.

Sable Island and *Guadalcanal.* Waterloo-class amphibious assault ships. Carries twenty aircraft and 2,000 marines.

Jim had been doing this for the past two days. Going around the base, memorizing the names and specifics of every LAW weapons system he came across. He tried to convince himself it was to become familiar with the equipment and capabilities of his new allies. In reality, he did it to try and get his mind off everything that had happened since their escape from Elizabethtown.

He clenched his fist, thinking about Doug, how he looked just after Chuck's death. He expected him to cry, or at least be angry, maybe blame him for his brother's death. And why not? Chuck had been a civilian. Jim should have insisted he leave with the prisoners. But after Chuck blew off Demon Alpha's head, after he fought the Shreth'kil without flinching or cowering like he had at the church, Jim started thinking of him as something of a soldier.

And look what happened because of it.

But Doug didn't blame him. In fact, Doug did nothing. He just sat against the wall opposite of Chuck's bed, and continued to sit there when they wheeled the body down to the morgue.

Now, Doug sat in the psych ward of the base hospital, barely moving or talking.

Jim thumped his fist against his leg. One cousin dead, another catatonic.

More faces floated past his mind's eye. Captain Williams, Duguid, Wierzbowski, Hafaz, Vasquez, Carpenter.

"Impressive, aren't they?"

He looked over his shoulder. Kenaevya walked over to him, wearing slate gray fatigues, her hair tied in two thick braids.

"Huh?"

"The ships. I may not be a sailor, but I never failed to be awed looking at one of our Emperor-class carriers, thinking of all the firepower it possesses."

"Yeah. They're impressive." He turned back, his eyes fixed on another ship. *Jellicoe.* Acivya-class destroyer. Primary mission, anti-submarine warfare.

"I have some news about the prisoners," Kenaevya said, now standing by his side. "The Royal Governor of Iceland is asking citizens to house them until more permanent living quarters can be arranged. There's already a long list of people willing to do this."

"That's good." So far, all the surviving prisoners had been living in a hastily-erected tent city on one of the base's training areas.

"It was worth it, wasn't it?"

Kenaevya gave him a quizzical look. "What do you mean?"

"The mission. It was worth it, right?"

"Of course it was. How can you ask that?"

"How many people did we lose? How can I not ask it?"

"They were soldiers. We're all soldiers. No matter if you wear a LAW uniform, or U.S. Army uniform, or Israeli Defense Forces uniform, we all accept the risks that come with it, and we're all prepared to make the ultimate sacrifice to protect the people of our countries, or Earths, or the entire multiverse."

"And what about Chuck?" asked Jim. "He never wore any of those uniforms. The only uniform he wore was the one for his college baseball team."

Kenaevya's jaw tightened. She laid a hand on his shoulder. "He became a soldier by default, and acquitted himself admirably. You should be proud of him."

"I'd rather have him be alive than be proud of him." Jim sighed and shook his head. "I've lost people before. Not that it ever gets easy. But this time . . . one of the things they tell you in training is never make the fight personal. But I did. I failed those people back at the church, I failed Hannah, and I was bound and determined not to fail anyone else again. And look what happened. One of my cousins is dead and another one is locked up in a rubber room. Williams is dead. Duguid's dead, along with twenty other LAW troopers. Hell, one of your cruisers is at the bottom of the Gulf of Mexico because I had to get my way."

He waited for Kenaevya to say something. Instead she looked at him in silence. What could she say? Right now he was a living, breathing example of the old saying, "Pride goeth before the fall."

"Come." She spun on her heel and strode off.

"Where are we going?"

"Come," she repeated in a more demanding tone, never breaking stride.

Grunting in annoyance, he took off after her. They hiked past clusters of block-shaped, utilitarian buildings, eventually making their way to a field covered by rigid, domed tents. Several white vans and trucks were parked among them, bright red crosses painted on their sides. Even on a world so drastically changed by a Scandinavian Empire that ruled much of Europe and North America, they still had an International Red Cross. Volunteers went from tent to tent handing out care packages to the freed prisoners.

As Jim and Kenaevya entered the tent city, he watched a group of boys and girls kicking around a soccer ball. Two men clutched care packages as they conversed. Trading, perhaps?

"Ah! There's the one." Kenaevya veered toward a tent on their left. "Excuse me, Mrs. Oliver? It's Major Kenaevya and Major Rhyne. May we come in?"

The tent flap drew back. Jim's eyes widened when he recognized the woman.

It was Amanda's mother.

"Hello. Thank you so much for coming by." She shifted her gaze to Jim and smiled. "Amanda's been asking for you. Major Kenaevya said you've been recovering the last two days. How are you feeling?"

"I'm fine, thank you."

They stepped inside. There wasn't much to the interior. Two cots, two trunks, a little pile of care packages, and two metal folding chairs that had seen better days. Amanda sat next to one of the trunks, coloring on a piece of paper. She looked up at him and beamed. "Major Rhyne!"

Amanda leapt to her feet and barreled into him, hugging him with one hand while holding the piece of paper with the other.

"Hey, kiddo." He patted her on the back with his left hand. "You doing okay?"

"Uh-huh. This place is neat. Mommy took me for a walk and I saw the ocean and all the big boats and the big mountains. And they had snow on them. Will they let me play in the snow?"

"I'm sure you'll be able to one of these days."

"Yay! Oh, I made this for you 'cause you saved me and Mommy from the ugly monsters."

She handed him the folded piece of paper, which turned out to be a hand-made card. The front had a bunch of crudely drawn pictures of flowers and a smiling sun. When he opened it, the inside read, "Thank You, Major Rhyne. Love, Amanda and Mommy."

He couldn't help but swallow. "Thanks. I really appreciate it."

"I don't think I've thanked you enough for the way you've taken care of us," Mrs. Oliver said.

"You're welcome." Kenaevya nodded. "I know this isn't much, but hopefully soon you and your daughter will be able to stay in a real home. Some of the citizens of Reykjavik are opening their homes to you and the others."

Mrs. Oliver's eyes glistened. "Bless you. You've all been so kind."

Amanda hugged him again. Mrs. Oliver also hugged him, then Kenaevya, before they left their tent. Jim looked back, thinking of Amanda at the church, how he had feared the worst had happened to her. But by some miracle, she had survived. He and the LAW had kept her from being turned into food for the Shreth'kil. Because of him, and Kenaevya and Valerie and One Cent and Doug and Deathswipe and all the others, especially the ones who didn't make it back, she actually had a future.

He then gazed around the tent city. All of these people had futures because of what they had done.

"So ask yourself again," said Kenaevya. "Was it worth it?"

Jim exhaled slowly. "Hard to say no when that little girl's hugging you, isn't it? I just hope all the ones we lost would feel the same way."

"They would. Trust me on this. Many of us in the LAW Armed Forces have had people we knew and cared about taken away by the Shreth'kil and turned into food." The veins on her neck stuck out for a few moments. Jim guessed she was thinking about her late husband and son.

She continued. "Believe me, given the opportunity to free even one prisoner of the Shreth'kil, they would take it, no matter how great the risk. And the last I heard, the Shreth'kil's offensive in Pennsylvania and Virginia has stalled, and our forces and yours managed to keep them from taking control of Albuquerque. I'd like to think our mission in Elizabethtown inspired everyone on your Earth to fight harder. So in the end, despite our losses, we did do the right thing."

Jim looked at her for a few seconds before taking hold of her hand. "You're right." He kissed her on the cheek.

They walked back to the hill overlooking the bay, gazing out at the LAW ships, and the crystal blue water beyond them.

"So what happens with you now?" he asked.

"My squad and I will rest for a few days, then drill and prepare for the day we go back to your Earth and liberate it."

Jim nodded. "I'll be going with you."

"I expected as much."

"Meantime, what do we do until we go back to work?"

Kenaevya stepped in front of him, a wry grin on her lips. "We can use this time to get to know each other better. We have a beautiful, scenic island to explore, and I'm certain there are many inns we can stay at that have very large and very comfortable beds. Does that sound appealing?"

Jim cocked an eyebrow and squeezed Kenaevya's hand. "Sounds good to me."

THE END

ABOUT THE AUTHOR

John J. Rust was born in Hamilton Township, NJ, where he graduated from Nottingham High School and Mercer County Community College. After receiving a communications degree from the College of Mt. St. Vincent in Riverdale, NY, he worked for New Jersey 101.5 before moving to Arizona to become a radio sports reporter and play-by-play announcer. Some of his previous science fiction stories include "The Last Soldier" in the anthology *What If? A Collection of 14 Short Stories,* and "The Art of Fear" starring the ghost of Edgar Allan Poe in the anthology *Halloween Dances with the Dead.*

17049757R00132

Made in the USA
Charleston, SC
24 January 2013